ECHOES AND SHADOWS

North Beach. Garreth pursed his lips. Lane always found her supper there. Maybe Irina had discovered the same hunting ground. And maybe someone had seen her.

He parked just off the Embarcadero at the foot of Broadway. From there he walked up toward Columbus, and within a few blocks had plunged into the show he thought about so often while watching Baumen's Friday- and Saturday-night cruisers. Baumen must have tempered his memories, though, because he did not remember the sounds, lights, and smells as being this overwhelming . . . a bright sea of neon signs, jewel strings of headlights and taillights from four lanes of traffic, rumbling motors, honking horns, human voices calling and laughing, the raucous voices of barkers rising above all others as they shouted the virtues of the shows in their particular clubs at the humanity swarming along the sidewalks. The crowds jostled Garreth, people wearing everything from ragged jeans and torn sweat shirts to evening clothes, smelling of sweat, tobacco, alcohol, marijuana, perfume and cologne, and . . . blood.

Look for these Tor Books by Lee Killough

BLOOD HUNT
BLOODLINKS

Bloodlinks

Lee Killough

TOR HORROR

A TOM DOHERTY ASSOCIATES BOOK

BLOODLINKS

Copyright © 1988 by Lee Killough

First Printing: May 1988

A TOR Book

Published by Tom Doherty Associates, Inc.
49 West 24th Street
New York, NY 10010

ISBN: 0-812-52064-5
Can No.: 0-812-52065-3

Printed in the United States of America

0 9 8 7 6 5 4 3 2 1

For PAT and JANE, and
the fans who asked for
more of Garreth Mikaelian

Burning Bridges

1

He dreamed of death, and undeath. Inspector Garreth
Mikaelian stood backed against the wall of an alley in
San Francisco's North Beach, pinned by the hypnotic
gaze of eyes glowing like rubies, unable to move even
enough to ease the pressure where the handcuffs
looped over his belt pressed into the small of his back.
Red light glinted in the vampire's hair, too . . . not a
beautiful woman, some distant part of him noticed,
but she used her long, showgirl legs and mahogany
hair to seem like one.

"You're going to like this, Inspector." She gave him
a sultry smile. "You'll feel no pain. You won't mind a
bit that you're dying."

There was pleasure in the touch of her cool lips, and
it persisted even after the kisses moved down his jaw
and became bites that pinched his skin in hard, avid
nips. High-heeled boots made her five-ten height
tower above his five-eight. Lassitude held him passive
while she tipped his head back to reach his throat
better.

Her mouth stopped over the pounding artery. "Lovely," she breathed. "Now don't move." Her tongue slid out to lick his skin. She stretched her jaw. He felt fangs extend, then she bit down.

A spasm of intense pleasure lanced through him. Catching his breath, he threw his head farther back and strained up against her sucking mouth.

Presently, though, as cold and weakness spread through him, concern invaded the ecstasy, a belated recognition of something unnatural, wrong. Evil. Fear stirred. He started to twist away sideways, but to his dismay he could not move. Her body slammed into his, pinning him helplessly against the wall . . . despite the fact that he outweighed her by a good fifty pounds. The fear sharpened.

Use your gun, you dumb flatfoot, a voice in his head snarled.

Her grip blocked him from reaching the weapon. He sucked in a breath to yell for help, but her hand clamped over his mouth. In desperation he sank his teeth into it. Her blood scorched his mouth and throat . . . liquid fire.

The vampire sprang away, ripping out his throat in her retreat.

He collapsed as though drained of bone as well as blood.

She laughed mockingly. "Good-bye, Inspector. Rest in peace."

Her footsteps faded away, leaving him face down in his blood. Leaving him to listen in helpless terror to heartbeats and breathing that gradually slowed, stumbled, and stopped.

Garreth woke, shaking.

Sitting up in bed, he leaned his forehead against drawn-up knees, waiting for the adrenalin rush to subside. Shit. How many times did that make for the damn dream this week?

Except that it could not be called a dream exactly. A

dream was something one woke from, returning to the ordinary. For him that would be his San Francisco apartment, and joining his partner Harry Takananda in the homicide squad room at the S.F.P.D.'s Bryant Street Station. Instead . . .

Garreth raised his head to look around the den-come-efficiency above Municipal Court Clerk Helen Schoning's garage in Baumen, Kansas—wood paneling, leather chairs, kitchenette, and closet forming one side of the corner bathroom. The uniform hanging on the open door, tan shirt with dark brown shoulder tabs and pocket flaps to match the trousers, belonged to the Baumen Police Department. Despite heavy drapes, which left the room in midnight darkness, he saw every detail clearly, even to the lettering on the shirt's shoulder patch. The daylight outside pressed down on him like a great weight. And his throat already tickled with increasing thirst.

He did not wake these days, but merely exchanged one nightmare for another. The vampire was memory, not dream. She had existed . . . Lane Barber, born Madelaine Bieber seventy years ago in this little prairie town where he tracked her, where he had killed her. But not destroyed her.

Falling back against the pillow to the accompanying grit of dried earth in the air mattress beneath the sheet under him, he sighed. In all honesty, he had to agree that Baumen probably deserved better than to be called a nightmare. Everyone believed the cover story he used to justify asking questions about Lane, that his father had been her illegitimate son. They accepted him as one of the Biebers, albeit a strange one, no doubt because he came from California. The eight-P.M.-to-four-A.M. shift despised by Baumen's five other officers suited his needs perfectly, and the rolling hills around pastured plenty of cattle who never missed the blood he took from them.

Vampires did not *have* to drink human blood.

5

It was a quiet town, unnoticed by the rest of the world, a good place to hide, to bury himself—he smiled wryly—at least until someone began wondering too much about his quirks and why he never aged.

And then? When he wanted to leave this nightmare, what did he wake up to? Where did he go?

The pressure of the unseen daylight outside shifted. Approaching sunset. *Rise and shine, my man.* Garreth swung out of bed and after folding it back into a couch, headed for the bathroom.

He shaved without turning on the light so his eyes would not reflect red. A sharp-boned face with sand-colored hair and gray eyes stared back at him from the mirror, boyish-looking despite the mustache he had grown, and still a stranger's face even a year and a half after replacing the beefier one of his younger days. *No, boys and girls,* he mused, running the humming razor around the edges of his mustache, *it isn't true that vampires don't reflect.*

As he dressed, the tickle in Garreth's throat grew, flaring to full-blown thirst. Taking a thermos from the little refrigerator, he poured some of the contents into a tall glass and leaned against the counter to drink.

The cattle blood tasted flat and bland, like watered-down tomato juice, never satisfying the appetite, no matter how much he drank. But he refused to become what Lane had been, preying on people, drinking them dry whenever she felt it safe to do so, and breaking her victims' necks to keep them dead. He scowled down into the glass. Since he got along on animal blood, that was all he would use! He just wished . . .

Garreth finished off his breakfast in a gulp and rinsed out the glass in the sink. *I just wish I could like it.*

2

Garreth's key let him in through the back door of the police department's end of city hall. Chief Danzig and Lieutenant Kaufman had both been gone since four o'clock, when Nat Toews—pronounced "Taves"—the evening officer, came on duty, but as usual Danzig had left a written briefing. Sue Ann Pfeifer, the evening dispatcher and clerk-typist, looked up from the communications desk dividing the office and reached across it to hand Garreth the notes—warrants issued by the sheriff's office down in Bellamy and in surrounding counties, requests on activity to be watched, a bulletin on a nationwide manhunt for two men who had robbed a bank in California and then killed a highway patrol trooper in Nevada, a synopsis of the day's activity, items the shift sergeant in a larger department would have covered verbally at roll call.

"Nat's rattling doors downtown. Maggie radioed that she's on her way in," Sue Ann said. "Have a cookie."

Garreth grimaced. "I'm allergic to chocolate, remember?"

"I wish I was." She sighed, patting a generous hip.

The smell of her blood curled around Garreth, warm and tantalizingly salty-metallic, pulsating with the beat of the dispatcher's heart. Thirst flared in him.

Pretending to become engrossed in the briefing notes, he unzipped his fur-collared winter uniform jacket and strolled away from her back to a desk by the locker room, where the other odors permeating the office disguised the blood smell: sweat and gun oil, coffee, the eternal plate of donuts and chocolate chip cookies by the coffee urn, scents of urine and disinfectant in the four cells upstairs.

Item ten brought a groan of dismay. The bloodmobile visited Bellamy in two weeks. Not that again? "Does Danzig really want every one of us to drive down and donate?"

On the other side of the communications desk, Sue Ann smiled. "He says it's good public relations."

Vampire blood dripping into the veins of someone with a weakened immune system would *not* be.

Lane had believed in a vampire virus carried in the blood and saliva. According to her, a healthy person's immune system easily destroyed small innoculations of the virus. The virus triumphed, however, in a severely weakened body, invading every cell and altering the host's DNA. Anyone transfused with Garreth Doyle Mikaelian's blood would certainly live, but at what a price. Worse, some nurse or doctor might discover what the patient had become, might realize that far from being just myth, vampires actually existed.

He had to find some way out of donating.

A key clicked in the lock on the back door. Moments later Baumen's best-looking officer strolled up the short hallway between the locker room and Danzig's office. Grinning at Garreth, Maggie Lebekov tossed her cap onto a desk and combed the fingers of both hands through her curly cap of dark hair. "You'll have fun out there tonight."

He pushed aside the problem of the bloodmobile. "Rough shift?"

Her blue eyes crinkled. "Mine wasn't, but . . . it's the first Friday after Easter and all those virtuous abstentions for Lent are over with. Business is booming at the bars and private clubs. By midnight you'll have your hands full of DUI's. Oh, and take your slicker; there's rain headed our way."

"Damn." Kansas spring storms could be exhilarating with their roily purple clouds sweeping in from the west in a spectacular play of lightning and thunder, but on a night like this shift promised to be, rain meant only headaches.

Maggie followed him to the locker room. As he took his equipment belt and clipboard out of his locker, she wrapped her arms around him. The speedloader cases on her belt pressed into his back below his jacket. "What say I set my alarm for 0400 and come over to your place in time to soothe your aching body after the shift?"

The scent of her blood enveloped him, beating at him. Pretending he needed the room to buckle on his equipment belt, he moved out of her arms.

He ought to tell her not to come, he knew. It would be in her best interests to break off the relationship entirely. Over the year and a half they had been seeing each other, her nearness and the blood running warm and salty beneath her skin increasingly brought the hunger boiling up in him with such fierceness that the effort of denying it left him shaking. And yet . . . he could not face the thought of always coming home alone.

Hating himself for his weakness, he said, "I'll look forward to seeing you," and dropped a kiss on the tip of her nose. Maybe her presence would chase off the nightmares.

3

Rain coming in, indeed. Thunder rumbled to the west while he checked the equipment in the patrol car's trunk. Climbing into the car, Garreth racked the shotgun and switched on the ignition prepatory to testing the lights and siren.

All hell broke loose. Above him the siren screamed. Red and white lights flashing across the building and the other cars in the lot told him the light bar was on, too, and the left turn signal. Both the car and police radios blared at top volume and the windshield wipers scraped across the windshield at full speed. The air conditioner blasted him with cold air. A knee cracked against the steering column in his startled jump. With the pain, though, panicky confusion —what did he turn off first?—gave way to a return of rational thought. He switched off the key, then opened the door to lean out and glare back at the department's rear door.

"You're dead, Lebekov."

Maggie grinned wickedly from the top of the steps and jumped back inside.

Shutting off all the switches before he tried the ignition switch again, Garreth chuckled. But amusement faded by the time he pulled onto the street. The problem of the bloodmobile seeped back up. What could he do? He had manufactured a bout with flu the last time, so the excuse of illness had been used up. He needed something else this time.

"Bellamy S.O.," Sheriff Lou Pfeifer's voice drawled on the radio, calling his office. "Emma, call Dell Gehrt and tell him he has cattle out on 282 north of the river again. I almost hit one of them."

Garreth swung the car onto Kansas Avenue. The motorcade was in full swing, two lines of traffic on each side of the railroad spur running up the middle of Baumen's main street, teenagers from Baumen and surrounding farms and smaller towns driving cars, pickup trucks, and vans on an endless loop that stretched north to the Sonic Drive-In this side of the railroad station, across the tracks, and south past Baumen's three-block shopping area to the A & W near the edge of town before turning north again. The vehicles parked down both sides of the street and along the tracks belonged to patrons of Baumen's movie theater, open only weekends, and to adults drinking and dancing in the local bars and private clubs.

Garreth cruised south. His radio muttered sporadically, mostly with traffic from the Bellamy P.D. and sheriff's offices in Bellamy and surrounding counties. Around him kids honked horns at each other and shouted back and forth between cars. A few cars zigged around others to catch special friends, and he kept an eye on one pickup he remembered citing twice last month for jumping lights, but for the most part, traffic remained orderly, following its ritual pattern.

He passed Nat Toews checking the doors of businesses and honked a greeting at the stocky cop.

When the cruise circuit crossed the tracks and turned north, Garreth did, too. Presently a sleek black Firebird with four girls inside pulled up beside him on the inside lane. A blond girl in the passenger seat rolled down her window and leaned out, smiling.

"Hello, Garreth."

Garreth sighed. Amy Dreiling. Well, it was inevitable that he run into her sooner or later this evening. "Good evening, Miss Dreiling."

"Do you have to be so formal?" She pouted prettily. "You always called my brother by his first name."

Only to his face. For a long time Garreth had other names for the banker's son, which he used in private and with fellow officers. "Scott and I shared what you might call a professional relationship."

"If I buy a customized van and drag race and run stop signs with it like Scott did, will you call me by my first name, too?"

Mention of the van abruptly took Garreth back to another night on this street, an icy one two Thanksgivings ago with him struggling across the treacherous, deserted thoroughfare, bleeding and weak from arrow wounds Lane had inflicted. He held the beautiful vampire prisoner, helpless in the rosary he had managed to wrap around her neck. At the roar of a motor he looked up to see Scott's van and a pickup drag racing on the far side of the street. Inspiration flashed . . . a way to destroy Lane using this boy who continually dared the police to arrest the son of a city father. He hurled himself and Lane across the tracks into the van's path, snapping Lane's neck as he did so.

He remembered how the brakes screamed, followed by the shriek of metal as the skidding van wrapped around a telephone pole in a vain attempt to avoid hitting the two of them. Then fire enveloped it, set by Garreth to incinerate Lane's body.

13

Later, however, he had made friends with the boy, stabbed by guilt at the sight of a pale, frightened Scott facing charges of vehicular homicide in juvenile court. With the arrogance knocked out of him, Scott was not a bad kid. Garreth had actually come to enjoy having him ride along on weekends.

Garreth smiled politely at Amy. "You'll do better driving carefully. Good night, Miss Dreiling."

He turned right at the next corner and patrolled the side streets. It netted him two cars with expired tags and one without handicap identification parked in a handicap zone. It gave him satisfaction to call for a tow of the latter, then while waiting for the truck, he also wrote the car up for a broken outside mirror and missing lens on a taillight.

Thunder growled louder in the west.

Nat's voice came over the radio announcing he was back in his car.

The pace of the evening picked up. Garreth answered a complaint of a barking dog and vandalism on parked cars in a residential area. Between calls, his mind churned. What *was* he going to do about the bloodmobile?

Lightning flashed in the west now, accompanying the nearing thunder.

On a swing back down Kansas Avenue, Garreth spotted Nat parked at Schaller Ford and turned in to pull up window to window with the other officer's car.

Nat grinned beneath his mustache, a red bush matching his sideburns, though his hair was dark. "How's the groupie? I saw you flirting with her."

Garreth grimaced. "I don't know what's worse—a juvie daring us to pick him up or one inviting me to. Oh, speaking of juvies, our antenna-twister struck again. Three cars on Poplar. One of the neighbors saw some kids in the area, one matching Jimmy Pflughoff's description."

Nat scowled. "The little shit. If only we could catch him at it."

"He's hit Poplar three times out of five. How about planting a car there, something flashy and inviting, with fairy dust on the antenna?"

Nat arched a brow. "Fine. Now if we can find a night dry enough not to wash off the marker, what car do we use . . . a certain flashy red ZX?"

"You go to hell."

"Not devoted enough to sacrifice your own car, huh?" Nat grinned. "Speaking of flashy cars, there's someone new in town you ought to meet."

"What's *he* driving?"

"A Continental, but that isn't why you ought to meet him. The car just reminded me about him. He was at the Driscoll Hotel when I went by, asking Esther at the desk if a Madelaine Bieber lives around here."

Garreth fought an irrational desire to run. *Don't be ridiculous. What do you have to be afraid of?* Nothing . . . except questions that might revive others he preferred everyone to forget. He knew Lane was dead but to everyone else she had mysteriously disappeared. She had been disguised as a man that night. After the fire, of course, what remained of her body had been unrecognizable and Garreth volunteered no information about her identity. Why should Anna Bieber have to learn her daughter was a killer?

Garreth forced a casual tone. "Did he say why he's looking for Mada? Who is he?"

"He's English. His name's Julian Fowler and he's a writer. I told him no one's seen Miss Bieber for over a year but he still wanted to talk to her family. I sent him over to your great-grandmother."

Despite the knots in his gut, Garreth felt a rush of relief. Now he could stop pretending calm. "What? You sent a stranger we don't know anything about to visit an old woman who lives alone? You should have had him talk to me!" He slammed the patrol car into gear and gunned backward in a tight Y-turn.

"What could you tell him?" Nat yelled after him. "You only met her once. I'm not stupid, though. I looked over his identification before I gave him the directions. He's—"

"I'm still checking on Anna," Garreth interrupted.

4

The Englishman must have rented the car in Hays. Pulling up at the curb in front of Anna Bieber's house, Garreth's headlights shone on an Ellis County tag on the sleek gray Lincoln in front of him.

Garreth keyed his mike. "407 Baumen. I'll be out of the car on high band at 513 Pine." Sue Ann would recognize the address.

He moved up the walk and climbed the steps to the porch in long, urgent strides.

Anna Bieber answered his knock, her face lighting with surprise and pleasure. "Garreth! How nice. I wasn't expecting to see you until Sunday."

The radio on his hip muttered. Garreth smiled through the screen at the old woman—thin with age but still straight-backed and sharp-eyed. "I thought I'd just drop by for a minute. This Englishman is visiting for a long time this evening, isn't he?"

Her smile went knowing. "Ah. That's why you're here." She shook her head. "Thank you for your

17

concern, but Mr. Fowler is a charming gentleman." Like so many people in the county descended from the Volga Germans who settled the area, her accent gave "is" and other plurals a hissing pronunciation. "Don't be such a suspicious policeman all the time."

"Con men are also charming." A distant part of him noted wryly that his anxiety for her had become genuine, as though he were actually her great-grandson and not just playing a role. "Grandma Anna, what does he want with Mada?"

"He's a writer researching for a book about World War II."

Lightning flashed, brightening the yard, followed several seconds later by a long drumroll of thunder. The wind picked up. Garreth's radio spat a report of a tree knocked down across a road by lightning in Ellis County.

"Why don't I come in and meet Mr. Fowler?" Garreth asked.

"Why don't you," Anna replied dryly. She unhooked the screen and pushed it open.

Garreth followed her through the hall into the living room. He left his jacket on for the appearance of huskiness its bulk gave him, and did not regret the choice when the visitor on the couch set his teacup on the coffee table and stood. Julian Fowler stretched up a good six-foot-plus, an athletic-looking man in his late forties with light brown hair, pale blue eyes, and the kind of peculiarly English face that had probably been pink-cheeked in his youth but had now aged enough to gain character and masculine edges. He looked vaguely familiar, though Garreth could not imagine where he had seen Fowler before. The Englishman's gaze raked him, too.

"Mr. Fowler," Anna said, "I'd like to have you meet my great-grandson, Garreth Mikaelian . . . Mada's grandson."

The visual autopsy ended abruptly. Fowler grinned

in delight. "Really?" He pumped Garreth's hand. "Splendid. I don't suppose you'd know where your grandmother's got to?"

"I'm afraid not." Garreth rescued his hand and gave the Englishman a tight smile. "Excuse me, Mr. Fowler, but I don't quite understand what you want with Mada when you're doing a book about World War II. Shouldn't you be looking at military records?"

Fowler chuckled. "The book isn't *about* World War II, it just takes place during it. It's fiction. All my books are."

All his books? Garreth started. Fowler. Of course! Now he remembered where he had seen the face . . . on the back of a book his first wife Judith was reading. "You write under the name Graham Fowler."

The Englishman shifted his shoulders, as if embarrassed. "Actually it's as much my name as Julian is. Julian Graham Fowler. I use it because my publisher is of the opinion that Graham sounds more appropriate than Julian for a writer of thrillers. It's just for books and promotional tours, however. Otherwise I'm Julian."

Garreth raised his brows. "I'd think using Graham would open more doors."

"That's quite true. Unfortunately, it also attracts attention when I need solitude." Fowler grimaced. "Tell me, what do you think happened to Mada? Mrs. Bieber says the chief of police believes she was abducted by accomplices of a man killed in town that night."

"As a hostage in case they were pursued. That's what he thinks, yes."

"And you?"

Garreth shrugged. "I can't see abduction. We never found a body."

"Could she have simply run away?" Fowler frowned thoughtfully. "It's rather a habit of hers, isn't it . . . first haring off to Europe with that college

19

professor, then abandoning him in Vienna, not to mention dodging Hitler's army and all."

Cold knotted Garreth's gut. "How do you know so much about her?"

Fowler blinked. "She told me. I met her once, you know, in the south of France after the war. That is, my parents did. I was just six at the time." He smiled. "I went mad over her. She was the most smashingly magnificent creature I'd ever seen. When she visited with my parents, I was underfoot the whole time, hanging on her every word. She had marvelous stories about traveling around Europe with a Polish woman just before the war."

Garreth caught his breath. That would be Irina Rodek, the vampire who Lane told him brought her into the life.

"But the story I remember best was the one about escaping from Warsaw just ahead of Hitler's forces. She made it so real, like being there. When my publisher suggested that I try a World War II story, naturally I thought about her." Garreth had the feeling that Fowler had forgotten everyone else in the room. He stared dreamily past them. "We have a young girl coming from a sheltered, insular background, suddenly exposed to the sophistication and desperate glitter of pre-war Europe, and then caught up in the violence of the war itself. Everything would be seen through her eyes, a romantic vision at first, then increasingly sophisticated, but although still politically naive. Gradually, however, she understands what's happening and is terrified by it until finally, stripped of all innocence, honed into a practical, shrewd woman by the needs of survival, she triumphs." He focused on Garreth. "So I dredged up every detail I could remember her mentioning about her background and came looking for her, to talk to her and learn more about—" A clap of thunder shook the house, interrupting him. Fowler jumped. "My God. We're under seige."

Garreth had to smile. "Of a sort."

Lightning crashed outside, making the lights flicker. Rain drummed against the house. Garreth kicked himself for not bringing the slicker in with him.

The radio on his hip sputtered: "Baumen 407. 10-93, Gibson's."

An alarm at the discount house. The lightning had probably set it off, but it had to be checked out.

He backed toward the door. "Sorry we can't help you. I wish you luck on the book." Just not enough to learn what had really happened to Lane in Europe.

5

Wind drove the rain before it in blinding sheets. Swearing, Garreth dived down the steps and across the lawn toward his car. But even that short a distance left him soaked. In the car he pushed dripping hair back out of his eyes with a grimace and peeled off his jacket, tossing it into the back seat. With his broadened temperature tolerance, the chill of the rain did not bother him, but water running down his neck did, and he hated the feel of the sodden trousers plastered to his legs.

None of which improved at the Gibson store. His slicker and hat did nothing to protect his cuffs and Wellingtons from further soaking while he walked around the building checking doors amid the crash of thunder and the shrill clamor of the store's alarm. For a wistful minute he considered how much drier and more comfortable it would be searching the building from the inside, but with regret he discarded the idea as too risky and waited outside until Mel Wiesner, the manager, arrived to shut off the alarm. If Wiesner had found him inside, it would be impossible to explain how he had managed that with all the doors locked.

The shift wore on . . . two bank alarms, both, like the Gibson's alarm, apparently set off by lightning; power lines pulled down by a fallen branch where Garreth sat until a KPL truck and crew arrived to take care of them; fights in two bars; opening a car for a woman who had locked her keys inside at the Shortstop, Baumen's single convenience store. None of the activity could quite make him forget about the writer or the bloodmobile, however. Through everything, both problems gnawed in the back of his mind.

Lightning and thunder eased. The rain settled into a steady drizzle.

Toward midnight the cruisers along Kansas Avenue had thinned to a last stubborn few. But the closing bars had begun emptying their customers onto the street and the combination of alcohol and wet pavement produced two minor fender benders and several near accidents. One of the latter erupted into a fight as the drivers, both big, burly men, piled out of their cars, enraged by the damage almost inflicted.

Garreth broke up the fight by stepping between them, and while they stared down at him, astonished at being pushed apart by someone so much smaller, caught the eyes of each man in turn. "Don't you think that's enough? There's nothing to be upset about."

Rage faded from the men's faces. "I guess you're right." They eyed Garreth with puzzled frowns, clearly aware that something had happened to them, but not sure what or how.

Garreth gave them no time to figure it out. "Then why don't you both go home?"

With pats on their shoulders, he steered the two sodden men toward their cars and stood in the street watching until they drove away.

Someone chuckled behind him. "The Frisco Kid strikes again. I'd sure like to know how you make them roll over and wag their tails for you."

Garreth glanced around. It was after midnight already? Ed Duncan grinned at him from the other patrol car. The grin made the morning-watch officer look strikingly like Robert Redford, a resemblance Garreth knew Duncan cultivated. Garreth sent him back a wry smile. "It's a gift that comes with me blood."

"Okay, if you don't want to share with—hey, podner, we've got a live one!"

Garreth followed Duncan's gaze to a car weaving its way down the lane line on the far side of the tracks. ~~The light~~ bar on Duncan's car flashed to life. "I'll pull him over. You test and breathalize him."

Garreth frowned. "Me? It's your stop. You do it."

Duncan grinned. "But you're already drowned and I just got a trim and blow dry this afternoon."

Usually Duncan did not bother him, but tonight the remark scraped the wrong way across Garreth's nerves .He said shortly, "Tough nuts. You want the fucking DUI? You haul your pretty blow dry out of the car into the rain and write him up yourself."

He turned away.

"You got an attitude problem, you know that, Mikaelian?" Duncan snapped after him. "You think you're so goddamn much better than the rest of us, a real hotshot, because you were a detective and worked in a big city department! But *I* never froze and let a partner get shot."

The jab hit dead center. Garreth stopped short, pain twisting his gut.

"And I wonder about you . . . skinny like that and coming from San Francisco. Maybe we ought to warn Maggie to watch you for night sweats."

With that parting shot, Duncan gunned the car away across the tracks, lights flashing.

6

The rain either sobered everyone up on the walk to their cars or inspired cautious driving. After the private clubs closed at two, their parking lots cleared without incident. Garreth checked the Co-op, Gfeller Lumber, and other businesses along 282 on the east side of town, then made a sweep through the city park up by the river and around the sale barn and rodeo grounds, disturbing half a dozen parked couples.

The rain continued unabated but radio traffic faded to near zero. For five and ten minutes at a stretch, only the soft hiss of static came over the air. Garreth yawned. Now came the hard part of the shift—staying awake.

He turned around to head back south on 282.

Then in the distance, brakes and tires screeched.

Garreth held his breath, straining to hear through the drum of rain on the car. The sound stretched on for what seemed infinity before ending abruptly in a scream of crumpling metal and an animal shriek of agony.

25

Swearing, he flipped the light bar switch and stamped on the accelerator. The sound came from the north. Over the bridge was out of city jurisdiction but something cried out in pain-edged grunts, and who else was there to check it out?

"407 Baumen. Investigating possible 10-47 on 282 north of the river. Advise S.O."

Half a mile past the bridge his stomach jolted floorward. Dark, square shapes loomed through the rain on the road, shapes the human eye would never see until on top of them. Angus cattle. Those Lou Pfeifer had reported earlier? One sprawled on its side groaning, rumen and intestines spilling onto the asphalt.

Garreth swung onto the shoulder, radioing for a wrecker and ambulance. The car that hit the Angus lay upside down in the ditch, a little Honda, or what remained of it after ploughing into a ton of beef at fifty-five or more miles an hour. And north beyond it, a human form hung across a barbed-wire fence . . . feminine in outline . . . motionless.

The stench of rumen contents and blood washed around him with the sound of the cow's agonized grunts as Garreth scrambled down into the muddy ditch to peer into the car. He ignored the thirst they triggered in him. The ditch was filled with two or three inches of water and another girl remained in the Honda. She did not move, either. He smelled no more than the normal blood smell about her, though. By lying flat and reaching in through the slot left of the front window, he could reach her wrist. A faint pulse fluttered under his fingers.

She was alive at least.

He splashed up out of the ditch to the girl on the fence, and cursed softly. This one must have gone out through the windshield. Her face had turned to bloody hamburger. With only pulp remaining of her nose, she gasped for breath, open-mouthed, in liquid, bubbling sounds with a blast of blood smell on each expiration. Cold bit into Garreth's spine. The girl's throat was filling with blood draining down from her nose.

"I need that ambulance *now!*" he shouted into his portable radio.

"It's on its way," Doris Dreiling, the morning dispatcher, reported.

But how long before it arrived? Baumen had no regular ambulance service, just one owned by the hospital with a couple of personnel assigned to it on each shift, and when a call came, those individuals could be in the middle of other duties just as pressing.

Garreth gnawed his lower lip. Maybe if he laid the girl on her side, the blood would drain out of her mouth and let her breathe.

All the warnings against moving accident victims echoed loudly in his head as he gingerly lifted the girl loose from the barbs impaling her and eased her to the ground. On her side she did seem to breathe easier. He covered her with his slicker against the rain.

A shrill cry mixed with the groans of the injured cow. "Help! Someone help!"

He whirled. The girl in the car had regained consciousness. He slid back down beside the vehicle and stretched out in the muddy water where the girl could see him. "Take it easy, miss. I'm a police officer."

"Get me out, please!"

Not even vampire strength could move this car the way it had wedged into the ditch. What would happen to the girl inside if it were moved anyway? He had no way to assess her injuries.

"There's a wrecker on the way, miss. We'll have you out in a few minutes."

"No! Please, I want out now! My legs and back— this thing." She began thrashing, pounding at the steering wheel pinning her.

"Don't move! It's important that you lie still and wait for—"

But panic kept her from hearing. She continued fighting and screaming. And up near the fence, the bubbling of the other girl's breath grew worse.

"Miss. Miss!" God, if he could only catch this girl's eyes. Where the hell was Duncan? He needed help. Grabbing the girl's arm, he shook it. "*Goddamn it, listen to me!*"

Miraculously her screams softened to whimpers. But she continued pushing at the steering wheel and would not look in his direction.

He lowered his voice soothingly. "What's your name, honey?"

It seemed an eternity before she answered. "Kim." The nails of her other hand dug at the wheel. "Please, please help me."

"Kim, listen to me. I know you're scared but you'll be all right if you just lie still and wait for the wrecker. Will you do that while I go help your friend?"

"Sheela?" The arm in Garreth's grip jerked. "Oh, no! Where is she?"

"She was thrown out of the car." He let go of the girl's arm. "That's why—"

"No!" Her fingers clamped around his wrist.

"Kim, don't worry. I'm not going far, just up the bank. Your friend—"

"Don't leave me!" Her fingers dug in with fear-driven strength.

The gasps by the fence became gurgles.

His heart lurched. Tearing loose from the girl in the car, Garreth scrambled backward and clawed his way up the slippery ditch to the fence. Lying on her side no longer helped.

He groped for his radio. "Baumen, where's . . . that . . . ambulance!" The girl needed immediate suction to clear her airway.

"En route. It should be there anytime."

28

The girl's breath gurgled.

Garreth stared down at her in anguish. His own breath rasped through a closed-tight throat. Below, her friend in the car continued to scream in hysteria. "Anytime" would be too late. "Anytime" now she would be dead, drowned in her own blood.

She choked.

Unless he did something.

He bit his lip and grimaced at the prick of his unextended fangs. *No.* Rain washed down his face and splashed on the slicker covering the girl.

The injured cow grunted, each cry punctuated with a thrash of its legs.

Garreth pushed sodden hair out of his eyes. No, he could not do that. He would not touch human blood. Must not.

Desperately he peered toward town, but no emergency-vehicle lights showed through the rain.

The girl choked again.

His gut knotted. He should not touch her, and yet . . . if he did not, she would die.

"All right!" he shouted, though at whom Garreth had no idea. Fate, perhaps, or Lane's ghost. "All *right.* Just this once."

He knelt at the girl's head, lifted her chin, and crouched over her. His mouth fastened over hers, sucking. He would spit out the blood, would—

Then it filled his mouth.

Every cell of him screamed in joy. The hot, salty-metallic liquid flowed over his tongue with a richness animal blood never had. A richness his instincts had been craving since the moment he woke in the San Francisco morgue. Garreth could not turn away and spit. Something else snatched control of him. He swallowed.

The blood burned like fire in his throat, but a fire that cooled, not seared, soothing the other fire of thirst. And from it, warmth spread outward through the rest of him, warmth and a crackling surge of energy. All awareness of the rain, the mortally injured cow, and the screaming girl in the car faded to the distant edge of perception. Garreth sucked and swallowed again and again, ravenously, greedily relishing every drop.

Then, also dimly, he became aware of a siren wailing, rising above the cries of the trapped girl.

The chest of the girl at his knees heaved, drawing in a convulsive breath.

A hand touched Garreth's shoulder. "We'll take over now."

Fury boiled up in him. *No, not yet!* He clung, snarling, to his prey.

The hand pulled at him. "Mikaelian!"

The sound of his name ripped through the urge controlling him. Garreth suddenly saw what he was doing. In horror, he flung away, jumping up and backing until the fence stopped his retreat. Barbs pricked him but he barely felt them. *Animal! Is this the way you serve and protect, feeding on a helpless girl?*

One of the ambulance attendants glanced up from examining the girl. "You've got her airway clear. Good work."

Good work? Garreth grimaced bitterly. They had no idea how he had done it, or that he had taken such pleasure in the act. A pleasure that part of him still felt, savoring the taste lingering in his mouth. That part of him also pointed out with some smugness that for the first time since he entered vampire life, all hunger had been satisfied.

Red lights flashing on the highway toward town caught his eye. The wrecker. That reminded him of the car in the ditch.

The girl in it was still screaming. He hurriedly slid into the ditch and lay down beside the car again to reach in and catch her hand. "Kim, honey, it's all right. I'm back."

To his ears, the reassurances he murmured at her sounded inane, but perhaps all that mattered was the sound of his voice and being touched by someone. The girl calmed. He made no attempt to leave again, just lay holding her hand, two of them alone in the rain and cold and mud. Thank God the wrecker was coming. The water in the ditch felt deeper, and the girl's hand had gone icy.

Then abruptly the solitude vanished. The ditch swarmed with people: the wrecker crew, one attendant from the ambulance, a deputy sheriff from Lebeau, the town north, and a tall, beefy man who Garreth recognized as Dell Gehrt. Someone shot the cow and put it out of its agony.

Garreth continued holding the girl's hand through the jolts and bumps of winching the car up on the shoulder and while it was cut apart to free her.

Finally the ambulance screamed away with its two patients. Garreth collected his slicker from where it had been pulled off the girl and slipped back into it to protect the seat of his car from his messy uniform. Then, leaving the deputy to finish up at the accident scene, he headed back to town.

7

Garreth had never been so glad to finish a shift. Despite the energy from the girl's blood, exhaustion dragged at him as if the sun had risen.

Doris Dreiling's plump, motherly face peered at him with concern over the top of the communications desk. "Are you all right? You look like you could use some fortified coffee."

That meant brandy in it. She kept a bottle in her desk—against regulations—for just such occasions. Lien used to meet Harry and him at the door with rum-laced tea, he remembered wistfully. What a lifesaver that had been sometimes. Now he smiled wryly. *Now I'd have to have Doris drink the brandy and take the shot from her.* "Thank you, no. I'm fine."

"How are the girls?"

The girls. He sighed and peeled off his slicker. "The one from the car just has a broken ankle and some broken ribs. For which she can probably credit her seat belt. The other one . . ." He grimaced at the blood and mud smearing both sides of his slicker. It would have to be washed thoroughly before it could be worn again. "They don't know yet. She might have brain damage, or never regain consciousness. X-rays showed a severe skull fracture with fragments in her brain. The helicopter from Fort Riley picked her up a few minutes ago to fly her to the KU Med Center for surgery."

Mud crusted his equipment belt, too. And probably filled his holster and gun. He dropped it all on the floor for dealing with later. Right now he sat down at a desk and rolled a form into the typewriter to start on his reports.

A key clicked in the back door. Duncan stamped in. "God, what a miserable night. Doris, sweetie, would you consider making up a thermos of your fortified coffee to go? Jesus!" He stared at Garreth. "You're a mess, Mikaelian. It must have been some fun up there."

Garreth typed on without looking up. "Where were you? I could have used some help."

"Sorry. I was on the way when I got a flat, and by the time I changed the tire, you didn't need me anymore. I could hear on the radio that the ambulance and wrecker and a deputy sheriff were there. So, kind of tough out there on your own, is it . . . even for the Frisco Kid?"

Garreth stiffened, anger flaring in him. The smug tone told him there had been no flat. It was merely Duncan's alibi for not backing him up.

He looked up, and either the anger showed in his face or his eyes reflected the light because Duncan retreated several steps. Garreth made no attempt to follow, however. He just said with deadly quiet, "I think the question is the ethics of letting personal differences between officers jeopardize civilian lives. Now if you'll excuse me, I'd like to finish this paperwork and go home."

Bending over the typewriter again, he saw by the

flush rising in Duncan's face that the shot had hit dead center. But as Duncan slammed out of the office, Garreth wondered unhappily whether he had solved their problem or only made it worse.

8

Rather than mess up the inside of his car, Garreth left the ZX in the city hall lot and walked home. What did it matter being wet a little longer? Halfway to Helen Schoning's house he realized he did not really want to go home. What would he do there but think about the accident and remember the taste of the girl's blood?

He turned south at the next corner. Minutes later he walked up the main drive of Mount of Olives Cemetery. Obelisks and other ornate headstones of the older graves near the gate bore names like Dreiling, Pfeifer, Pfannenstiel, and Wiesner. And Bieber. Garreth passed them all, striding on until he reached a grave on the far west side that bore no headstone or name, just a metal stake with a laminated card: UNKNOWN MALE D. 11/24/83.

Garreth knelt beside it. How small a grave it seemed for so tall a woman. Not that much of Lane remained after the fire. He began pulling the new spring growth of dandelions and other weeds sprouting in the grass around the edge of the plot. The rain-softened earth made the task easy; even dandelion taproots came up. Garreth still worked carefully, avoiding the thorns of rosebushes on the grave.

The memory of Maggie's voice whispered in his head. *This is crazy, Garreth. The man was a cop hater. He tried to kill you and Ed Duncan. Yet you look after his grave like your mother is buried there. Why?*

A lot of people wondered the same thing, Garreth knew. "He was also someone's son," he had replied for Maggie's and everyone's benefit.

New leaves showed on the canes of the rosebushes. Soon there would be buds, then, hopefully, a profusion of blossoms. Blood-red American Beauties. What more fitting for Lane?

Thinking about her here, he usually pictured, not the vampire, the killer, but Mada Bieber, the child she had been ... angry and tormented, her unusual height and quick temper making her a pitifully easy target for the ridicule of other children. He ached for the child and for all she might have been if hatred had not driven her to beg Irina Rodek for the vampire life as a way to wreak revenge on the humanity she despised. He talked to the woman, though.

"You would have laughed seeing me tonight." He carefully worked a weed free, making sure he had its roots, too. "I can just hear you: *See, lover, that's what this life is about. Human blood is what we're meant to drink. They're our cattle, not the four-legged kind. So stop being so stubborn and unnatural. Stop trying to be human and join your people.* You'd like me to become like you." He jerked out a dandelion. "It would mean you'd won after all."

With her rich, mocking laughter echoing in his head, he continued cleaning the grave until growing light and a sudden drag at him announced dawn. Garreth sighed. Time to go before he fell asleep on the cool, inviting earth, or early bird citizens saw him and wondered why one of Baumen's finest was running around looking as if he had wallowed in a pigsty.

He might already be too late for the latter. The sound of running footsteps carried across the cemetery. By the time Garreth managed to push to his feet, a man in sweats appeared out of the drizzle up one of the paths. So intent was his effort, though—blowing steam at every step, his face grim with eyes focused inward—that he passed close enough to touch without ever seeing Garreth.

Surprise made Garreth call out. "Good morning, Mr. Fowler."

The writer started violently and flung around white-eyed, then let out a gusty breath of relief. "It's you, Officer Mikaelian. You gave me a bit of a turn. Disheartening, isn't it? We think we're such civilized, rational beings and then something appears out of nowhere in a cemetery and we jump right out of our bloody skins."

"Yet you chose to run through the cemetery. Isn't it a cold, wet morning for exercise?"

"Yes, well, I suppose, but I'm British, aren't I?" Fowler smiled wryly. "I'm used to weather like this. And I've been addicted to running since Alistair Cooper."

Garreth blinked. "Who?"

"A spy character of mine who used marathon running as a cover. I started running to learn what it felt like." He peered at Garreth. "What about you? Surely it isn't part of your normal patrol to be out here dressed and looking that way. If you don't mind a personal observation, you look like hell."

"It's the way I always look when I've been walking in the rain after pulling sixteen-year-old girls out of what's left of their car."

Fowler sucked in his breath. "Bloody shame. I keep a flask in the car for myself after a run on a day like today. You're welcome to a nip."

His gaze slipped past Garreth as he talked. Garreth turned but saw nothing except Lane's grave. His chest tightened. "Something wrong?"

Fowler blinked. "What? Oh. No, nothing. The rosebushes just caught my eye. You know that's how legend says you keep a vampire in his coffin."

Garreth hoped his expression looked like surprise and not guilt. "I thought you used garlic or drove a stake through his heart."

"That's all the cinema shows, yes," Fowler said and snorted, "but real vampire lore says to drape the coffin or grave in mountain laurel or roses. The thorns supposedly have magical power against vampires."

Garreth kept his face expressionless. "I'll remember that."

Fowler circled around him to lean down and touch the new green growth on one bush. "The word 'vampire' is Balkan in origin, of course, but vampires aren't. They can be found mentioned as far back as Babylonia under the name *Ekimmus*. The Greeks had them, and the Chinese." He turned to lift a brow at Garreth. "Your Irish forefathers had them, too."

Dearg-due. Yes, I know. It still hurt remembering Grandma Doyle hissing the term at him. "Interesting. I take it you're into vampires?"

Fowler smiled. "It's purely professional interest. I used to write horror novels. But what a fool I am, nattering on when you're standing there looking positively frozen. Why don't you come back to my car for that nip. Then I'll give you a lift home."

Garreth grimaced. "I haven't eaten anything in hours. I'm afraid alcohol would put me flat on my butt and you'd have to *carry* me home. I'd rather walk anyway. Home is close; everywhere in Baumen is close. Thanks anyway."

"As you wish. Well, then, I hope there's someone warm at home waiting to help you thaw—what is it?"

Garreth stared at Fowler in horror, suddenly remembering. *Maggie!* He had completely forgotten about her! "I'm in deep shit. Pray for a miracle, Fowler, or the next time you see me, I may *really* be a ghost."

He spun away, and despite the exhausting drag of daylight on him, began to run.

9

His single hope all the way home was that Maggie had not come over after all, but one quick look through the garage door windows shot that down. Her Bronco with its SHE-PIG license sat parked in his side. *I'm dead.*

He crossed his fingers and silently climbed the outside steps. Maybe she had fallen asleep waiting and did not realize how late he was.

No such luck. The door opened even before his key touched the lock. Maggie stood in the opening, fully dressed.

Garreth opened his mouth. Only no words came out except a guilt-stricken: "Maggie . . ."

"Garreth!" She threw her arms around him. "Where the hell have you been?"

He gaped at her in surprise. "You're not angry?"

"Angry? Of course I am. I'm furious. I've been frantic. My God, you feel like ice. Come in and get out of those clothes and into a hot shower this instant." Hauling him in by the shirt front, she shut the door and began unbuttoning his uniform shirt. "When you didn't come home, I called the office. Doris said you'd left ages ago and she was worried because you'd left both your jacket and slicker and when she looked into the parking lot, your car was still there, too. Where did you go?"

The scent of her blood curled around him, bringing up the taste of the girl's blood in his mouth. He pulled loose and bolted around her for the bathroom. "Just walking. Did Doris tell you about the accident I worked tonight?"

She followed him. "She told me. Walking where, for God's sake? I got dressed and drove all over town. You weren't anywhere."

The smell of her was making him dizzy with longing. He shut the door between them. "I ended up in the cemetery."

"Again? Why? Isn't that what we have each other for, to talk to and work out these job stresses?"

"Yes, but . . . I forgot you were here."

As soon as the words were out he wanted to kick himself. *Open big mouth; insert big flat foot.* An ominous silence answered from the other side of the door. Garreth stripped off his clothes and jumped into the shower.

The bathroom door banged opened. Maggie jerked back the shower curtain and turned off the water. "You *forgot* I was here?" she asked quietly.

He grimaced. "I'm sorry."

The blue eyes bored into him. "What else happened besides the accident?"

"I don't know what you mean." He could not talk about the writer and bloodmobile with her.

Her lips tightened. "Okay, you want to shut me out, I guess I can't do anything about it."

The hurt in her voice ran through his gut like a knife. "Maggie, I'm not—"

"Yes, you are," she said sadly. "You always do.

41

Somewhere in every one of our conversations there's a wall and part of you is shut away on the other side. You're very skilled at putting up diversions to hide the wall, like when you worm out of dinner invitations, but I see it anyway. I keep hoping that one of these times we'll mean enough to each other that the wall will come down. But maybe not."

"Maggie, I'm sorry." He wanted to hug her, to take her in his arms and soothe her hurt and somehow make it up to her for not loving her as well as she deserved, but the scent of her blood beat at him. He was afraid to touch her. "I don't know what else to say."

She sighed. "I don't, either, Garreth. Maybe until we do—"

"Maybe what we both need is sleep," he interrupted. "There's that movie in Bellamy you've been wanting to see."

"*Witness*."

"Yes. Why don't we go Monday, just have a good time? Then we can talk afterward."

She stared hard at him for several minutes before replying, but finally she nodded. "All right, we can try."

When she had gone, Garreth turned on the cold faucet and leaned back against the stall with the icy water pelting him. *We can try.* Her tone held no optimism. He bit his lip. He was going to lose her. It would be better for her, but he would lose one of his fragile ties with humanity, and he would have nothing to come home to but the apartment and the ghosts waiting there.

Lane's laughter echoed in his head.

10

He dreamed of fire. He stood in the shade of a tree at the edge of the artificial island in the city's Pioneer Park. High overhead a summer sun blazed in a heat-bleached sky. Lane lounged on the railing of the old-fashioned octagonal bandstand in the island's center. A blood-red dance costume cut up to her hipbones showed off the full length of her showgirl legs. Even in the shade her hair shone rich mahogany, and her eyes gleamed red as fire.

"Come here to me, Inspector," she crooned. "Blood son. Lover. I need you. We need each other."

"The hell I need you," he yelled at her. He wanted to leave the island, but the wooden bridge lay in the full blaze of the sun. Just looking at it made him feel weak. If only he could find his mirror-lensed trooper glasses. Somehow he had mislaid them, though. He searched all his pockets in vain. The thought occurred to him that perhaps Lane had taken them.

"But you do need me, lover," she called. "You don't want to be all alone."

"I'm not."

She laughed. "You're referring to your human friends? Don't be foolish. They don't want you. See?"

She pointed. Following the direction of her finger, he caught his breath. Massed at the shore end of the bridge stood Duncan, Maggie, Maggie's father in his wheelchair, Anna Bieber, Nat, Sue Ann, Chief Danzig, and Helen Schoning. And Julian Fowler, too.

"All in favor, say *aye*," Duncan said.

"*Aye*," the rest of them chorused.

"Carried." From a box of kitchen matches in his hand, Duncan struck one and tossed it onto the bridge.

"Maggie, stop him!" Garreth yelled.

Maggie turned away.

Smiling thinly, Duncan struck another match. "What's the problem, Mikaelian?" He tossed the match. The plank it struck began to smolder. "All you have to do is come over and stamp them out."

Garreth tried, but the moment he stepped out of the shade, the sun struck him down like a sledgehammer. He reeled backward into the shade, pain blinding him.

Duncan struck another match and tossed it. A second plank caught fire. "I don't see what's so difficult. Just walk over the bridge and join us. Anyone can do that. Any human."

But Garreth could not. The sun held him pinned in the shade of the tree. He could only stand and watch helplessly while his single link to those on shore blazed up.

"You see, lover?" Deceptively soft arms wrapped around him from behind. Sharp teeth nipped his ear. "You're mine. I'm the only one who'll have you. I'm the only one who understands. Now aren't you sorry you murdered me?"

11

Sunset woke him. Garreth scrambled gratefully out of sleep and stumbled out of bed. In the bathroom a note on the mirror greeted him: MAGGIE TONIGHT. DON'T FORGET THIS DATE.

As if that would save the relationship. True, she had been friendly enough when he saw her Saturday and Sunday, but there had been a certain reserve.

At least he had done better with her than Duncan. An attempt Saturday to smooth things over with the other officer when he found Duncan parked in the Schaller Ford lot had met a chilly reception. "So the department is too small to afford a feud?" Duncan snapped. "Too bad." Gunning his car, he pulled away in a scream of tires.

Then there had been Sunday and Julian Fowler. Garreth found the writer in Anna Bieber's living room when he arrived after dinner to take her to evening mass. The fact that the writer accompanied them to church did not bother Garreth. As usual, he found the service soothing, quite the opposite from the physical agony that Lane, raised in a strict faith, had experienced around religious objects. Afterward, though, having tea at Anna's, Fowler kept asking questions about Lane. What had Mada been like as a child? How had she changed when she finally came home again? Did she ever mention the names of friends in Europe or fellow performers she worked with? Did Anna save letters from her? Did she remember the return addresses and postmarks?

Cold crawled along Garreth's spine. The man asked questions like a detective. In the right quarters, the answers were likely to bring him too much knowledge . . . too much for Garreth's safety and peace of mind.

"You sound like you're planning a biography," he had said. "I had no idea you had to know so much to write fiction."

Fowler smiled. "Oh, yes. I have to make it sound realistic, after all."

Garreth had spent the evening sidetracking Anna into reminiscences of Lane's childhood and had come home exhausted.

And today had one strike against it already. After two days of feeling no hunger, thirst burned in his throat with a fierceness that the entire remaining contents of the thermos scarcely blunted. The cattle blood tasted even thinner and more unsatisfying than usual.

He surveyed himself wryly in the mirror on the closet door—black turtleneck shirt, tan corduroy sports coat and slacks. *What the well-dressed vampire wore to a good-bye date.* Saluting his image, he turned and left to wait at the station for Maggie to get off duty.

12

The late show ended around eleven. They walked out of the theater into an overcast night that, although chilly, smelled of spring—damp earth and hints of green. Clean smells, free of any blood scent. Garreth drank them in.

"Did you like the movie?" Maggie asked.

"Of course. It's a good flick." He lied, but how could he tell her the truth? Movies were always difficult for him at best, sitting there drowning in the smells of blood from other patrons, tortured by thirst and sometimes by deadly whiffs of garlic, which left him suffocating, the air in his lungs hardened like concrete. Tonight, too, one of the blood scents had carried the sour smell of disease. It set him itching. But most uncomfortable had been the painful chords the movie rang in him as the big-city detective hid in the alien culture of a rural community. Detective John Book had one big advantage, though, which Garreth envied. When it became clear he did not belong, at least that cop had another world to return to.

Garreth had parked in the next block. They started to cross the street, only to stop short at the wail of a siren. A Jeep wagon painted with the sheriff's star shot past them from the side street and into the parking lot of the courthouse across from the theater. The stocky driver vaulted from behind the wheel to race into the two-story law enforcement wing of the courthouse.

Maggie stared after him. "That's Tom Frey."

The undersheriff. The hair twitched on Garreth's neck. "I wonder what the trouble is."

Serious discussions of their relationship could wait. As one, they changed direction toward the court-house.

Both the Bellamy P.D. and sheriff's office shared the wing. A broad counter with a glass and metal grill along it partitioned the main office. Behind it, Tom Frey's black AmerInd eyes glinted grimly as he glanced from a walrus-mustached officer to a tall, lean man who looked as if he belonged on horseback working cattle—Sheriff Louis Pfeifer.

". . . heard the trouble buzzer," the officer was saying, "and ran down from the jail, only as I came out the stair door, someone hit me from behind. By the time I could get up again, this turkey had fished the car keys out of my pocket and was dragging Emma outside with him. He had a gun. I called Wes in 512 on the radio right away and he's tracking them. They're headed northwest."

The sheriff spun. "Tom, get on the horn to the Russell and Rooks S.O.'s, then call our deputies. Have them spread out north and west, but keep back. We don't want Emma hurt."

The undersheriff reached for a phone.

"Can we help, Sheriff?" Garreth asked.

The tall man looked around through the glass at them and smiled. "Who says there's never a cop around when you need one? Our dispatcher's been kidnapped. Why and how he got past the counter, we don't know. Give me your radio, Clell."

The officer lifted it out of the case on his belt. Pfeifer handed it to Maggie through an opening in the glass. "Head toward Schaller and help 512 keep track of that car."

Garreth and Maggie raced for the ZX.

As they reached it the radio crackled with alerts issued by the Russell and Rooks S.O. dispatchers for the Bellamy P.D. car carrying a male of unknown description and a female that the dispatchers described.

Then another voice said, "512 Bellamy. Subject is headed north from County Nine at Droge Corner."

"Lincoln Street takes us out to Nine," Maggie said. "But I don't know where Droge Corner is."

With no siren or lights to clear the way for him, Garreth drove carefully as far as the city limits, then stamped the accelerator. "Watch for anything that looks like a corner."

"That ought to be fun in this dark." Maggie tightened her seat belt.

A harsh male voice came on the radio. "If that pig following me comes anywhere near, I'll kill this bitch."

A woman yelped in pain.

Garreth's headlights caught a sign with names and distances to various farms. The top name read: DROGE.

"Garreth—" Maggie yelped as they hurtled past.

He was already hitting both gas and brake and hauling at the steering wheel to spin the car in a one-eighty turn. He gunned back for the corner, reached it still accelerating, and somehow still made the turn anyway, wheels screaming, gravel from the new road scattering beneath his wheels. Maggie whooped like a banshee.

"512, turning east five miles from last turn."

"Get away from me! I'm warning you!"

Garreth swore. He had not noticed his mileage at the turn. "How are we going to know which corner it is?"

"Relax," Maggie said. "These roads are section lines, remember, exactly one mile apart."

She counted crossing roads; he concentrated on keeping the car on theirs and, when it came, making the turn without piling them into a heavy stone fence post at the corner of the field.

"I see them!" Maggie hissed.

He did, too . . . small ruby points of light far ahead, and two more points half a mile beyond those. The farther lights swerved and vanished.

"512. Turning north—"

Maggie hit the transmit button on the hand radio. "We have you, 512."

"You've got one last chance to get away from me or this cow dies."

A female voice came on moments later. "Bellamy S.O. Fall back, 512."

The taillights grew larger and brighter as Garreth gained. He watched them swerve into a turn. He followed and, shortly after that, drew up alongside.

"Roll down the window, Maggie." When she did, Garreth shouted across to the Bellamy officer, "Drop back and mark that corner. I'll follow him from here."

"Orders are—"

"He won't see me, I promise." He shut off his headlights as he passed the patrol car.

Maggie gasped.

The road stretched before him in a distinct gray ribbon, as if through twilight. On it ahead of him, growing ever brighter, shone the taillights of the stolen police car.

Maggie clung to the radio. "I can't see a thing. How can you?"

He hesitated only a moment before answering. "I never told you but I'm a werewolf."

"Terrific. I've been dating a fruit loop." The car fishtailed and she swallowed audibly. "How fast are we going?"

"I'm afraid to look."

Her stream of language had to come out of her father's oilfield days.

The lights ahead swerved off onto another road, then another, and finally into a lane which consisted of two wheel ruts with a grass-grown center. Far up the lane, perhaps half a mile, Garreth made out the blocky shapes of buildings, one tilting crazily.

He downshifted to slow the car, then stopped with the hand brake to keep the brake lights from giving their presence away. "Maggie, I'll follow on foot from here."

"On *foot!* Garreth, you can't—"

He climbed out. "Take the car and go back to wait at that last corner for the others. I'll leave my jacket on this fence post to mark the lane. Get going."

"Do you have a gun?"

"Of course." He patted his ankle holster, and before she could protest further, took the radio from her, peeled off his sports jacket, and dropping it over the fence post beside the gate, sprinted up the lane after the fading lights of the car. His breath swirled thick and white around him in the chilly air.

The lights vanished.

Garreth stretched his stride. Had they gone over a rise? Around a corner? He had almost reached the buildings. He slowed, still looking around for the car. The lane led on past. Could the kidnapper have continued?

No, voices carried on the night wind, whispers so low that no normal ears could have heard them . . . a woman's, frightened and weeping, a man's, hissing angrily. "Stop whining, you bitch, or you're dead."

Garreth tilted his head, testing for direction of the sound. The house with its multiple doors and windows gaping empty, or in the dark cave of the tilting barn? A car could be hidden from sight in there. The barn, he decided. The wind brought him scents of human blood and sweaty fear mixed with the odor of moldering hay.

Circling behind the house, he climbed through two barbed-wire fences to the rear of the barn. The windows, empty of glass, were high and small. The doors had been blocked up sometime in the past. Garreth nodded in satisfaction. The kidnapper should feel himself safe from the rear, then. The sealed door gave no protection from a vampire, though.

He pressed against the door. Everything in him wrenched sharply, then he stood inside between disintegrating stacks of hay. A tall, raw-boned man with a heavy thatch of dark, wiry hair sat against the bales in a position where he could watch the lane. Beside him huddled the dispatcher, a short, plump woman in her late thirties, held down by an arm twisted behind her back.

Now what? Garreth plucked at his mustache. As soon as he revealed his presence, the man would open fire. The trick was to make sure he did not shoot his hostage first.

But what would happen if the kidnapper shot and hit *him*? Theoretically, if a vampire could pass through a door, an object could pass through him without harm. Wooden stakes excepted. Theoretically.

There was only one way to learn. *Watch the idiot cop put his head in the lion's mouth.*

52

Laying the radio on a hay bale, he stepped forward. "You're under arrest, turkey."

The kidnapper whirled, the muzzle of his gun flashing fire.

He shot well for having only sound to aim at. A small, wrenching pain lanced through Garreth's chest. Reflex brought his hands clutching at the point of pain, but a moment later he realized he felt nothing else, no weakness, no bleeding.

The kidnapper fired again, and once more Garreth felt only that single small pain similar to the one of passing through doors. Good enough. He grinned. "Try again, turkey." Then he charged.

Cursing, the kidnapper tried to empty the gun, but had time for just two more shots before Garreth reached him. Wrenching the gun away, Garreth rapped the butt across the side of the kidnapper's head. The man dropped in his tracks.

Beyond him, the dispatcher huddled on the floor. She had to be terrified, hearing the gunfire and collapsing body but unable to see who had gone down.

Garreth spoke before touching her. "Emma, it's all right. You're safe. I'm Garreth Mikaelian, Baumen P.D." Then he picked her up.

"Mikaelian. You're 407." Burying her head against his shoulder, enveloping him in a smell of blood and terror-sweat, she burst into tears. "What an idiot I am. When he went down in the waiting area, I thought he'd fainted. I didn't even think; I just opened the counter door and ran out. Of course it was a trick. He grabbed me around the neck and dragged me back inside the office. He demanded the keys to the cells, to get his brother out, he said. I pretended to be getting them and hit the button that rings an alarm at the guard's station up in the jail. I knew Clell Jamison had just brought someone in and was up there, too. The bastard figured out what I'd done, though, and he dragged me over to the stair door and hit Clell when he came down. Did he kill him?"

"Jamison is fine."

Garreth led her back to where he had left the radio. "Mikaelian to Bellamy S.O. Situation resolved. Hostage unharmed."

In minutes the old farmyard had filled up with cars and flashing light bars, representatives of law-enforcement agencies in three counties—police, sheriff and deputies, highway patrol.

His ZX was there, too, and Maggie, throwing her arms around him, drowning him in the smell of her blood. "You took him by yourself? Are you all right?"

"Of course." He slid away from her so she would not smell the powder burns on his shirt. "He fired a couple of shots at me but he's a lousy shot in the dark." Luckily the powder burns did not show up on the black turtleneck. "Do you have my coat?"

She handed it over. "Are you sure you're all right? There are holes in your shirt."

"Front and back. Yes, I know. I had to crawl through two barbed-wire fences." Smiling, he carefully buttoned his coat across the holes.

13

Pounding woke him. At first he thought it was part of his dream, hammering on the barn being unaccountably built by a swarm of Amish men at the land end of the bridge from Pioneer Park's island. He did wonder when the entire group turned and began shouting in unison: "Mikaelian! Mikaelian, goddamn it, wake up!" Amish would surely not curse that way. These could not be real Amish.

Then he noticed that though they stopped pounding when they yelled at him, the pounding noise went on. Their voice sounded familiar, too.

"Mikaelian!"

The voice and pounding were real . . . outside his door. He clawed his way up out of sleep to squint at his clock. He stared in outrage. Eleven-thirty!

The pounding sounded ready to break through the door. *"Mikaelian! MIKAELIAN!"*

"I'm coming!" He staggered to the door and opened it half the width of the safety chain.

Through the crack and the glare of light outside, he recognized the burly form of Lieutenant Byron Kaufmann filling his porch. "Helen Schoning and her mother weren't kidding about how sound you sleep," Kaufmann grumbled. "I've been making enough noise to wake the dead."

Garreth leaned his forehead against the crack, sighing. "So you have. What do you want, Lieutenant? I just got to sleep."

"Sorry, but I'm supposed to bring you down to the station."

"At *this* time of day?" While he unchained and opened the door, Garreth's mind raced, hunting serious transgressions.

"Relax." Kaufmann strolled in past him. "There are just some reporters waiting for you."

"Reporters?" Garreth's gut knotted. He shoved the door closed. "Shit."

"Jesus, it's dark in here."

Garreth switched on a lamp. "Why do they want to talk to me?"

Kaufmann grinned at him. "Don't you realize who you collared last night? Frank Danner."

The name sounded vaguely familiar. Garreth had shaved before he identified it, though. Then he stared at Kaufmann. "One of the bank robbers who killed that Nevada trooper? They're in Kansas?"

Kaufmann rolled his eyes. "Don't you read your briefing notes?"

"I've been off for two days."

"Don't you watch the news? Two days ago Frank and his brother Lyle shot a Colorado trooper. Every cop in the country wants them. And you nailed Frank without a scratch to you or his hostage. Danzig says wear something professional-looking."

Garreth reluctantly put on a suit and tie, and after a moment of hesitation went to the refrigerator. Instead of filling a glass, though, he drank directly from the thermos, freshly refilled from the Gehrt Ranch herd after taking Maggie home last night.

They never had talked.

Kaufmann eyed him. "That's health-food stuff, I suppose."

"Liquid protein and additives." Perfectly true. He added sodium citrate to keep it from clotting. But let Kaufmann think he meant vitamins and brewer's yeast. Despite the knots in his stomach, Garreth could not resist adding slyly, "Try some?" He held out the open thermos. "It's very healthy. Makes you live forever."

As he hoped, Kaufmann refused with a shudder and he returned the thermos to the refrigerator.

They trotted down to the patrol car in the driveway. "Why don't I just follow you in my car?" Garreth asked.

"Danzig remembers how camera shy you were after our round with the bow-and-arrow cop killer. He wanted to make sure you showed up. I'm also supposed to brief you on the way."

Why became obvious as Kaufmann filled him in. The Bellamy P.D. had arrested Lyle Danner without realizing who they had. Early in the evening he had tried to rob a liquor store, only the owner had been in the back room when Danner pulled a gun on the clerk, and the owner had called the police from an extension. Then he sneaked out to jam a shotgun in Danner's back and hold him until the police arrived. Danner gave the name William Dane when he was booked, which came back negative when checked through the National Criminal Information Center in Washington.

"So the arresting officer tossed Danner in a cell to wait for the fingerprint check and his court appearance and thought nothing more about him," Kaufmann said. "But when Pfeifer and Chief Oldenburg saw 'Dane' and the guy you collared together in jail, their descriptions clicked. Someone woke up the editor of the *Bellamy Globe* to tell him what had gone down and in nothing flat he had it on the wire and people out to collect more details. A whole group of reporters complete with minicam showed up at our office half an hour ago asking to talk to you."

Minicam. Garreth slunk down in the seat. *Damn.* "Does the chief want me to say something in particular?"

"Just avoid making us sound like hick cops who stumbled over these fugitives in spite of ourselves."

There should be nothing to this interview, Garreth told himself. With all the mass murderers, serial killers, and terrorists in the news, no one cared about a couple of men who had only robbed a bank and killed two law-enforcement officers, let alone had any interest in a small-town cop who happened to be part of capturing one of them. At most this would be something for the local news out of KAYS in Hays. Still, he felt like a prisoner marching to execution.

At city hall Danzig charged out of his office, a big man still built for the football he had obviously played in school, still impressive despite his waistline trying to match the width of his shoulders. "What the hell took so long? I have them waiting in the city commission meeting room." He led the way through the door connecting the office to the rest of city hall and down the corridor.

To Garreth's relief, the group consisted of only five, and he already knew Jeanne Reiss from the *Baumen Telegraph.* The others were from the *Bellamy Globe,* the Hays paper, and KAYS.

"Would you mind removing your sunglasses so we can see your face better?" asked the TV cameraman.

And record the flare of his eyes if he tilted his head wrong? Garreth left on the glasses. "I work a night shift. My eyes aren't photogenic at this time of day. Just why do you want to talk to me anyway? Frank

Danner's capture resulted from a coordinated effort of several law-enforcement agencies. I was just one of many officers involved."

From his place by the door, Danzig nodded approval.

The *Globe* reporter, an attractive brunette woman named Catherine Heier, raised an eyebrow. "You were the one who followed the kidnapper's car without headlights to keep him from spotting you behind him, and then tracked him to that farmyard on foot and faced his gun in the dark. That was very brave."

Garreth shrugged. "It's my job and no more than any other officer would have done in my place."

Each reporter took a turn. Had he realized at all who he was after? Would he have changed his tactics if he had? How had he felt with the kidnapper shooting at him? Predictable questions, he thought. Stupid ones. He did his best to answer politely.

Then the *Globe* reporter said, "You seem to have as many lives as a cat when it comes to brushes with death."

Garreth tried not to stiffen. "You mean that incident with the killer archer a couple of years ago?"

"And the one in San Francisco where you were found in North Beach with your throat mutilated and erroneously thought dead."

How the hell had she found out about that? He glanced at Danzig, who frowned a denial.

"No, your chief didn't tell me," Heier said. "I came into town before dawn and met one of your fellow officers. In the course of chatting, he made remarks about the circumstances of your departure from the San Francisco Police Department that piqued my curiosity."

Duncan! It had to be. Garreth held his face expressionless.

Behind the reporters, Danzig did not bother. He stiffened, his mouth thinning to a grim line. Duncan would pay for talking to a reporter instead of referring her to the chief, Garreth saw, but that did nothing to help right now. Damn the man! Garreth asked evenly, "Are there more questions about Frank Danner?"

But the reporter was not about to be distracted. "I called a friend of mine who knows someone on the *Examiner* out there, who in turn knows someone in the police department, and it turns out that your colleague misunderstood the facts. Which delights me, because the true story is much more interesting than the one I thought I'd get. I'd like to talk about that with you, Officer Mikaelian."

"I *don't* want to talk about it," Garreth replied. "It's totally irrelevant to Danner's capture. Now if you'll excuse me, I need to go home and sleep before I come on duty tonight."

Heier tried to follow him. "We have a great human-interest story here."

Which would make life in Baumen very awkward if she turned up the difference between his actual re-corded parentage and the one he claimed locally. He produced a weary sigh for her benefit. "I don't think much of it, Ms. Heier. I lived it. It was painful. It was traumatic. And I prefer to forget about it."

14

He should have known that was too much to ask. It was obvious the moment he walked into the office before his shift.

Sue Ann grinned at him over the communications desk. "Hello, celebrity."

And Danzig still sat in his office. "Did you see the news?"

Garreth stopped in the open door. "No. How bad was it?"

Danzig smiled. "Not bad at all . . . a minute of KAYS footage on the national news, mostly Sheriff Pfeifer and Chief Oldenburg, but they did mention you as the officer who disarmed Frank Danner, and showed you for a couple of seconds, saying how you'd only done what any other officer would have done. Locally," —his smile broadened to a grin— "you rated about the same amount of time, but Ms. Heier managed to get herself on with a guest editorial about how people forget what a dangerous job law enforcement can be and how dedicated we cops are to stick with it. You, needless to say, were her prime example."

Garreth groaned.

Danzig shook his head. "I don't understand you. Most people would love a moment of fame."

"I'm not most people."

The saving grace was that tomorrow everyone would forget it. In the meantime there was tonight to survive. Bill Pfannenstiel, the aging officer who worked relief and replaced Nat Toews tonight, teased him every time they passed, and everyone else he met wanted details about the incident in North Beach. Why had he ever thought he could hide in a small town? Lane knew what she was doing sticking to cities. In San Francisco only colleagues and a few close friends would have known or cared about his part in the arrest.

Here even Julian Fowler stopped him in front of the hotel. "I saw you on the news. That's fascinating. It'd make a great novel, *The Lazarus Incident* or some such title. May I talk to you about it sometime?"

"I'll think about it," Garreth replied.

Maggie tracked him down, too, at the Shortstop, buying a cup of tea. "Hey, TV star. You looked great." She followed him back out to the car and when he climbed in, leaned down to the window. "Very professional."

Her blood scent coiled tantalizingly around him. The smell of it brought back the memory of the girl in the accident. He fought hunger. "Thanks. I wish they'd picked on someone else, though."

Her stare showed the same disbelief that Danzig expressed. After a moment she said slowly, "What *is* behind that wall you're so afraid of someone seeing, I wonder?"

"I'll talk to you later," he said, and backed out of the parking space.

BLOODLINKS
In the rear-view mirror he saw her staring after him. Was it imagination that she seemed to be standing at the far end of a bridge going up in flames?

15

A note waited on Garreth's door when he reached home after the shift, in Helen Schoning's bold, square handwriting in dark green ink on pale green paper.

Garreth,
   Your old partner in San Francisco called after you left for work. No wonder you were such good friends. He's a delightful man; great fun to flirt with. He wants you to call him back as soon as possible.

                                        Helen

Garreth pulled down the note and smiled at it as he unlocked the door and went inside. He had opted to keep his phone an extension of Helen Schoning's instead of putting in a private line, and times like this he never regretted the choice. Having missed Garreth, Harry Takananda had probably found it much more pleasant talking to Helen than he would have leaving his message on a machine.

Only one small chill marred the thought of talking to Harry, wondering what he wanted. Call him back as soon as possible did not sound like a social call.

Garreth glanced at the clock. It was too early yet; they would still be asleep.

He changed out of his uniform, showered, and drank a glass of blood, then settled into the easy chair with a book and read until he knew Harry would be getting ready for work. He punched Harry's number.

Lien Takananda answered. The sound of her voice spread warmth through Garreth and brought a quick image of her, wrapped in her comfortable old terry robe, her black helmet of hair streaked with gray but her face still smooth as a girl's. Her voice also reminded him of the hours she had spent patiently talking at the wall of misery enclosing him after Marti died, battering through it, forcing food into him, dragging him back into life.

"Lien, this is Garreth."

"Garreth?" Her voice warmed even more. "Hello! Oh, it's good to hear your voice. How are you?"

Guilt stabbed him for not having called more often.

Harry's voice came on another extension. "Is this really Garreth Doyle Mikaelian? So you still remember our number after all. I wondered if maybe you'd forgotten since you never call and now you're a nationally famous cop."

Garreth pictured Harry, too, black eyes glinting with mischief, belt straining to hold in a waistline spread by Lien's excellent cooking and the copious amounts of sugar Harry always added to his coffee. Garreth winced. "You saw that story out there, too?"

"Oh, yes, Mik-san, though I have to admit you were a bit hard to recognize with that funny stuff on your upper lip. When did you grow that?"

"I think you're thinner than the last picture you sent us," Lien said. "Are you taking care of yourself?"

"Lien, you sound like a mother; quit fussing at him," Harry said.

"I'm not fussing. I just want to be sure he's all right. You looked so uncomfortable, Garreth."

"What he looked like, honorable wife, was the stereotype of the hard-assed cop. Garreth, couldn't you have taken off the dark glasses? You've sure become addicted to those things."

"Terrific," Garreth said in pretended disgust. "Is this what you wanted me to call you for, insults?"

"Call. Oh, no. I called because after the item about you and the Danner brothers, I thought you might be interested in another fugitive who's surfaced: Lane Barber."

Shock jolted Garreth. Lane! "Surfaced? What do you mean?" That was impossible. Neck broken, burned, buried under roses. Impossible! He sat bolt upright, fingers digging into the phone receiver. "Has —has someone seen her?"

"Not her personally," Harry said, "but last week we found the apartment she moved into after lamming out of the one on Telegraph Hill. There's been a man in and out and it's only a matter of time until she shows up, too."

Guilt pricked him again, but this time because he could not tell Harry they were wasting time and manpower. "That's great," he lied.

"Yeah. I wish you were here. You deserve to be in on the kill . . . so to speak."

Garreth started, prodded by an idea. Time away from here might be just what he needed . . . to avoid the bloodmobile and Fowler and that reporter, to think about his relationship with Maggie. "Maybe something can be arranged. I'll get back to you this evening."

Not until he had already hung up did it occur to him to wonder: If Lane's ghost haunted him here where she had lost to him, what might it do where she had been strong and triumphant?

Echoes and Shadows

1

In the morning light, San Francisco rose bright and inviting above the waters of the bay. A feeling of homecoming enveloped Garreth as he drove across the Oakland Bridge, countering the day's lethargy and the headache from sunlight sneaking around the edges of his trooper glasses. At the same time, however, he felt as if he drove into cold and shadow. Lane's laughter echoed in his head and foreboding lay like lead in his gut. Was he wrong to be coming back?

He had refused to think about it until yesterday, and the question was easily shoved aside in the rush of preparing to leave Baumen, in the strain of trading shifts with Maggie and working a day shift on Saturday in order to leave that evening. Certainly he had no time to doubt while driving cross-country, not with watching the rear-view mirrors and road ahead for cars with light bar silhouettes. The vast open stretches of I-70 and I-80 had been too tempting to resist and he turned the ZX loose, slowing down only for the mountains and when instinct suggested troopers might be around.

Which had brought him rolling into Davis and up to his parents' house early Sunday evening, and to his surprise, into the middle of an unexpected family reunion.

"Hey, we couldn't waste this chance to celebrate the current family hero," his brother Shane said, and dragged him from the car into the crushing hug that always made Garreth pity anyone meeting Shane on the line of scrimmage.

Not only had Shane come from Los Angeles with his wife and daughters to join their parents and Grandma Doyle—Shane looking content and healthy, obviously satisfied with giving up playing end for the Rams for a position on their coaching staff —but Garreth's ex-wife Judith was there, too, with his son Brian, and her husband. The scents of blood and sweat from the inevitable Sunday family scrimmage washed around him, making Garreth glad he had taken a long drink from his thermos before reaching the house.

Phil Mikaelian wrapped a beefy arm around his shoulders. "That was a damn fine piece of police work catching Frank Danner, son. I'm proud of you."

No praise meant more than a few words from this cop who Garreth had grown up worshipping. He grinned happily. "Thank you, sir."

"But it doesn't look like you're taking time to eat," his mother said. "Or can't your Maggie cook?"

"Mom, I eat enough."

"His sport is running, remember, not football," Grandma Doyle said.

"Not football?" Shane's wife Susan pretended shock. "Esther, are you sure you brought the right baby home from the hospital?"

Judith and Dennis greeted him less boisterously, Judith with a light kiss, her husband shaking hands.

Brian, tall and husky enough that he looked twelve instead of ten years old, held out a hand, too. "Hello, sir. Congratulations."

Such formality from his own son stung, even as Garreth recognized that he could hardly expect more when he saw so little of the boy. Judith had been right to have Dennis adopt Brian.

Still, it felt like—it felt like someone had tossed another match on his bridge. Suddenly all pleasure drained from the evening. Even at home, surrounded by laughter and chatter, he stood alone.

By the end of dinner the swirl of blood scents and the strain of playing with his food to hide the fact that he ate none of it left him feeling suffocated. He fled to the dark and peace of the backyard. Sitting down in one of the lawn chairs, he breathed deeply. The air smelled wonderfully of nothing but flowers, grass, and earth.

Presently the back door clicked and footsteps moved across the porch. The scent of lavender drifted to him on the night air.

He looked around. "Hello, Grandma."

She crossed the lawn to sit in the chair next to his. "It's a lovely night."

That was all she said for a long while. They sat in silence, not the strained one there would have been with his father or Shane, who both treated silence as a void to be filled, but a sharing of solitude, each wrapped in separate thoughts and reluctant to intrude on the other. If he had to be alone, Garreth reflected, Grandma Doyle was a comfortable person to be alone near. If she felt any horror at what he had become, she was careful never to show it, yet she did not appear afraid of mentioning it either.

She broke the silence by mentioning it. "You handled dinner very well. I hardly noticed meself that you weren't eating anything."

He smiled wryly. "Thanks. I'm glad I don't have to

keep it up for more than a couple of meals in a row, though."

"You're going on to San Francisco in the morning then?"

"Yes."

She reached out to lay a hand on his arm. "Don't."

Cold slid down his spine. "Do you have a feeling about it, Grandma?" Grandma Doyle's feelings had been a source of amusement for friends and some neighbors over the years, but no one with any experience with them ever laughed, not even tough cop Phil Mikaelian. "What kind of feeling?"

"There's danger waiting there, and maybe death."

He smiled wryly. "I thought you said I'm already dead."

Age had not slowed her hands. She thumped him on the head with her knuckle just as fast and hard as she had when he was a boy. "I won't be taking backtalk from you even if you are grown and *dearg-due*. Perhaps you're dead, or it's as you say and just a different kind of living, but there is a true, final death for even your sort, and it's waiting in San Francisco."

"From what? Can you see?" He rubbed the sore spot on his head.

She sighed. "No, I can't. There's a woman involved, though, a woman with eyes the color of violets."

The words echoed in Garreth's head as San Francisco loomed nearer across the bridge. A violet-eyed woman and death. He stared across the bay. Was he a fool to go there? He could still turn around on Treasure Island. But the city called to him, echoing with the past . . . Marti, Harry and Lien, good times and love, friendship. Bridges whole and strong.

He kept driving.

2

Leaving the terminating I-80 at Bryant Street and pulling into the police department parking lot was like slipping into familiar old clothes. All the months away might never have existed. His feet automatically followed the familiar path into the building and up the elevators to the homicide section where the faces were exactly as he remembered: Rob Cohen with half glasses riding the end of his nose, Evelyn Kolb with her ever-present pump thermos of tea on the corner of her desk, Art Schneider. Schneider appeared to be wearing the same brown suit he had the day Garreth cleaned out his desk. And the room smelled the same beneath the blood scents—coffee and cigarette smoke and the acid tang of human bodies sweating in frustration and anxiety.

One new face at a desk near the door looked around from talking to a red-eyed female citizen. "May I help you, sir?"

"I'm looking for Harry Takananda."

The detective glanced around the room. "Sergeant Takananda and Inspector Girimonte aren't here right now. Can someone else help you?"

Girimonte must be Harry's new partner. Garreth did not recognize the name. "Maybe. Thanks. Hi, Evelyn, Art," he called.

The double takes around the room were classics. "Mikaelian?"

"My God." A grinning Schneider loped around his desk, with Kolb and Rob Cohen close behind. He pumped Garreth's hand. "Harry wasn't kidding when he said we wouldn't recognize you."

Cohen slapped his shoulder. "If you're an example of Kansas cooking, remind me not to eat there."

"*I* think he looks *great*." Kolb sighed. "What's the name of your diet?"

Garreth grinned back, warmth spreading through him. This was like another family reunion. And why not? The department had been his family, too, the homicide inspectors his brothers and sisters. "You're all looking great, too."

"Well, well. The wanderer." Across the room Lieutenant Lucas Serruto had appeared in the doorway of his office, as dapper as ever and still with the dark good looks of a TV cop-hero. "Of course, we all want to welcome Mikaelian, but remember that we're here to serve and protect the taxpayers of San Francisco. Let's get back to it as soon as possible. Mikaelian, grab a cup of coffee and join me when you're through saying hello." He disappeared into his office again.

Garreth followed in five minutes or so with a mug of Kolb's tea.

Serruto motioned him to a chair. "That Danner business was a good piece of work. I take it you're enjoying rural life?"

"Oh, yes." Garreth sank gratefully into the chair. Lord, he hated daylight. "You might say cattle are in my blood now."

As Serruto's brows rose, Garreth kicked himself for the wisecrack, but the lieutenant did not pursue the subject. He leaned back in his chair. "Don't think I'm being hostile, because it really is nice to see you again, but let's have something straight from the beginning, Mikaelian. Despite the understandable score you have to settle with Lane Barber, she isn't your case any longer. You don't work for this department now. You're just a guest, a ride-along. Remember when you resigned and we had a chat about how much I dislike vigilantes? I still do. So leave all action in this case to official personnel. Is that understood?"

The lieutenant had not changed a bit. "Understood." Garreth sipped the tea. Its heat soothed the burning in his throat. "Do you mind if I ask how you found the apartment, though?"

Serruto smiled wryly. "The way we get most of our really big breaks—sheer blind luck. We had a hit-and-run and when we found the vehicle and checked it against the list of cars involved in other accidents and crimes, lo and behold, the computer announced that the vehicle identification number matched the one on the car you found in the Barber woman's garage. We hoped we'd get a lead backtracking the car through the used-car lot where the hit-and-run driver bought it, but she sold it the day after she attacked you, using her Alexandra Pfeifer alias and the Telegraph Hill address. So that went nowhere. But when the lab examined the car for evidence on the hit-and-run, they found a section of apartment rentals from the want ads down behind the passenger seat. The yellowing indicated it had been there a while so we took a chance and checked every apartment listed."

Garreth leaned forward. "Some neighbor or leasing agent identified the Barber woman's picture?"

Serruto grinned. "Give the man a cookie. We found a guy she'd sweet-talked into carrying a box of books up the stairs for her. She hadn't even disguised herself, just used an alias, Barbara Madell, and put her hair up under a kerchief." He paused. "That bothers me. It's as if she wasn't trying to hide at all. As if she wanted to be found."

The words reverberated in Garreth's mind. Lane *had* wanted to be found, he realized suddenly, only not by the police. She had known that by just tearing out Garreth Mikaelian's throat, instead of breaking his neck, he would become a vampire. She was expecting him to come after her, was waiting for him. By finding her, he would prove his suitability to be her lover and companion. Only she had overestimated him. He never thought to look for her car, had never found the planted apartment listings.

Garreth sipped his tea without either tasting it or feeling its warmth any longer. If he had done as she expected, had followed the trail she laid and found her here in San Francisco while he was still frightened and confused by what he had become—and she so knowledgeable and assured, so seductive—how different the outcome of their confrontation might have been. A twinge of regret stirred in him. Whatever she might have made of him, he would at least not be alone now.

Belatedly he realized that Serruto had said his name several times. "I'm sorry. What?"

An elegant dark brow rose. "That's my question. Did you fall asleep? It's impossible to tell through those glasses. I thought you'd want to know there's someone trying to attract your attention." He pointed toward the squad room.

Harry waved wildly from the other side of the glass forming the upper half of Serruto's office walls.

Garreth leaped out of the chair for the door.

Outside it, Harry enveloped him in a fierce hug. "I wasn't expecting you until tomorrow, Mik-san. What did you do, confuse the highway numbers with the speed limit?"

With the arms also came the scents of Harry's after shave and the salty warmth of his blood. A vein pulsed visibly in the older man's neck. Garreth broke away, covering by pretending it was to eye his old partner with mock concern. "Lien's still starving you I see, Taka-san."

Grinning, Harry slid his thumb inside his belt. "Not lately, as she would say. Oh, I'm forgetting introductions." He turned toward a woman behind him. "Old partner, meet new partner. Garreth Mikaelian, Vanessa Girimonte."

Girimonte made Garreth think of a panther—long, lithe, and mahogany dark with hair cropped to velvet shortness. Even her name purred.

He held out his hand. "Glad to meet you."

"Likewise." She shook his hand, then stepped back, dark eyes dissecting him. Reaching into the breast pocket of her slack suit jacket, she pulled out a pencil-thin cigar and lit it. "I don't know, Harry. For me the lean, hungry look and mirror glasses add up to menace, not boyish charm, but I suppose you can still be right. If the old adage about cold hands holds true, he definitely has to be warmhearted."

Garreth winced. "Harry, don't tell me you've been trying to sell her on me."

Harry grinned. "I want you two to be friends." He picked up his coat. "Come on, we'll show you the hideout."

Girimonte frowned. "Now? Harry, we—" She broke off as he raised his brows. "Go ahead. If you don't mind, though, I'll stay here to get our woman's description in circulation and see what possibles missing persons has."

"Sounds good." Harry headed for the door. "See you later. A fine officer," he said in the corridor, "except maybe a workaholic. A bit like you that way, Mik-san. I think she also has ambitions of being chief someday."

"She didn't seem too happy about you leaving. What are you working on?"

Harry grimaced. "The usual assortment . . . a liquor store clerk shot during a holdup, some nut case who walked into a clinic in the mission district Friday afternoon and opened fire with a shotgun—killed a nurse and wounded three patients—and a woman found in Stow Lake this morning."

"Then you shouldn't have to bother with me right now. I'm tired from the drive anyway. I'll find a hotel, then this evening we—"

"Hotel!" Harry interrupted. "Nothing doing. You're staying with us." He punched the elevator button.

Visions of a solicitous Lien plying him with an endless succession of the dishes he used to love ran through Garreth's head. The situation would not be like last night at home, where everyone was so busy talking that they paid no attention to anyone else's appetite or lack of it. Lien would notice he ate nothing. And she would try to find out why. Panic flickered in him. "I don't want to put you to any trouble."

Harry rolled his eyes. "You're not putting us to any trouble. You'll be saving my hide, in fact, because Lien will have it if you *don't* stay with us."

The argument echoed familiarly in Garreth's head. Harry had always said the same thing when dragging him home to dinner with them. He found himself reacting the same, too; mention of Lien melted away his resistance. How could he refuse anything to someone he owed so much?

He sighed as the elevator doors opened and they stepped inside. "All right. You have a guest." He would work out something—perhaps hypnotize her into thinking he ate normally. "Now tell me about Lane's apartment."

3

She had gone to ground almost under their noses, just moving west of her old Telegraph Hill apartment. Harry parked with his wheels turned into the curb to keep them from rolling down the steep street and pointed at a house half a block below, a two-story blue Victorian structure with bay windows and white gingerbread.

"She has the second floor."

Seeing the house gave Garreth a sharply uneasy feeling, compounded by a sense of being late for an appointment and that he stood on the edge of a trap. The knowledge that the trap could no longer be sprung somehow changed nothing. Perhaps it was still a trap. The house tugged at him.

"She hasn't been around for months but you still think you're close to catching her. Why?"

"Her downstairs neighbor, a guy named Turner, the guy who ID'd her, says there's a guy with a key who had been coming in Sunday afternoons to collect Barber's mail and check the apartment, and once a month with a cleaning woman. Then starting just before we found the apartment, Turner noticed the mailbox being emptied every couple of days. He knew it was still the guy and not Barber doing it, because he met the guy at the mailbox one evening. The guy didn't say so but Turner got the feeling he was hoping to find Barber in. He must have some reason to think she might be showing up."

Garreth started. Lane had a friend? Someone close enough to entrust with keeping an eye on her apartment? His pulse leaped. Another vampire? He could not understand a vampire choosing daylight visits, but would Lane trust one of the humans she despised and preyed on? Vampire or human, though, neither jibed with her claims of loneliness when she was asking him to become her companion.

She could have lied, of course.

"Have you talked to this guy?"

"We will as soon as we find him." Harry sighed. "So far all we have is a description: fifties, five-ten, 180 to 190 pounds, gray at the temples, blue eyes, mustache, and glasses. He's never given Turner his name and since we've been around, Turner hasn't seen him to get a car description or license number. I was about to talk Serruto into a stakeout for him when I called you. After you said you were coming out—"

"You thought you'd let me volunteer for the job," Garreth interrupted dryly.

Harry grinned.

"You know Serruto's told me I'm only riding along on this. Period."

"So we won't tell him." His ex-partner's eyes widened with innocence. "It isn't as if you'll actually be *doing* anything, just sitting here for a couple of days until you get a license number, or happen to tail the car home. Any citizen might do the same. Of course, you'll pass the information on to me for action."

"Of course." Would he? Did he dare give Harry

someone who knew Lane well? "Let me trade cars with you. My red beast isn't exactly inconspicuous."

"You don't say." Harry grinned. Digging into his trousers, he produced the car keys. "We'll go back for it as soon as we've visited Armour, Hayenga, and Kriszcziokaitis."

Garreth blinked.

"Accountants," Harry said. "I started wondering how the rent and other bills are paid with Barber gone. Maybe this guy does that, too. So I contacted the landlord to find out." He started the car. "His accounting department finally called back on Friday. The rent check comes from Armour, Hayenga, and Kriszcziokaitis. I was going to talk to them then, but—"

"But a wacko walked into that mission clinic with his shotgun and upset your schedule," Garreth finished for him.

Harry nodded. "Let's go see them before anything else interferes."

4

The accountant firm's tastefully understated offices occupied most of a skyscraper floor in the middle of San Francisco's financial district, and judging by the directory inside the double glass doors, it included several generations of Armours, Hayengas, and Kriszcziokaitises.

Harry eyed the sculpture and original oils around the reception area and dragged in a deep breath. "Smell the money."

The stunningly beautiful receptionist directed them down the corridor to the office of one Margrethe Kriszcziokaitis, a handsome woman in her forties, to argue out what they wanted.

Ms. Kriszcziokaitis smiled politely. "Sergeant Takananda, I understand your situation and I would like to help, but I just don't know what I can tell you. I know nothing about this Barbara Madell."

Harry sent back an equally professional smile. "But your firm has been paying her rent for over a year and a half. I respect your desire to maintain the confidentiality of your clients, but I remind you that the woman is a suspect in a murder case."

Ms. Kriszcziokaitis tented her fingers. "The woman

isn't our client, strictly speaking. We only pay her bills."

"Then you must know where she is. How does she give you her instructions?"

"She gives us none, Sergeant. The instructions come from another party."

Harry straighted. "Someone else's money is paying her bills? Whose?"

The accountant leaned back in her chair. "I'm sorry. I'm not free to divulge that information, Sergeant. Unless, of course, you come back with a court order."

Harry's expression never changed but his body language told Garreth how hopeless Harry considered that possibility. He stood. "Perhaps we will. Thank you." Leaving the office, he muttered to Garreth, "Do you think it's the guy?"

"She's a beautiful woman. What do *you* think?" But this time Garreth knew he lied. There could be only one possible person paying, the person who had so much money to spend. *A woman with hypnotic powers can learn a great many investment tips from the business giants she beds,* Lane had told him. "Damn." He felt his pockets. "I think I dropped my notebook in there. Go on and I'll catch up with you at the elevator."

He stepped back into Kriszcziokaitis's office. As she looked up with a frown, he pulled off his glasses and caught her gaze. "A moment more of your time, please. Tell me, is a Madelaine Bieber paying Madell's bills?"

The accountant's pupils pulsated with an inner struggle. It lasted only a moment, however, before she surrendered. "Yes. She's a very old and respected client."

"How old?"

"She's been with us since 1941."

That sounded about right. "And in that time she's

paid the bills for a number of young women, hasn't she?"

"Yes."

All of them Lane herself with different aliases. What a convenient solution to the problem of finances through numerous identity changes.

"Please write down the name of her bank for me." The money belonged to her family; they should be able to find it.

The accountant scribbled on a memo pad and ripped off the sheet.

Folding the sheet and putting it away in the inside pocket of his sports jacket, Garreth smiled at her. "Now please forget that I came back and we had this conversation."

He slipped out of the office.

Outside the reception area, Harry held the elevator, calmly ignoring the glares of the passengers. "Hard time finding the notebook? Strange. I don't remember you having one in there at all."

The doors closed and the car started down.

Garreth grinned while conscience stabbed him over the lies and half lies to come. *I'm sorry, Taka-san; you deserve better.* "What sharp eyes you have, Grandpa. No, it was just an excuse to spend more time in there and hint we know who Lane's patron is. She didn't turn a hair, though. She's one cool lady."

Harry glanced sideways at him. "Why didn't you ask her before we left?"

Garreth gave him a thin smile. "You don't want to know I'm doing anything except riding along." *And I don't want you hearing Lane Barber's and Mada Bieber's names together. You'd go hunting the connection between them.*

5

Watching Lane's apartment had to be the most un-comfortable stakeout of his career, Garreth reflected. Between the boredom of inactivity and weariness from the sleep he had missed since leaving Baumen, daylight dragged so heavily that he felt as if he moved through molasses. Despite his glasses and the shade of Harry's car, his head also throbbed from the sunlight. If only he had come in summer, when heat in the central valley would be pulling sea air in through the Golden Gate and blanketing the city in thick, beautiful fog. That might make the day bearable, and the jumble of police calls coming over Harry's scanner interesting instead of irritating.

What are you doing here anyway, Mikaelian? The object of agreeing to this was to fail, so the police would not learn the name of Lane's friend. He would do best at that by being somewhere else, such as Harry's house, so he could not possibly see the man arrive. With Lien gone, either working at her studio or teaching her grade school art classes, whichever she did on Mondays, the house would be empty. He could be sleeping. He ought to be. So why was he suffering this daylight vigil in Harry's car up the hill from the blue house?

A rich laugh echoed in his head. *Because I want you here, lover.*

Staring down at the house, he knew it was true. Lane had meant him to find it, and her trap still retained its power.

Garreth fought the house's pull by laying back in the seat, closing his eyes, and forcing himself to listen to the scanner. For a while it worked. The radio traffic brought a flood of memories, of patrolling in uniform, of becoming an inspector and working for robbery, then homicide. The radio and car sounded and felt so familiar he could almost believe he had never left. When the radio announced, "Inspectors 55," Harry's and his old number, it even brought him automatically upright, groping for a mike to roger the call.

That shattered the illusion. He had no mike. Inspectors 55 were now Harry and Girimonte. And the blue Victorian house sat down the street whispering its siren call at him.

Garreth climbed out of the car and sauntered down the street. What the hell? Without Lane around, what harm could there be in going down for a look?

At the house steps he resisted the urge to glance around for anyone watching him. Few people questioned someone who appeared assured and going about his business. Hesitancy or furtiveness, however, caused suspicion. Passing the door of the lower apartment, pain burned at the edge of perception, warning him of the fire that would sear him if he attempted to enter the dwelling uninvited. Upstairs, however, the hallway and door remained cool. Rooms ceased to be a dwelling if they were empty or the occupant had died.

Still, he hesitated outside. *Watch the visiting cop get arrested for breaking and entering.*

But he was not breaking in. He pressed against the door.

Wrench.

Darkness filled the apartment—delicious, cool darkness without a single ray of daylight leaking in through the blackout drapes over the bay window. That alone told him a vampire lived here. The darkness of Lane's other apartment the first time he visited her in his human days remained indelibly imprinted in memory. He had been blind, groping his way uncertainly until she turned on a lamp.

Now he saw perfectly well and reveled in relief from the sun. Despite feeling Lane around him. She might not have lived here long, but she had imprinted herself firmly on the room, from her old-fashioned taste in furniture—overstuffed couch and chairs, a wicker basket chair, colonial-style desk and chair—to personal belongs. The type tray on the wall held an assortment of stones, animal teeth, marbles, a rodent skull, and other small treasures she had collected as a child. Books and toys filled bookcases built in on either side of the fireplace: children's books, others on the occult, music, history, and medicine; old dolls; a cast-iron toy stove; a miniature tea set. Original oils and watercolors Lane had bought around the world hung on the walls while several small sculptures stood between old photographs on the mantel. Anna Bieber had identical photographs in her home, a wedding picture of her and her husband and another of Lane seated with her next youngest sister and a girl cousin on the running board of an old touring car.

The room echoed so strongly of Lane's presence that Garreth found himself holding his breath, waiting for her to appear, smiling seductively and offering him the world if only he would give up his ties to humanity.

An envelope leaned against one of the sculptures on the mantel. He noted it and started to turn away, then stopped short. Precise, square handwriting on the outside said: MADA. He stared, his breath caught somewhere in the middle of his chest. Someone had been here who knew her real name?

Even as he imagined Harry coming in with a search warrant and stumbling across the note, his hand reached for it.

The square handwriting continued on the sheet of thick, cream-colored stationery inside.

Dear Mada,

   I wish I could bring this myself, but since I have not yet been invited in, Leonard is delivering it. Contact me as soon as possible. It is urgent. I regret not being able to be more specific, but this is a matter better not detailed in writing. For the moment, I can be reached at Leonard's.

Irina

Garreth shoved the note into his coat pocket along with the memo bearing the name of Lane's bank. No, this note must not be left where Harry might find it. It had clearly been written by another vampire.

Another vampire.

Remembering when Lane had talked about the vampire who made her, he took the note out to read the signature again. Could this Irina be Irina Rodek? A beautiful woman, Lane had said, describing her, exquisite as a Dresden figurine, with sable hair and eyes. . . .

His grandmother's warning rang in his head and cold trickled through him. Irina Rodek had eyes the color of violets.

Now the echoes in the apartment seemed less those

of Lane than the clang of a closing trap.

It took several seconds to realize that the metallic sounds were real, but not in the apartment. They came from the lower hall. Garreth caught his breath. Someone had closed a mailbox. Leonard?

Footsteps hissed across tile.

Garreth spun, looking for a place to hide. The man must not find—

The thought broke off at the bang of the front door. Cursing, he sprinted for the apartment door. The man was leaving!

Wrench!

In the hallway he vaulted over the railing onto the middle of the stairs and half scrambled, half fell down the rest of the flight to the lower hall. A car started outside. Jerking open the front door, Garreth raced across the porch and down the steps. As in his dreams, the brilliant sunshine slapped him like a hammer. He fought through it to the street, swearing every step of the way. The visitor was the man Harry wanted. What he saw of the man as the car pulled away matched the description Harry had given him. But there was no chance to reach Harry's car in time to tail the man, no time for anything more than catching the BMW's license number.

Only when he had it written down on Irina's envelope did he remember that his object had been to miss the man. He laughed wryly. Foiled by cop reflexes.

Or had he done the right thing after all? Garreth fingered the envelope. If Irina really posed the threat his grandmother's feeling indicated, he dared not stumble around in ignorance. He must learn something about her, in which way she might be dangerous, and exactly how deadly. So he needed this Leonard.

He trudged up the hill to the car and started it. The

scanner crackled to life. If only he had been able to tail the man. Then he would know who Leonard was and still be able to pretend the stakeout had failed. With just a license number, though, he had to tell Harry so his old partner could run a registration check on the car for the name and address of its owner.

Then again, he reflected, listening to the scanner, maybe not.

6

It took almost fifteen minutes to locate a black-and-white unit with a familiar face in it. Pulling up alongside on the passenger side, he rolled down his window and shouted across at the patrol car's driver, "Kostmayer. Dane Kostmayer. Hey, remember me, Garreth Mikaelian?"

The driver glanced over, frowning, then started. Another classic double take. Grinning, he motioned Garreth to turn up a side street. Once parked, both officers climbed out of their car and Kostmayer loped back to meet Garreth at the rear bumper with a staggering slap on the back.

"Mikaelian, you old devil. What've you been doing with yourself? I heard you quit after your partner got shot."

Garreth nodded. "I'm still a cop but in a smaller department." He pulled out his Baumen badge and ID.

"I'd say smaller." Kostmayer snorted. "So what are you doing back here? Vacation?"

Garreth nodded again. "Visiting Harry Takananda and looking around . . . and until I spotted you and got distracted, I was tailing one gorgeous lady."

"Tailing?" Kostmayer's partner said.

"We were drinking coffee at tables next to each other at Ghirardelli Square and started talking. We hit it off great, but when she left I realized she hadn't given me her name. So I jumped in my car—"

"Your car?" The partner pointedly eyed the California plate on the front bumper.

Garreth shrugged. "Harry's car. He loaned it to me to use while I'm here. I was hoping to catch her and ask her name, but then I spotted you and got distracted. Now it looks like I've lost her."

Kostmayer shook his head. "That's too bad. Sorry."

"Except . . ." Garreth smiled. "I got her license number. It's a personalized plate: PHILOS. Do you suppose I could ask for a little favor?"

Kostmayer and his partner exchanged glances and grinned. "Sure thing. Run it, Ricardo."

The partner slid into the car. Garreth heard him call the dispatcher.

"I really appreciate this, Dane."

"A favor for an old friend. What's it like working in Baumen, Kansas?"

They chatted until the partner climbed back out of the car. "You didn't tell us she was driving a BMW. She also has a Pacific Heights address. That's nice taste in women, Mikaelian." He handed Garreth a page from a notebook, scribbled with a name and address. "But it looks like your lady is married. The car is registered to a Leonard Eugene Holle."

Garreth eyed the paper with pretended disappointment. "Maybe she's his daughter? Anyway, however it turns out, thanks again. I owe you one."

"We'll get together some evening before you leave and you can buy me a beer."

He stood watching while the two officers climbed back in their car and drove away. Then, grinning in satisfaction, he headed for his own car. Now to have a little chat with Mr. Holle.

7

The short burp of a siren behind him several blocks later brought a quick rush of anxiety—was Kostmayer coming back for something?—which quickly escalated to low panic with a glance in the rear-view mirror. The flashing light behind him came not from a light bar but the pop-on bubble of an inspector's car. Had Kostmayer's partner used Garreth's name in checking the registration? Had word of it reached Serruto?

Biting his lip, he pulled over. The other car stopped alongside. He found himself looking into the long face of Dean Centrello, and beyond him to a grinning Earl Faye at the wheel, his hair as much of an unkempt mane as ever.

"Small world, isn't it?" Faye asked.

Garreth groaned inwardly. A chance meeting. That bitch Lady Luck. He had had to *hunt* for someone to talk into running his registration, but when the last person he wanted was a fellow cop, two former colleagues fell over him before he even managed to leave North Beach.

He forced a smile. "Hi, guys."

Centrello shook his head incredulously. "It really is you, Mikaelian."

Faye said, "I told you so. If you'd watch the evening news like a normal person instead of insisting your family eat supper around a table and talk to each other, you'd have recognized him, too." He grinned at Garreth. "Hey, man, it's good to see you again. Where you headed?"

Garreth shrugged. "Just driving."

"Oh, I thought maybe you'd made the guy who's been visiting the Barber chick's apartment. Harry said you were watching the place this afternoon."

A string of profanities ran through Garreth's head. So much for secrecy. With Faye's motor mouth, Serruto would know about this meeting before the end of the day. "All right, yes. I got lucky, too. I have the man's name and address. I was just headed back for Bryant Street to tell Harry."

"That's two breaks for Takananda today," Centrello said.

Garreth raised his brows and breathed a sigh of relief that neither man appeared to notice that driving west was a strange way to reach Bryant Street to the south.

"Someone dropped a dime on the mission clinic shooter," Faye said. "He and Girimonte are out now picking up the turkey. Hey, we're headed downtown, too. Follow us on in and we can catch up on old times while you wait for Harry."

Garreth saw no way to refuse without arousing curiosity, if not suspicion. He gave them his broadest smile. "Sure. Great."

Riding up in the elevator at Bryant Street, he felt the same prisoner sensation he had meeting the reporters in Baumen. Faye and Centrello seemed oblivious to his discomfort, though. If anything, Centrello's expression contained envy. "Harry says you're into running these days. It's sure thinned you down."

"Sometimes I think about running," Faye said, "and then I start wondering why should I deliberately inflict pain on myself and deprive my brain of oxygen? I remember this case last year. We were called out to the Great Highway early one morning for a body in the northbound lane by Golden Gate Park. More of a grease spot really. The dude is squashed flat. Almost every bone broken. And the first car must have dragged him . . . smeared blood and skin down the highway for a good hundred feet."

Garreth could not help smiling. Faye always relished a story with gory detail.

The elevator stopped. They stepped off. Faye never missed a syllable. "He must have been hit by a dozen cars before people realized what was going on and someone blocked the lane so the traffic would go around. He turned out to be a runner. Went clear around Golden Gate Park every morning—did it for years. We figured he was a hit-and-run, but you know what the post turned up? He'd died of a heart attack. He was dead before the first car hit him. Can you beat that? Here's this dude running miles every day and in great shape, then all of a sudden . . ." Faye snapped his fingers. "Think about it, Mikaelian."

Garreth chuckled.

The amusement died in an icy drench of dismay as they walked into homicide. He stopped short, staring.

In Serruto's office, Julian Fowler stood up, smiling.

Garreth swore silently. What was the writer doing here?

Fowler came out of the office, followed by an attractive young woman and a poker-faced Serruto. "I dare say this is a bit of a surprise, Mikaelian."

The height of understatement. Garreth dragged his

feet loose from the floor to move farther into the room. "I . . . thought I left you in Kansas."

Fowler grinned. "Sorry, no. I followed you. Or to be perfectly accurate, I preceded you. I flew out on Friday, after Anna told me that you were going on holiday. Thanks to Miss Kirkwood here and the rest of the public relations section, who have been splendid help, I'm ready to start my research."

The young woman smiled. "It's a pleasure to work with such a well-known writer."

The air in Garreth's lungs felt as thick as if tainted by garlic. Research! That had to mean records of the case, the report of fingerprints found in Lane's Telegraph Hill apartment, prints identified as Madelaine Bieber's from the records of her 1941 arrest for assault, and photographs of Lane obtained from her agent. "You don't mean you're still thinking of writing about this case?"

"Too right!" Fowler's light eyes glittered. "It's absolutely fascinating. You're going to make a marvelous protagonist."

Every detective in the room turned to stare except Serruto, who leaned against the side of his office door with arms crossed and gaze fixed on the far corner of the ceiling.

Panic welled up in Garreth. His one protection against someone realizing that Mada Bieber and Lane Barber were the same person was their apparent age difference. Fowler's background in horror legends, though, made him one man capable of seeing the real truth in the facts, of seeing how Lane could be Mada and what she was . . . and by extension, what Garreth Mikaelian had become. He made his voice sound casual. "What about the war story you came over here to research?"

Fowler shrugged. "That'll wait." He raised a brow. "You're bloody reluctant, I must say. Most people would love to be written about." One brow arched. "I can make you immortal, you know." Both brows skipped. "You find that amusing?"

Garreth bit back his wry smile. "No." *Just redundant*. "Mr. Fowler, I'm not most people. Count me out of your project."

The woman from public relations frowned. "Officer Mikaelian, the department has agreed to extend Mr. Fowler every possible courtesy."

"I don't work for this department," Garreth pointed out. "Lieutenant, may I wait for Harry in your office?"

One corner of the lieutenant's mouth twitched. He waved Garreth by, then followed him inside and closed the door. "I'm glad someone else doesn't want to join the circus." He eyed Garreth. "You look exhausted. Are you that out of shape for stakeouts?"

Garreth started. "What stakeout?"

Serruto ticked his tongue against his teeth. "What stakeout. Mikaelian, I can see the parking lot from my window. I watched you drive out in Takananda's personal car. Why would you use a vehicle other than your own except to be less conspicuous, and why would you want to be inconspicuous except—"

"All right." Garreth sighed. "Yes, I was watching the apartment for Harry."

"And?"

Garreth showed him Holle's name and address. "Here's the guy who's been looking after the apartment. I swear I did not accost him and interrogate him, Lieutenant, sir. I didn't even tail him. I only took down the license number and ran a registration check."

"Good boy." Serruto glanced toward the squad room. "Ah. Ms. Public Relations has taken her pet away and the conquering heroes have returned." He opened the office door.

Harry and Girimonte swaggered into the squad room. Harry shook clasped hands above his head.

"We got the turkey! He's signed, sealed, and delivered to the jail."

Thumbs went up around the room.

"Did you get the gun, too?" Serruto asked.

Girimonte lit one of her sleek cigars. The sweet smell of it drifted past the lieutenant to Garreth, temporarily drowning the blood scents. "Of course. It's at the lab." She blew a perfect smoke ring.

Harry headed for the coffeepot. On the way he caught Garreth's eye. "How was your sightseeing this afternoon, Mik-san? Has the old town changed much? Glad to see the cable cars back?"

Garreth grimaced. "Forget the subterfuge, Harry. Serruto knows everything." He slid around Serruto out of the office to hand the notebook page to Harry. "However, I did see the individual we hoped I would."

Harry's sheepish wince vanished in a grin. "The luck of the Irish." He passed the page to Girimonte. "Well, partner, let's run Mr. Holle through records and pay him a visit, unless you're hot to start on the shooter's paperwork?"

"Hot for paperwork?" Girimonte blew another smoke ring and bared her teeth. "Harry, honey, I have absolutely no interest in starting any of it without you. We've got all night to write reports." In one sinuous motion she stubbed out her cigar and headed for the door.

8

Holle's house matched the BMW for quiet elegance
—faintly Gothic, three and a half stories of red brick
with pointed windows gleaming gold in the late afternoon sunlight and an entrance of broad double doors
set into a pointed stone arch. Eyeing it, a sharp pang
of apprehension stabbed Garreth. He found himself
reluctant to leave the car. A reaction to his grandmother's warning, or perhaps a feeling of his own? Or
was it more from this sense of being just a ride-along
that had grown in him riding in the back seat, like a
civilian or prisoner, while Harry and Girimonte up
front gleefully rehashed their capture of the mission
clinic shooter, reliving a shared experience Garreth
had no part of. Another match burning on his bridge.

Garreth forced himself out of the car. Misgivings or
not, he had to hear Holle's answers, and head off
dangerous ones.

Fire licked at him as he approached the doorway.

A middle-aged woman in a light gray dress answered the bell. A strong scent of perfume drifted

from her. After studying Harry's identification with a frown, she opened the door wide. "Please come in. I'll see if Mr. Holle is available."

The flames in Garreth snuffed out.

She left them waiting in a baronial-looking hall of wood paneling and a soaring ceiling while she disappeared up the broad staircase.

Girimonte rolled her eyes. "Jesus. I like Emeraude, but that woman smells like she bathes in it. I wonder how a servant gets away with so much perfume."

A few minutes later, when a man matching Harry's description of Lane's caretaker came down the stairs, Girimonte's question had an answer. Leonard Holle reeked of cologne himself, a spicy male scent but still so strong it overpowered even the blood smells around Garreth. Holle could not have smelled a pigsty next to him.

He put on his glasses to take their badge cases and read the identification. "Inspector Girimonte, Sergeant Takananda, and . . ." His brows rose at Garreth's silver oval shield with its blue seal of Kansas in the center, so different from the seven-pointed stars the other two carried. He looked up with a smile. "You're a long way from—" Both sentence and smile died in a start.

Panic washed through Garreth. That was recognition flaring in Holle's eyes, and since it had not come until he looked up from the ID to Garreth himself, it had to be recognition not of who but *what* he was. And it could not be because Holle himself was also a vampire. Beneath the heavy scent of his cologne was a blood smell. Lane had had none.

". . . from home, Officer Mikaelian," Holle finished. He handed back the badge case.

"Officer Mikaelian has special knowledge in this case and is working with us as a consultant," Harry said.

Holle's eyes did not leave Garreth's face. "What case is that, Sergeant?"

"Do you suppose we might sit down somewhere to discuss it?" Girimonte asked.

Holle blinked. "Oh. Of course." He glanced toward an archway and the living room beyond, golden in the late sun shining through the front windows. "I think we'll be most comfortable in the library." Turning toward the stairs, he led the way up to the next floor.

Breathing came no easier. Holle *did* know. The library had drapes as heavy as those in Lane's or Garreth's apartments. With the doors slid closed, the only light came from a lamp that Holle switched on.

He waved them to deep leather easy chairs around a fireplace and took another for himself. The leather, smooth and cool and smelling faintly of saddle soap, squeaked as Garreth settled in. Around them, bookshelves filled the walls from floor to ceiling.

Holle leaned back in another squeak of leather, stroking his mustache. "Now what's this about, Sergeant?"

"You've been collecting the mail at an apartment in North Beach belonging to a girl named Barbara Madell."

Holle hesitated only a moment before replying. "Yes. Is there some problem with that? I have her keys and can show you a letter from her asking me to look after the apartment while she's gone. I've done it often before."

"She's a friend of yours then?" Girimonte asked.

Holle considered. "More a friend of a friend, but she needed someone who could be expected to stay in one place so I ended up with the job."

"That's a bit unusual, isn't it?" Girimonte said. "Asking a near stranger to look after your place?"

Holle frowned. "Not among my circle. What *is* this about?"

"How long since you've seen her?" Harry asked.

The frown deepened. "I'm not sure. About a year and a half I suppose. Sergeant—"

"She's been gone that long and you've never worried? Or is *that* common in your circle, too?"

"It is with Lane. She's a singer and a footloo—"

"Lane?"

Holle rolled his eyes. "That *is* her name . . . Lane Barber."

"Then how do you explain the name on the mailbox?"

"Oh for God's sake! Names are a game with her. She's always changing the ones on her mailbox. Sometimes there are groups of them, all outrageous. Surely that can't be what this is about. As far as I know, using different names is no crime if there's no intent to defraud."

"What this is about, Mr. Holle," Girimonte said with a thin smile, "is murder."

Holle stiffened. "I beg your pardon?"

Harry leaned forward. "On August 30, 1983, a visiting businessman named Gerald Mossman was dumped in the bay with his throat cut and neck broken. We have evidence linking Lane Barber to the death."

"Lane?" Holle's jaw dropped. "That's impossible."

"Before he was killed," Garreth said, "someone drained him of blood. The autopsy found two punctures in his neck that the pathologist said could have been made by large-gauge hypodermic needles."

Holle stared hard at Garreth. "And you think a charming young woman like *Lane* would do such a . . . barbaric thing? Ridiculous! You should be looking for some demented cultist."

"On September 7 she attacked and attempted to kill Officer Mikaelian here, who was a member of the San Francisco Police Department at the time," Harry said. "She bit him savagely on the throat."

"I can hardly be mistaken about who attacked me.

How could you be unaware we were looking for your friend? The papers were full of the case at the time, complete with pictures of Miss Barber as a suspect."

"I—" Holle swallowed. Sweat gleamed on his forehead. The acid smell of it cut through the spicy sweetness of his cologne. "I was in Europe from the middle of August to the middle of September. I never heard anything about the case, I swear. When I came home, there was an envelope with keys and a letter from Lane saying she was leaving and asking me to look after her new apartment. I had no reason to think it was any different from the other times."

"Did she say where she was going?" Harry asked.

Holle shook his head. "I doubt she knew. I gather she just travels where the urge—or some man she's attached herself to—takes her."

"Suddenly you're visiting the apartment more frequently, according to her neighbors. Have you received word that she's due back soon?"

"No," Holle shook his head emphatically. "I haven't heard anything from her."

"Then why the increase in visits?"

For a moment Garreth wondered if he would answer. Holle's eyes flickered behind his glasses, as if his mind was racing frantically. His gaze slid back toward Garreth. "A friend of hers came to town and wanted to reach her. So I kept going over hoping Lane would have come back."

"What's the friend's name?" Girimonte asked.

Garreth held his breath. Holle had not contradicted him at the mention of hypodermic needles, though he must know that Garreth knew what made those punctures, and he was being evasive about the reason for checking Lane's apartment so often. Still, there was always a chance he might mention the name Irina.

"I—I'm sorry, I don't know," Holle said.

In relief, Garreth resumed breathing.

Harry frowned. "How the hell can you not know? You talked to this person, didn't you?"

To Garreth's astonishment, the panic in Holle evaporated. His face smoothed and his voice steadied. "I never met her before. Mutual friends in Europe had told her that I might know where to reach Lane."

"Exactly what is this circle of people you run with, Mr. Holle?" Girimonte asked.

Holle sighed. "Before my parents died and left me this house, I worked for one of the airlines as a ticket agent. There is a subculture among airline employees. Since we had free flight privileges, we often flew to different places for weekends—to a jazz festival or the Mardi Gras or the opening of a new opera. Just about anything. We stayed with friends when we got there. Except very often the friend wasn't someone we knew directly. Sometimes the friend's friend wasn't even home. It wasn't uncommon to be given a key, stay in the house, and leave without ever meeting the people who lived there. By the same token, friends and friends of friends of friends stay here with me while they're in San Francisco. I've stopped working for a living but I've kept my friends."

Harry's almond-shaped eyes narrowed. "And Lane's friend came by one of these indirect connections?"

"Exactly."

Garreth glanced around the darkened library. All those friends of friends could not be just airline employees.

"Yet she never told you her name?" Girimonte asked.

Holle sighed again, this time in exasperation. "Of course she told me, but I have a terrible memory that way. I don't know that it would help you anyway, since if she had any idea where Lane is, she wouldn't have come to me. If I remember her name, or I hear anything from Lane, I'll contact you immediately. I really can't believe Lane is involved in anything so . . . psychotic, and the sooner she can clear her name the better." Holle stood. "Is there anything else you need?"

"Not for the time being, no." Harry gave him an inscrutable Oriental smile. "But we'll keep in touch."

Holle's steps faltered only a moment as he crossed to slid open the doors. "Of course."

Smiling politely, he saw them down to the front door.

As it boomed closed behind them, Girimonte bared her teeth. "We ought to have leaned on him, Harry. You know he's lying."

And hiding a hell of a lot, Garreth thought. "But not lying about knowing where Lane is."

Harry nodded. "I'm pretty sure he didn't know anything about Mossman's murder or the attack on Garreth, either."

Girimonte scowled up at the house. "I'll bet he believes Barber did it, though, and what about that story of some friend looking for her?"

"Oh, I think that's true enough," Harry said. "The lie is he doesn't remember the friend's name. We may have to chat with him again about that, but for the time being, since records says he's clean, we'll leave him alone. Besides, we have reports to write, partner, which we'd better start if Garreth and I want to make it home before Lien's dinner dries up in the oven."

9

Lights by the front door and shining through the dark from the living-room windows above the garage welcomed them. *Another homecoming,* Garreth reflected, squeezing the ZX into the driveway beside Harry's car. How many evenings had he spent here? Dozens. Hundreds. After Marti died, it had been more home than his apartment had, a sanctuary from the stress of the job, from personal pain. He climbed over the gearshift and out the passenger door.

"Harry! Garreth!" Lien rushed out of the house with her salt-and-pepper hair flying around her face, throwing herself into her husband's arms first, then breaking loose to circle the front of the cars and give Garreth a fierce hug that almost smashed the trooper glasses in his breast pocket. The warm, salty scent of her blood flooded him.

Thirst seared his throat and closed like a fist around his stomach. Garreth fought for the control not to push her away.

Fortunately she released him and drew back, smiling. "It's so good to see you. This is just like old times . . . the two of you home after dark to a dinner kept from total mummification only by arcane Eastern cooking arts." Catching both their arms, she propelled them toward the door. "Honorable husband, you could at least have sent Garreth on ahead instead of making him wait while you finished your reports. I would have had time to find out all the personal news that bores you, like what his Maggie is like, and we could have finished off four or five rum teas and gotten comfortably smashed."

Harry grinned. "See the virtue of a Chinese wife? She still scolds, but with respect."

Lien pinched him through his suit coat.

Longing twisted in Garreth. The welcome and the fond bantering echoed so many other evenings. If only this one *could* be like those others.

Inside, Lien steered them past the stairs into the family room. They had changed it a little but the general flavor still remained—sleek, contemporary American furniture surrounded with Oriental touches, a Chinese vase here, a Japanese flower arrangement, shoji doors closing off the dining area, paintings by Lien with brush strokes as clean and elegantly simple as Chinese calligraphy.

Lien vanished through the dining room into the kitchen, calling back, "Your rum teas are on the coffee table. Relax while I heat dinner in the microwave."

Dinner. Garreth grimaced inwardly. *How are you going to fake your way through* this *one?*

He and Harry kicked off their shoes, shed their coats, and unclipped holsters from their belts. Harry plopped onto the couch. Picking up his cup of tea, he leaned back and propped his feet on the coffee table. "It really is like old times. Cheers."

Garreth curled up cross-legged in an easy chair. "Cheers." The odor of the rum wafted up from the tea, setting his stomach churning. He pretended to start a sip, yelped, and put the cup back down.

"Too hot?" Harry said. "Sorry."

"No problem. I'll just let it cool a bit." In the course of which he could "forget" to drink it at all. But there was still dinner to face. Could he even tolerate being at the table? The tantalizing smell of Lien's sweet and sour pork flooded the room, tearing him between longing at the memory of the taste and the nausea of his new preference's rejection of it.

Harry mentioned something about an evening several years earlier. Garreth nodded automatically, eyeing the patio doors. Perhaps a few breaths of night air would help clear his head and settle his stomach.

"Garreth," Lien called, "will you please come help me?"

Harry winked at him. "Careful, Mik-san. She just wants a chance to cross-examine you about your girlfriend and love life." He heaved to his feet and trailed after Garreth, still holding his teacup. "I'll come along to protect you."

Lien raised her brows at them. "I might have known both of you would come in. Very well, but no snitching bites before everything is on the table."

"Snitching bites? Us?" Harry said innocently.

Garreth smoothed his mustache. That was an idea. He feigned passes at the food while he and Harry helped move it into the dining area and sat down. And he kept talking, answering all Lien's questions about Baumen and Maggie at great length, telling every amusing anecdote he could think of, including Maggie setting up his patrol car. Lien seemed to have relaxed her rules about forbidding shoptalk, but he did not want to push his luck.

Lien shook her head. "I really believe the biggest danger you face on the street is other cops. I remember when this one was in uniform." She pointed at Harry. "Nickels glued over keyholes, lockers turned upside down, windows and doors of other patrol cars sealed with fingerprint tape with the officers inside, and then, of course, we mustn't forget the Fourth of July, that wonderful holiday when he could throw bottle rockets into other patrol cars as he passed them."

Harry grinned.

Garreth winked at him. "I guess I'd better never tell her about the time you and I unplugged the mike in Faye's and Centrello's car and it took them most of the morning to figure out why they couldn't roger their calls or reach dispatch."

Lien rolled her eyes. "*Boys* in blue indeed."

Miracle of miracles, she did not appear to notice that he only stirred his food around on his plate instead of eating it.

Then Harry, reaching for the pork a third time, stopped with his hand on the serving spoon to raise a brow at Garreth. "Hey, Mik-san, you're falling behind. Better clean up your plate before you lose your chance for seconds."

Now they were watching him. Garreth cursed silently. Could he possibly swallow one bite and keep it down for a few minutes? The lurch of his stomach said no. So did memory. That last solid meal he had eaten, in the hospital after Lane attacked him, had done an instant reverse. "That's all right. This is plenty. My eating habits have changed since I left." The understatement of the year.

Perfectly true, though. Yet guilt pricked him as if he had lied. *Well, aren't you?* By implication, by omission, hiding the truth and separating himself from two people he cared about. Starting a fire on his bridge he could blame only on himself.

10

He tried to sleep. With people here expecting him to live by daylight, he had to make himself rest at night. Surely he could manage that for a few days; he had done so in the beginning. The earth pallet and sheer tiredness should have helped, but his mind kept churning, tossing up images of Lane, Fowler, his grandmother, and Holle, of a small woman faceless but for violet eyes, of burning bridges and Gothic houses full of shadows and chill with danger. Garreth rolled over and pulled the top sheet up over his shoulders, but the images continued to spin behind his closed eyes, mixing together in endless varieties . . . Lane and the bridge, Fowler and the bridge, his grandmother and violet eyes, Lane and Fowler, Fowler and Holle.

Fowler and Holle! Garreth came wide awake, sucking in his breath. He sat up in bed. That could happen. Harry had no probable cause for requesting a search warrant for Lane's apartment, but Fowler's passion for details about his characters might well take him to Holle to charm his way into accompanying Lane's friend on the next visit to her apartment. Cold crawled up Garreth's spine. One look around —at the photographs duplicating some of Anna Bieber's, at the books inscribed to "Mada" and "Madelaine"—and Fowler would know what the police file on Mossman's murder might have already suggested, that Lane Barber and Madelaine Bieber were the same person.

Garreth had not looked into Lane's kitchen, but in her other apartment it had been empty, its cupboards barren of anything to cook in or eat from, not even a drinking glass. Lane, he knew, considered it a backstage area she never expected anyone to see and, therefore, not worth the trouble of stocking with props. What would it suggest to a horror writer, though, after reading the autopsy report on Mossman and seeing file photographs of Garreth's body and the wounds on his throat?

Garreth sucked in his lower lip. Fowler must not see the apartment. How to stop him, though? Attempting to keep the writer away from the apartment might draw his attention to it instead.

"Damn." His gut knotted. Throwing off the sheet, Garreth swung out of bed and paced the room. His grandmother was right; he should never have come back to San Francisco.

The urge to run beat at him. His suitcase sat invitingly by the dresser. All he had to do was slip away. Except it was too late to pack up and retreat. The very act of coming had brought the means for his destruction, and Fowler would still be here even after Garreth—

The thought broke off in a hurried reverse. Pack up? He grimaced. *You're a thick mick, you know that, Mikaelian? If there's a stake in your future, you deserve it.* He had been looking at the problem with Fowler from the wrong end. The solution was not preventing the writer from seeing the apartment, but keeping Lane's belongings out of his sight.

Relief and resolution washed away his weariness. Dressing, Garreth slipped out into the hall. Voices murmured in Harry's and Lien's bedroom. He glided silently past their door and down the stairs to the front door.

Wrench.

Outside, lights still showed in the houses along the street, each behind its narrow strip of grass and hedge. Except for a man walking his dog and an occasional passing car, though, the neighborhood was quiet. Garreth drew a deep breath, savoring the briny scent of the sea and the muted symphony of city sounds: distant traffic, barking dogs, threads of voices and music from nearby houses. Very different from night in the hills around Baumen, where a cow's bellow or coyote's yodel carried for miles in the stillness and the stars glittered cold and brilliant as ice chips overhead, but no less enjoyable.

Climbing into the passenger side of the ZX, he reached back behind the seat for his thermos. A few swallows finished off the remaining blood. Now the question was: Should he refill it and risk storage in Lien's refrigerator, or depend on nightly hunting with *its* attendant hazards?

That question could be answered later, he decided, crawling over the gearshift onto the driver's seat. Turning the key enough to free the steering wheel, he slipped the car into neutral and let it roll backward out of the drive, then he swung out and pushed it down the street. Harry knew the snarl of the ZX's engine too well to risk starting it in front of the house.

"Can't you get it started?"

Garreth spun to find the man who was walking the dog eyeing him from the sidewalk. The man's thoughts ran almost visibly across his face: *Man pushing car down the street in the middle of the night.*

Very suspicious. Possible car thief. Garreth thought fast. "The damn battery's down. I thought maybe if I got it rolling, that'd be enough to turn the engine over."

He gave the car an extra-hard push to make it move, then, jumping in, he cranked the key. The motor roared to life. With a smile and a wave at the man, Garreth drove away.

Two blocks later he let out his breath, but even then he made himself drive around at random for fifteen minutes, watching the rear-view mirror for patrol cars, in case the man with the dog had gone ahead and reported him as suspicious activity. Of the several black-and-whites he spotted, though, none showed any interest in him. Finally he headed for Lane's apartment.

11

Cleaning out the apartment went smoother than he had dared hope. The neighborhood was even darker and quieter than Harry's had been. Garreth parked at the curb, slipped soundlessly into the house and up the stairs through the apartment door to release the dead bolt from the inside. None of the furniture went, of course, just her personal possessions, as on her flight from Telegraph Hill. Four heavy cartons he found in the bedroom closet held everything—no doubt the very boxes she had used to move everything in. Four soundless trips downstairs had them all stashed in the car, albeit somewhat tightly, then he relocked the dead bolt from the inside and left.

Coasting down the hill before he started the engine, it struck Garreth that, of course, packing her effects was simple; Lane had planned it that way. She kept only what had personal meaning—mementos of her past and things of value and easy to carry—nothing cumbersome or that could be replaced with a charge card at any department store.

There was the small matter of what to do with everything once he had it out, of course, but he had had the drive over to North Beach to think about it. When he left San Francisco, he had stored his own belongings. Lane's things could join them. From the apartment he drove down to Hannes-Katsbulas Storage on the Embarcadero, parked, and slipped through the wire fence around the warehouse.

Less than fifty feet inside, three huge Rottweilers charged around the building, teeth bared.

Garreth stared straight at them. "At ease, fellows."

The dogs slowed, foreheads wrinkling.

"Sit."

They sat.

He patted each in turn on the head. "Good boys. Okay, come on with me. Let's go find the security man." And he trotted on with the three escorting him.

The security guard was having a cup of coffee in his office. Garreth's appearance in the doorway made him jump out of his chair, clawing for his gun. "Who the hell are you? How did you get in here?"

Garreth stared him straight in the eyes. "I have some things to put away. Will you please unlock the front gate for me?"

The gun barrel wavered, then returned to the holster. The guard moved to obey. In ten minutes Lane's cartons joined Garreth's in the compartment assigned to him.

Garreth did not linger. Just seeing the furniture, the boxes of his own books and photographs, and the big pastel an artist in the Cannery had done of Marti, set pain twisting in him. So many memories, sweet and bitter, were entombed here. Would he ever again have an apartment where it could all sit in the open? Did he ever want to? He locked the compartment.

At the gate he patted the dogs and caught the

guard's eyes one more time. "Please forget about this visit."

The padlock snapped closed through the gate chain with the guard's eyes staring through Garreth, already having forgotten him.

12

Driving north along the Embarcadero, Garreth
sucked in his lower lip. Now what? He still needed
information on Irina. Calling on Holle at this time of
night was probably not socially acceptable, however,
even if the man did keep company with vampires. His
thermos also needed refilling. Despite the risk of Lien
discovering the contents of the thermos, he decided
he preferred to have several days' food supply on hand
than to count on being able to slip out hunting every
night. But it was too early now to skulk around piers
after rats. Someone might see him. The traffic remained heavy along here and would be so until the
clubs in North Beach closed at two o'clock.

North Beach. Garreth pursed his lips. Lane always
found her supper there. Maybe Irina had discovered
the same hunting ground. And maybe someone had
seen her.

He parked just off the Embarcadero at the foot of
Broadway. From there he walked up toward Columbus, and within a few blocks had plunged into the

show he thought about so often while watching Baumen's Friday- and Saturday-night cruisers. Baumen must have tempered his memories, though, because he did not remember the sounds, lights, and smells as being this overwhelming . . . a bright sea of neon signs, jewel strings of headlights and taillights from four lanes of traffic, rumbling motors, honking horns, human voices calling and laughing, the raucous voices of barkers rising above all others as they shouted the virtues of the shows in their particular clubs at the humanity swarming along the sidewalks. The crowds jostled Garreth, people wearing everything from ragged jeans and torn sweat shirts to evening clothes, smelling of sweat, tobacco, alcohol, marijuana, perfume and cologne, and . . . blood.

Hunger surged in him, searing his throat. He shoved clenched fists into the pockets of his sports jacket. Were the blood scents really so much stronger now than he remembered from that first visit up here after his change, or was it that all blood smelled alike to him then? Experience had taught him the subtle differences between individuals, and between the clean, salty-metallic scent of healthy blood and the sour, bitter, or sickeningly sweet edge warning of pollution by disease and foreign substances.

Good thing you're not *hunting supper here,* he reflected. So many of the men and women pushing past him smelled of tainted blood, more than he had ever noticed in Bellamy or Baumen. It almost killed his appetite. Almost. Some people, which was obvious from appearance alone, had been indulging in drugs and alcohol. With others it was just as obvious their problem was disease. Some, though, looked outwardly so healthy. In Baumen, where he knew people, he could usually stop to greet someone like that and, in the course of a conversation, casually remark that the person did not look well and perhaps should see a doctor. Here, as in the theater in Bellamy, Garreth had to make himself let them go, even the man who passed him arm in arm with a healthy-smelling young man.

Watching the couple, Garreth suddenly listened to his own thoughts and grimaced bitterly. He walked up what he had always considered a vital, pulsing street, where he had always previously found excitement and color in the crowds, and what did he think about? Blood.

Setting his jaw, he made himself forget about his thirst and look at faces. Familiar ones began emerging from the crowd, mostly hookers, pimps, pickpockets, and assorted other vermin out from under their rocks for the night. Unlike previous visits to the area, though, they failed to recognize him in return. Several of the hookers even started to approach him, then veered off with a disgusted expression that told him they had belatedly spotted that indefinable something in his moves and carriage which stamped him *cop.*

Only one portly, well-dressed man failed to notice him; the pickpocket was too intent on prey, a couple at the corner with the flashy look of well-heeled tourists. Garreth watched the dip start forward to "accidentally" bump the man, and in the course of it relieve the tourist of his wallet.

Garreth glided close behind. "I wouldn't, Hick-ham," he murmured. "The tree of evil bears bitter fruit. Crime does not pay. The shadow knows."

Then, from the corner of his eye, while he pretended to focus on a display of sexy photographs outside one club, Garreth watched with an inward grin as the pickpocket flung around, looking in vain for a known face that had to be the source of the voice.

An instant later, glee passed into dismay. Beyond Hickham, pedestrians surged across the street at the light change. Among them came another familiar face—Julian Graham Fowler's.

Shit. Garreth spun away and hurriedly joined the crowd crossing to the next block up before the writer could see him. Of all people to meet. Not that it should be unexpected; every tourist visited North Beach sooner or later. What lousy luck Fowler chose tonight.

After half a block Garreth glanced back, and to his relief, saw no sign of Fowler. Even without the writer around, though, hunting Irina was a problem with nothing to go by but the description Lane had mentioned once in passing.

A mulatto hooker eyed him and brushed on past. He fell into step with her. This might be the place to start. "Don't rush off, honey. Talk to me."

She rolled her eyes. "We got nothing to talk about . . . Officer." She shook her head. "I don't know where vice finds you kids. Don't you have height and weight requirements anymore?"

Fine. Let her assume he was S.F.P.D. "I'm homicide, not vice. I'm looking for a woman who might have been hanging around the area the past week or so—small, dark hair, violet eyes. She isn't a professional, but she'll have been up here every night, hitting on a different guy each time."

The hooker snorted. "The amateurs cruise the bars, not the street."

"She has to walk through the street to reach the bars. You sure you haven't seen her?"

She thought a moment. "Violet eyes?"

"And dark hair. A petite woman, pretty. Foreign accent."

The hooker shook her head. "Nope. Sorry." She eyed him more closely and, smiling, moved closer. The scents of her blood and perfume caressed him. "You know, for being a cop and so skinny and all, there's still something kind of . . . interesting about you. Did you ever consider that just like you're not always on duty, neither am I?" Her voice went professionally husky. She leaned still closer, the warm, tantalizing scent of her blood setting hunger snarling in Garreth. "Your pistol starts weighing you down, little boy blue, come look me up." Her hand ran down his crotch. "The name's Anita."

If he stayed near her any longer, the hunger was going to take control of him and drag her into the nearest alley. "Anita," he echoed, then hurriedly moved away.

Distance helped him push hunger back into its cage. A passing couple helped more. The reek of garlic from what had to be their recent Italian meal snapped around his throat like a noose. Garreth did not collapse or choke enough to attract attention, but he leaned against a light pole for support while he fought for breath. By the time air moved freely through his lungs again, hunger had vanished in the profound pleasure of breathing.

He resumed asking about Irina. Questions to several more hookers and a number of barkers in the area all brought negative replies, however. No one remembered a woman of that description.

A glance at his watch showed fifteen minutes until the bars closed. Smoothing his mustache, he frowned thoughtfully and looked down the street, debating whether to try a few more questions or pack it in for the night and head for the piers.

The debate broke off as he felt eyes on him. Garreth turned to find a tall, lean young man in an Italian-cut suit glaring furiously. In one sweeping glance Garreth took in the carefully blow-dried hair, the silk shirt open halfway down the chest, and the bulging crotch of the tight trousers.

Garreth folded his arms. "What's your problem, cowboy?"

"You, Jack," the hustler snapped. "You're trespassing." His eyes flared red with the reflection of passing car lights.

Shock jolted Garreth. He sucked in his breath. A whiff of the incoming air told him no scent of blood came from the other man. "You—you're another."

The hustler closed on him. "Right, and this is my territory, Jack. There's plenty of game here for everyone, but you find some other block and fucking well stay there." Grabbing the front of Garreth's jacket and shirt, he jerked him almost off the ground. "Or I'll be forced to hurt you."

Every police officer learned to tolerate verbal abuse, but manhandling was another matter entirely. Garreth reacted without even thinking. A knee drove hard into the hustler's groin.

The man dropped into a groaning knot of pain on the sidewalk.

"Don't touch me," Garreth snapped. "Don't you *ever* touch me again, or *you'll* be the one hurt!"

People had stopped and were staring. Barkers for a couple of the clubs started forward.

Garreth whipped out his badge case for a quick flash at them. "Thanks, gentlemen, but I have it under control." He dragged the hustler to his feet and down the sidewalk. "Walk. We have things to talk about."

"We've got nothing to talk about." The hustler pulled loose from him and leaned against a building, grimacing. "I don't care if you are a cop. This is still my territory."

"I'm not after your fucking territory! Look, all I want is information."

"Information?" The hustler blinked, then frowned skeptically. "What kind of information?"

"About a woman . . . one of us. Small, dark hair, violet eyes. Eastern European accent. Have you seen or talked to her?"

"I don't think so, but then," the hustler said and grimaced wryly, "I don't move in exactly the same circles as some others of the blood around here."

125

The hair on Garreth's neck prickled. "Others? What circles?"

The hustler snorted. "Jesus. Where've you been living, Jack?" Then his eyes narrowed, a sly light glittering in them. "Say, maybe—"

"Ricky! Hey, Ricky," a female voice called. "Come on. I've got us a three—"

The voice stopped short. Garreth looked around and raised his brows at a blond hooker behind him.

She stared back, eyes hard, then focused past him on the hustler, her voice sounding casual. "A friend wants to buy the two of us a drink, Ricky . . . if you're interested."

After a hesitant glance at Garreth, the hustler said, "Sure I'm interested." He ducked around Garreth to follow her to a Continental at the curb. A man sat behind the wheel. As he climbed into the car, the hustler called over his shoulder, "I think maybe I can help you, Jack. Meet me back here in two hours and we'll discuss it."

13

Hunting quickly used up the two hours. Once he had recaptured the skill to hunt, Garreth slipped like a shadow through the darkness of the covered piers, using his hypnotic power on rats so he could pick them up to break their necks and slit their throats with a switchblade. It took only minutes to decide that he liked hunting around Baumen better. There he had the exhilaration of the run to and from the pastures, often with a curious coyote for escort, and blood from one cow would fill the thermos without harm to the animal, compared to the dozen or more rats that had to die here. The strain of keeping alert for sounds indicating possible discovery added no pleasure to the hunt, either.

Still, it was blood, and with both his stomach and thermos filled, he drove up to meet Ricky. The vampire was not there. Garreth waited, sure the hustler would show up sooner or later. The tone of his words made it clear that the discussion he had in mind was to fix a price on his information, and vermin like Ricky never wasted opportunities for making a buck.

After an hour Ricky had still not appeared, however, and Garreth gave up. The three-way trick with the hooker and her john must have proven more profitable than selling information to a cop. Driving back to Harry's house, he slid inside, stowed the thermos in the refrigerator, and slipped upstairs to fall into bed.

14

Pounding on the door and the sound of Lien calling his name dragged him back to consciousness. "Garreth? Garreth, we're leaving for work. Sleep in as long as you like, then help yourself to whatever you want for breakfast. I've left a message for you from *I Ching* on the kitchen table. Be sure to read it. We'll see you later."

So she still consulted the sage every morning to see what the day held for Harry, and today, for him. "Okay. Thanks," he mumbled.

Sleep in as long as he liked. He would. Sometime he had to see Holle, but afternoon would be soon enough. Late afternoon.

The thought trailed away as he sank back into sleep.

Sleep, not rest. He dreamed of stalking the hustler up Broadway. As he tried to catch the other vampire, however, he felt someone watching him. Lane? The spicy musk of her perfume curled out of the blood scents around him. He swore bitterly. Would her shadow never stop following him? Every time he turned around, he glimpsed her tall, red-haired figure, but when he pursued her, she became a small woman with violet eyes who vanished among the crowd before he could see her face.

Lane's voice remained, though. It called to him from every shadow. *Garreth. Lover. Come to me. Come to me, Mik-san.*

Mik-san?

In the dream he pounded his fist against a wall. Shit. That had to be a real voice calling him, not Lane's. Cursing wearily, he clawed his way back toward consciousness.

"Mik-san." The doorknob rattled in a futile attempt to open the door. A fist pounded. "It's Harry. Wake up, damn it!"

Maybe Dracula knew what he was doing sleeping in a crypt deep under the castle. From there no doorbell could disturb him, no matter how long and hard friends and salesmen from the daylight world leaned on it. Without opening his eyes, Garreth called through gritted teeth, "I have a loaded gun, Harry. In five seconds I am going to fire it through the door at whomever is stupid enough to be standing there."

"At last. I thought maybe you'd died in there, Mik-san."

The man not only woke him, but had the unmitigated gall to sound *cheerful!* "I'm not kidding, Harry."

"I'm not, either, I'm afraid. You have to get up. It's important. It's also three-fifteen in the afternoon."

Three— Garreth pried open his eyes, only to squeeze them shut again in pain. Sunlight flooded around and through the thin window shades. Struggling out of bed, he groped blindly for his sports jacket hanging on the closet door and fished his glasses out of the breast pocket. With them on, he stumbled over to unlock and open the door.

In the hall, Harry wore a grimly unhappy expression.

A chill slid down Garreth's spine. "What's wrong?"

Harry grimaced. "You're sure a hard man to wake up. When no one answered the phone, we thought you'd gotten up and gone out. Then the black-and-white spotted your car still here, so they tried knocking on the door. Without any response. So Serruto asked me to drive home and see if you were inside."

The cold in Garreth's spine deepened. "Why, Harry?" And why did he have this sudden vision of violet eyes peering out of the shadows at him?

Harry rubbed at a flaw on the paint of the doorjamb. "What do you know about a guy named Richard Maruska?"

Garreth frowned. "I've never heard of him. Who is he?"

Harry sighed. "A male prostitute. Faye's and Centrello's new case. Some people they've talked to say they heard a guy threaten him last night up in North Beach, a guy who claimed to be a cop and who fits your description, Mik-san."

Murder, Murder

1

Harry pushed open the door of the squad room. "Here he is. Now let's get this nonsense cleared up."

Heads swiveled in their direction. Fowler, standing by Faye's desk with his wrists cuffed behind his back and a pick in one hand, broke off in the middle of an apparent handcuff-escape demonstration for Faye, Centrello, and Girimonte, his brows arching expectantly.

From the doorway of his office, Serruto pointed at the glassed-in interview room in the opposite corner, and said, "Not you," to Fowler.

Fowler shrugged and went on working at the lock of the cuffs.

The detectives, the lieutenant, and Garreth filed into the interview room.

Blood scents quickly filled the confined space, washing warm and salty over Garreth, drowning him. He bit the inside of his cheek, but the pain did not provide enough distraction. He remembered how he crouched over the girl at the accident again, rain pouring over him and the taste of her blood sweet liquid fire in his mouth. Longing seared his throat.

Think about something else, man. Think about the hustler. How can he possibly be dead? A vision of a sharp wooden stake flashed in Garreth's mind. He twitched away from it. Harry would have surely mentioned something that bizarre.

"You call this nonsense, Takananda?" Serruto asked.

The blood smells still surged around him. Garreth felt sweat break out under his mustache. He fought the impulse to grab a chair and throw it through a window to flood the room with fresh air. Except that would let in more light, too. The weight of day dragged enough at him already.

Harry frowned from the lieutenant to Faye, Centrello, and Girimonte. "I told you before—he was sound asleep at my place all night."

Serruto sat down on a corner of the table in the middle of the room. "And what do *you* say, Mikaelian?"

Garreth forced himself to focus on the lieutenant. There was no point in trying to deny he had been in North Beach. Faye's and Centrello's witnesses had to be the barkers who saw his scuffle with the hustler; they would make him in a second in a lineup. He had shown them his ID, for God's sake. No, what he had to do was concoct a reasonable excuse for being there.

If he could only think . . . but his mind spun uselessly. All he could think about was the blood smells around him and the taste of that girl's blood.

Serruto folded his arms. "Well, Mikaelian?"

Fowler paced the squad room outside, free of the cuffs and obviously eaten by curiosity. Those inside the room stared hard at Garreth. Harry had growing concern creasing his forehead.

Think, man, think, Garreth snarled at himself. *At least buy yourself some time for it.* "Yes, I decked that hustler." He sent Harry an apologetic smile. "Sorry."

The betrayal in Harry's eyes went through Garreth's gut like a knife. "But—how—"

"How did I happen to be up there?" *Okay, now lie your heart out, Mikaelian.* "I've worked nights for a year and a half, Harry. After a couple of hours I woke up and couldn't go back to sleep. I went downstairs to read but couldn't concentrate on that, either. So I went for a drive and ended up in North Beach." He glanced at Faye and Centrello. "How did just a physical description and a claim of being a cop make you think of me?"

"The guy showed the witnesses a police ID, but the badge was an oval shield, not a star," Centrello said. "How many visiting cops can we have who look and dress like you?" He pointed at Garreth's yellow turtleneck and tan corduroy jacket.

"Tell us about the hustler," Serruto said. Steel edged the words.

That helped him forget about the blood scents. Fast. Garreth made himself shrug while cold crawled through him. "There's nothing much to tell. I was just up there walking around and he grabbed me. I kneed him without thinking. What would you have done?"

They said nothing but agreement flashed in every pair of eyes. None of them would have tolerated manhandling, either.

"After I picked him up it turned out he'd mistaken me for someone else. Then a blond hooker came along and he got into a car with her and another guy—a late-model Continental with California plates. I didn't catch all of the license number. Two-two-something with the last letters UW or VW. Didn't the barkers tell you about that?"

"Yeah," Faye said. "They also said Maruska called

137

something about being able to help you and meeting you in two hours."

"Help you with what, Mikaelian?" Serruto asked.

More steel. He gave the lieutenant a tight smile. "I don't understand why you're so interested in me. He didn't keep the appointment. I never saw him again. How did he die? Did his little three-way with the hooker and her john go bad?"

Serruto repeated evenly, "We'd like to know what he was going to help you with."

The only plausible lie that came to mind was one that Serruto would not like. Garreth used it anyway. "Lane Barber. The hustler thought he might have some information on her."

The lieutenant's mouth set in a grim line. "Mikaelian, I warned you about—"

"I'm not tracking her on my own! I swear. I just stumbled across this possibility while I was talking to the hustler. If it had panned out, I would have told Harry, just like I told him about Holle. So." Garreth made his voice casual. "How and where did the guy die?"

"Not in the middle of the three-way," Centrello said. "The barkers gave us the hooker's name and we've talked to her. She swears Ricky left her and headed back to meet you. His roommate came home this morning and found him in the bathtub. His throat had been slashed and his neck broken. Coroner says he died between three and six."

The nervous system destroyed. Of course. That was the only permanent death. But how did the killer manage it? No human could overpower a vampire at night.

Maybe no human had. Violet eyes floated in the shadows of Garreth's mind.

"Where's the gray turtleneck you wore yesterday?" Serruto asked.

"At the house." Grimy with dust from the piers, but at least not splashed with blood, not even rat blood. He had been very careful about that. The knowledge did not stop the chill of fear biting into him. "Hey, you don't seriously think I had anything to do with it."

They all glanced at each other. Girimonte's eyes narrowed speculatively. Harry looked down. Serruto said, "At the moment, Mikaelian, you're all we've got."

Adrenalin surged through Garreth, icy hot. Could he really mean that? "This is crazy. It's a case with more holes than Swiss cheese and you know it! I was never near the hustler's apartment, wherever it is, and you won't find anyone who's seen me there."

Centrello sighed. "Unfortunately no one we talked to in the building saw *anyone*. At that time of night they were all asleep."

"Then check my prints against the ones the lab—"

Schneider rapped on the door. "Harry, phone call for you. A Mr. Leonard Holle. He sounds excited."

Harry left to take it. Two minutes later he was back at a run with Fowler right behind him. "Barber's turned up! Holle went to check the apartment this afternoon and it's been cleaned out! He's waiting there for us."

A chorus of indrawn breath rolled around the interview room. Relieved breath, Garreth noted with relief of his own.

Harry smirked. "So we have someone else after all. Barber could have been in North Beach last night and heard Garreth's conversation with Maruska, then killed him to keep him quiet."

"Slitting his throat and breaking his neck are rather her style, aren't they?" Fowler asked. His eyes glittered.

Garreth bit his lip in dismay. Lord, what had he

done? Screwed up royally. The department would be wasting its time and manpower hunting the wrong person.

On the other hand, did he really want them finding Irina?

Serruto scowled at Fowler. "It could be Barber." He glanced at Harry. "I expect if it *is* Barber, you're going to want a piece of this hustler case. Faye, Centrello, do you have any objections to giving it all to him?"

The two exchanged glances, then, grinning, shook their heads. Girimonte rolled her eyes and used a short, very unladylike word.

Serruto's mouth twitched at the corner. "Sorry, Girimonte. Okay, Takananda, you have it, but keep a tight leash on your ride-alongs, both of them."

2

Violet eyes. Irina. Garreth chewed his lower lip. If Lane were alive, she would have had an excuse for killing the hustler, but what could Irina's motive be? Why would *she* be so desperate to keep her whereabouts a secret? Could it relate to that mysterious matter mentioned but not discussed in her note to Lane? He frowned at Holle's back on the apartment hall stairs ahead of Harry and Girimonte. The man reeked of cologne today, too. Girimonte and Fowler grimaced at the heavily spiced air sinking back down the stairs around them, but Garreth welcomed its masking of blood scents; it let him concentrate on thinking. He had to talk to Holle. If only he could get the man alone.

"This is a surprise to you?" Harry asked.

"Absolutely, Sergeant," Holle said. "The mailbox hadn't been opened. I took one of those letters addressed to 'occupant' out of it before coming upstairs. Then when I opened the door . . ." He unlocked the door and swung it open. "See for yourself."

Garreth let the others go first and watched from the doorway while the others stared around.

"There's still furniture," Fowler said. He sounded disappointed.

Harry nodded in satisfaction, however. "But no books or pictures or other personal belongings." He peered into the kitchen. "No dishes or pans, either. It's just the way she decamped from the Telegraph Hill apartment."

Girimonte frowned. "Do you suppose it's worth calling the lab boys to see if she left prints this time?"

Harry snorted. "Fat chance. With our luck with her, all we'd find would be the Bieber woman's prints again."

Shit, Garreth groaned inwardly.

Fowler's brows rose. "Ah, yes . . . the mystery woman in the case, even more elusive than your Miss Barber. Have you found any trace of her? I didn't see mention of it in the case file."

Harry grimaced. "None. It's like all that exists of her is fingerprints and that old arrest record."

"Peculiar, isn't it?" With a final twitch of brow at Garreth, Fowler turned away to run a finger along the edge of a bookshelf.

Garreth blinked. What the hell kind of game was the writer playing? He had read the file and seen Mada's name, yet obviously intended to say nothing of what he knew about Madelaine Bieber of Baumen, Kansas. Why? "Mr. Fowler, will you step—"

"I wonder what made Barber bolt," Girimonte said. She looked straight at Garreth. "How could she know that we knew about her new apartment? You didn't happen to mention it to that hustler, did you, Mikaelian?"

He frowned back. "Of course not."

Harry sighed. "Well, I don't see any point in hanging around here any longer. I'm not sure what good having the lab go over the place would be, even if Barber did leave prints. It'd only tell us she's been here. But keep it locked and don't disturb anything please, Mr. Holle. We might change our minds later."

"As you wish, Sergeant."

They locked up and left the house. Holle's car sat parked in a space near the bottom of the block. He left the group to head down for it.

"Excuse me," Garreth said. "I'll be right back." He hurried after Holle. This was his chance at the man. Falling into step with him, Garreth said, "I have one question . . . about Irina Rodek."

Holle's start of dismay sent triumph through Garreth. *Gotcha!*

A moment later, however, a mask slammed across the man's face. "I beg your pardon. Who?"

Holle wanted to play games? Garreth hissed inwardly in annoyance and cursed the glare of sunlight that kept him from pulling off his glasses and ending the nonsense by trapping Holle's gaze and using his hypnotic power on the man.

Very well, they would play it out straight. He let himself sigh. "Mr. Holle, you know very well that Irina Rodek wrote the note you left in Lane's apartment."

Holle started. "How could you get in—" He bit off the sentence.

To keep from revealing that he had recognized what Garreth was and that he knew Garreth should not have been able to enter the apartment? Garreth gave him a thin smile. "Get inside to see the note? I'm not barred from this apartment. Is Irina staying with you?"

Holle fought his face back into composure. He arched a brow. "Why should you think that?"

"I can't imagine that you and your housekeeper pour on the perfume because you like it. Isn't it to mask your blood scent for the comfort of guests such as Irina?"

The acid odor of nervous sweat cut through the spicy sweetness of Holle's cologne, but his voice went icy. "Officer—Mikaelian, isn't it?—you are obviously a man with a serious psychological problem. And since you have no authority to be questioning me, this conversation is finished." He spun away.

Garreth walked back up to the others. When he reached them, Harry said, "It looked like you hit a nerve. What did you say to him?"

Garreth shrugged. "Nothing really, just that I hope he isn't hiding anything because cops take it personally when other cops are attacked as Lane attacked me." This evening he would make some excuse to get out of the house and slip over for a look at Holle's while there was a chance Irina or traces of her still might be there.

"It took you a rather long time to say it," Fowler remarked.

Girimonte's eyes narrowed. "Yes, didn't he?"

Harry glanced at his wristwatch. "Lord, look at the time. We'd better get back to the office and do the day's reports. We don't dare be late tonight."

"Oh, yes. The party," Girimonte said, then grimaced. "Damn. I'm sorry, Harry."

Garreth started. "Party?"

Harry sighed. "It was supposed to be a surprise. We've invited most of homicide and some of your other old friends in the department over for a little buffet tonight in your honor."

"Party. I don't know what to say." Yes he did: shit. A cop party. There went his chance to go out for the evening. He would be lucky if it shut down before dawn.

Harry smiled at Fowler. "Why don't you come, too.

I promise you'll hear all the war stories you can ever hope for."

Fowler beamed. "That would be lovely, Sergeant. Thank you very much."

"Just lovely," Garreth echoed.

3

As he anticipated, between all the conversations and the liberal intake of liquor, the party's noise level rose steadily toward deafening. Lien nonetheless moved through the crowded dining and family rooms with the smiling serenity of the perfect hostess, a state of mind no doubt helped by the removal of everything remotely breakable from the rooms and a warning posted on the stairs that any intruders upstairs would be summarily shot. Fowler, too, was obviously enjoying himself, all smiles, eyes missing nothing. Garreth could imagine a recorder whirling in the writer's head: making notes on dress and behavior, following Del Roth's drunken efforts to convince Corey Yonning's wife of the therapeutic value of adultery, capturing details of family and department gossip, hearing a debate on the Giants' chances at the pennant and World Series this year, and the war stories Harry had promised.

His own face ached with the effort of smiling. He hated himself for it. All these people had been his good friends. He should be delighted to see them as they were to see him. Between the relief of darkness and the smells of food, liquor, and tobacco smoke overpowering the guests' blood scents, he felt physically comfortable. Yet he longed for everyone to leave so he could slip away to visit Holle's house.

You know you're widening the gap, don't you? You're throwing matches at the bridge.

The note Lien gave him as they came home burned in his trouser pocket, too.

"You forgot to pick up the message from *I Ching* when you left earlier," she had said, handing him the sheet of memo paper.

One glance at the note knotted his gut. Hexagram forty-four, Coming To Meet. He did not have to look at the text Lien had jotted under the heading. He knew it by heart. Coming To Meet had been the hexagram she threw for him a few days before he first met Lane Barber. *The maiden is powerful. One should not marry such a maiden.* Meaning that he should not underestimate that which looked helpless and innocent. He had, of course. He consistently underestimated Lane. The mistake had destroyed and almost killed him. But there would be no such carelessness with Irina.

"What did you really say to Holle, Mikaelian?" a voice shouted at his elbow.

Garreth looked around at Vanessa Girimonte, who looked more pantherish than ever in a figure-hugging black jumpsuit. He sipped his glass of soda water. "I already told you."

"Bullshit." She pulled one of her long cigars from the jumpsuit's breast pocket and lit it. "Harry will believe anything you say because you're his old partner and a substitute for the son he never had. Everyone else in the squad wants to believe you, too, even Serruto. But you're nothing to me; I don't know you. I'm not sure I even like you. You pick your words like someone on the bomb squad handling a suspicious package."

The memo sheet crackled in his pocket. Garreth gave Girimonte a thin smile. Here was another woman he had better not underestimate. "That's an interesting comparison."

"It's even more interesting that you don't protest it." She puffed her cigar. "I wonder why you're really out here. Not to be in on Barber's capture. If you cared anything about her, you'd show some anger when we talk about her, or at least satisfaction at the leads on her. You're just cat-nerved twitchy, especially around Fowler. I don't suppose you'd care to tell me why."

He met her gaze steadily. "There's nothing to tell."

She smiled. "Maybe we'll see." Her gaze focused past him. "Hello, Mr. Fowler," she called. "Enjoying the party?"

Garreth made himself look around slowly.

The writer grinned. "It's marvelous. Tell me, though, are American parties always so loud?"

Girimonte dragged at her cigar. "Cop parties are."

"Yes, well . . . it ought to make good color for the book. Speaking of which," Fowler said to Garreth, "I wonder if I might have a word with you."

Yes, they did need to talk. Garreth glanced at Girimonte, who eyed them speculatively. "Somewhere . . . quieter." Somewhere private.

Fowler nodded. "Quite."

Garreth took him upstairs to the living room.

Fowler strolled over to the bay window and stood gazing out. "It's a lovely city. Simply lovely. I wonder how you could bear to leave it." After a few moments he turned. "Interesting coincidence, isn't it, your grandmother in Baumen having the same name as a woman here involved with the murderous Miss Barber?"

Garreth kicked off his shoes and sat down cross-legged on the couch. "Why didn't you mention it to Sergeant Takananda or Inspector Girimonte?"

Fowler came over to take the easy chair at right angles to the couch. "I thought I'd chat with you first. Seeing Mada's name in the case file makes sense of a lot of things that puzzled me before. See if I've got it right. There's only one Madelaine Bieber and she was never your grandmother. That's just a cover story. Somehow you tracked her down to Baumen. Since there's nothing in the case file, I'd say you stumbled across the lead after you resigned." He raised a questioning brow.

Garreth felt every cell of him freeze, waiting. "Go on."

"You settled in as Anna Bieber's great-grandson to wait for Mada, hoping that when she showed up again she would lead you to Barber . . . who is what, her *real* grandchild?"

The sentence took a moment to sink in. When it did, it left Garreth weak with relief. Fowler had not stumbled onto the truth about Mada and Lane after all! *Thank you, Lady Luck!* Aloud he said, "A late-born daughter, I think. They have to be closely related. The photograph in Mada's arrest record looks so much like Lane."

"Which explains the fingerprints in the apartment. Mada probably helped the girl move out. After all, no one on stakeout was expecting a middle-aged woman. It also explains Mada's disappearance. She wasn't kidnapped; she recognized you at her mother's house, and after she confirmed it talking to you, she bolted."

Garreth took up the lie happily. "Right. But I couldn't tell anyone because then it would come out that Mada was an accessory to murder and the mother of a murderess. I couldn't do that to Anna."

Fowler smiled. "She is rather an old dear." The smile faded into a thoughtful frown. "I wonder if both

Mada and the girl are in some blood cult."

"Oh, yes, I'm sure of it," Garreth said with a straight face.

The writer's eyes lighted. "You know, if you and I put our heads together, we might crack this case. Wouldn't *that* make an ending for the book?"

A hell of an ending. Garreth said, "I told you, I'm not interested in being in a book." He stood up and started for the door.

Behind him, Fowler said casually, "Blackmail is such an ugly word, but let me remind you, old son, you've withheld evidence in this case. I don't think your Lieutenant Serruto would approve of that."

Garreth spun back. "I can't go hunting Lane on my own. The lieutenant would have my head for that, too."

Fowler crossed his legs and smoothed the fabric of his trousers over the upper knee. "I'll settle for your cooperation then. You know, going over the case file with me, telling me what you felt and thought at various points."

Garreth ran a hand through his hair. Maybe working with the writer would be one way to control what he learned. "All right."

Fowler chuckled. "You don't have to sound like I'm an executioner. It isn't painful, becoming immortal. Really it isn't. I promise."

4

The party ended about three-thirty, after the second, somewhat apologetic, visit by a black-and-white. "Hey, Harry, we don't want to lean on you, but your neighbors are going to bitch about favoritism if we don't look like we're treating you the same as any other loud party. So turn it down, okay?"

Lien smiled at the officers and went into the family room to whisper something in Evelyn Kolb's ear. A few minutes later Kolb and her husband left with loud good-byes, and soon everyone else began drifting out, too. Garreth sighed inwardly in relief.

When the last guest had gone, Lien bolted and chained the front door and leaned against it, shaking her head. "Honorable husband, I think we're getting too old for this. Leave everything. Letty can deal with it when she comes in tomorrow morning. I hope you enjoyed yourself, Garreth."

"It was great fun seeing everyone again." He kissed her cheek. "Thank you both very much."

Upstairs, though, he scrambled into a sweat suit and running shoes and paced impatiently, waiting for Harry and Lien to settle down for the night. It seemed to take an eternity. Once he heard their bedroom door close, he bolted his on the inside and moved through it to glide silently downstairs to the refrigerator for the meal he had not been able to drink during the party. Then he slipped out through the locked front door.

Tonight he did not even consider driving. A man about to commit burglary needed an alibi. His bedroom door and the front door both locked from the inside and his car parked in the drive all night should make it appear he could not have left.

He regretted having to leave the car, but not much. As his legs stretched and the street streamed backward beneath him, he gave himself over to the exhilaration of running. Forget where he was going and why. Forget burning bridges, the hustler, and violet eyes watching him from cold shadows. For the moment, nothing mattered but the sea-scented air filling his lungs and the power surging through his legs, giving him the heady feeling that he could run forever. He ran soundlessly through the empty residential streets, a shadow, a phantom.

Leaving the Sunset district, he crossed Golden Gate Park, then angled on north and east through Richmond into Pacific Heights. The houses lay dark and the streets deserted except for an occasional civilian car or patrolling black-and-white, which Garreth avoided by moving off the street into shadows by houses or parked cars while the unit passed.

No activity showed in Holle's house, either. Garreth watched it from the shadow of a doorway across the street for five minutes just to be sure. With a look both ways up the street, he strolled across and listened at the front door. Nothing moved inside.

Wrench.

The hall stretched out before him, twilight bright in his night vision, empty but not silent. The house creaked and groaned in the voices of old stone and aged wood. Beneath the lingering traces of cooking odors, Emeraude perfume, and Holle's cologne, it breathed out the scents of its existence, too: varnish, wood, smoke from the fireplace, lemon oil. Garreth glanced around, from the paneling and paintings to the stairs and soaring ceiling. Where did he start looking? Right here?

Still moving silent as a shadow, he walked through the living, dining, and breakfast rooms, and into the kitchen. None of those rooms had heavy drapes. In the kitchen, though, he eyed the refrigerator. The chances of finding anything significant in it were probably slim at best. With a whole city out there to draw on, vampire guests had no need to store up blood for an extra day or two. Obtaining extra from people was not quite like bleeding a cow, either. People noticed the loss of three or four pints at one time. Still . . .

He opened the refrigerator.

Holle kept it well stocked for humans. He even kept a selection of chilled wine.

Garreth started to close the refrigerator, then stopped. He pulled the door open again to peer at the wine. Something looked odd about those bottles. After studying them for a minute, he realized why. Four of the eight had no seals. They had obviously been opened and recorked. But the recorked ones all stood in the rear.

Garreth reached back for one. Pulling it out, he blinked. A strip of red tape crossed the commercial label, lettered in black: RAW SEA WATER. DO NOT DRINK! Further examination found that the other three without seals had the same warning.

Odd. Garreth hefted the bottle. He could see someone keeping brine for marinating or cooking seafood, but why would anyone have four bottles of real sea water? There was no telling what pollutants it carried. No one could pay him to drink it! He shook the bottle.

The dark liquid inside moved sluggishly.

Garreth's neck and spine tingled. That was no sea water. He worked the cork free and sniffed at the opening.

The scent from it raised goose bumps all over his body. Human blood!

He stared down at the bottle, hunger searing him. Human blood, ready to drink without having to attack anyone. Hurriedly he returned it to the refrigerator and retreated from the kitchen. No. He could not afford to indulge his appetite.

On the second floor none of the rooms but the library had heavy drapes. At the rear of the house the scents of blood and Holle's cologne wafted around the edges of a locked door along with the sound of a sleeper's breathing. The room must be Holle's. The third floor, all bedrooms, had two occupied rooms at the front, neither locked. The sleepers in both smelled of blood. The next room stood empty. The two rear rooms by the service stairs, though, had been turned into an apartment for the housekeeper. The scent of Emeraude filled them, and the housekeeper herself slept soundly in the bedroom.

He climbed the service stairs to the top floor in the attic. The old servants' quarters there had apparently been turned into more guest rooms. The front ones were unoccupied. Two locked doors closed off storage rooms. Sliding through the doors, he found light from the street shining in the dormer windows to light stacked cardboard boxes and a jumble of old chairs, lamps, and some racks of clothing hanging in zippered plastic bags.

Two rooms at the back remained unchecked. He

opened one door. Heavy drapes covered the dormer window. Quickly Garreth examined the bed. Earth filled the plastic mattress cover. The delicious relaxation he felt running his hand over it told him that even before the gritty shifting inside did.

Pay dirt. The room could be meant only to accommodate a vampire.

Only one room remained.

As he opened its door, Garreth froze with his hand on the knob. A spicy muskiness lingered in the air, a perfume he remembered only too well. It had curled around him with such inviting sweetness that Thanksgiving night on the island in Baumen's Pioneer Park.

He fought to breathe. No! Impossible. Lane could not have been here! Could she?

But what did he know . . . really? Books with vampire lore could hardly be called authoritative. Beyond that, he had only personal experience and what Lane had told him. How could he trust what she said?

After a few minutes, panic ebbed, and as reason replaced it, it occurred to him that along with everything else Lane had learned from her mentor, Irina, she might also have adopted the other woman's perfume. What he smelled could be traces of Irina, not Lane.

His paralysis dissolved. Swiftly he examined the room. It had the same heavy drapes and earth-filled mattress cover the room next to it did. Both closet and dresser drawers had been cleaned out, but the spicy scent lingering in them, too, told him they had been used recently. Perhaps as recently as today.

He closed the door and glided downstairs to the next floor, through the door of Holle's room. Sitting on the edge of the bed, Garreth shook the sleeping man's shoulder. "Wake up, Mr. Holle; we have things to talk about."

Holle woke with a start. "What—" He blinked,

squinting up at what his dark-blind eyes must see only as a vague shadow beside him. "Who are you? How the hell did you get in—"

"I'm Garreth Mikaelian. So you know how I got in."

Holle sat up. "Then take yourself out the same way."

"Not until I know where to find Irina Rodek." Garreth switched on the bedside light. "Mr. Holle, look at me and tell me you don't know where she is."

Holle squeezed his eyes tightly shut. "I don't know."

"Look at me!"

"Sorry." Holle smiled faintly. "You're obviously young in the life. You don't have the power yet to command by voice alone."

"Someone around here has power, though," Garreth said grimly. "Great power. Last night that someone killed a man named Richard Maruska. Maruska happened to be one of my kind."

Holle's eyelids flickered but remained closed. "*Killed* him?"

"Broke his neck. At night. How many humans could do that?" Garreth watched Holle lick his lips as the statement sunk in, then added, "He was supposed to meet me to tell me how to find Irina."

Sweat beaded Holle's forehead. "Irina couldn't have killed him. She—" He broke off.

"She what?" Garreth prompted. "Tell me about her. And tell me about yourself. How long have you known vampires really exist? Do many humans know?"

But Holle only pressed his lips into a line and turned his head away.

"You're obstructing a murder investigation, Holle."

The man snorted. "Conducted in the middle of the night by an officer without authority who breaks into my house and bedroom? I wonder what Sergeant Takananda would think if he knew about it."

Cold chased down Garreth's spine. He came back, "Who's going to tell him? You? The man with bottles of a very unique and bizarre vintage in his refrigerator and earth mattresses on two of his guest beds? You can't risk close scrutiny any more than I can."

Holle licked his lips again. "Then we have reached an impasse."

"Not really. You say Irina can't be guilty. Fine. Let me talk to her and see for myself."

The stubborn set returned to Holle's jaw. "I told you before, I don't know where she is. She left and didn't say where she was going."

The experience from years of talking to reluctant subjects told Garreth that without more leverage, this was all he would pry out of Holle. He stood, sighing. "Okay. If you *happen* to remember something and care to confide it, in the interests of justice and public safety, you can reach me through Sergeant Takananda. Though it doesn't really matter. With or without your help, I'll find Irina."

The way to start, he decided on his way downstairs, was with a look at the murder scene. Maybe that would give him a lead. Even if he had free access to the case reports, doubtful under the circumstances, they might not help. For all the crime lab's competence, their examination could have overlooked something that had significance only to a vampire.

Holle's phone directory on the hall table listed a Richard Maruska with a Western Addition address. Not the best of addresses, Garreth noted, but there were worse, and it was close. He would have time to reach it and still be back at Harry's before dawn.

Footsteps whispered overhead.

Garreth froze. They came from the guest room. One of the guests heading for the bathroom to take a leak? No, he realized a moment later. The footsteps, so quiet that human hearing would not have detected them, were coming downstairs. The guest must have heard him!

Making sure he moved soundlessly this time, Garreth raced for the front door and slipped out through it with a sharp wrench. On the street he breathed easier, but he lost no time breaking into a lope and heading south toward the Western Addition.

5

Between siding overdue for repainting and hallway stairs deeply worn in the center, the house had seen better days. The vertical row of mailboxes just inside the street door gave 301 as Richard Maruska's apartment. But it was the other name on the mailbox that startled Garreth: Count Dracula. A chill slid down his spine. How could the hustler be so— Then it hit him—oh, the roommate—and he remembered stories that officers on vice told about a homosexual hustler who styled himself a vampire, coming out only at night, always dressing in formal evening clothes and an opera cape, affecting a Bela Lugosi accent. Climbing the worn stairs to the third floor, Garreth reflected that Ricky must have found the arrangement very amusing, a real vampire living with a counterfeit one. Did "Dracula" know or suspect the truth?

The door of 301 had a police seal across it. Fingering the broad strip of yellow tape with inner fire licking at him, Garreth swore softly. The whole place was sealed. That meant the roommate had to be staying somewhere else for the time being and could not invite him in.

He turned away. On the other hand, just talking to the roommate might turn up something, and maybe he could work out something for getting into the apartment. In the meantime, he decided, glancing at his watch, he had better head home.

6

Dragging himself out of bed into the press of daylight after little more than an hour of sleep was pure agony, but Garreth forced himself up. He had to ask Harry about the hustler's roommate before Girimonte was around to question his curiosity.

Harry looked in no condition for casual chitchat, though, when Garreth stumbled into the kitchen. He glanced up, winced in obvious pain, and buried his nose in his coffee cup again with a groan.

Lien set a plate of eggs and hash browns on the table. The smells from it curled up around Garreth. Harry groaned even louder.

Shaking her head, Lien slid the plate to her place. "I think honorable husband has quite a head on him this morning." She somehow managed to look as if she had had a full night's sleep. She smiled at Garreth. "What about you? Can you face food?"

"God, no. I'll just make myself some tea." He filled a cup from the kettle on the stove and dropped in a tea bag out of the canister on the cabinet next to it.

"Be sure to eat at noon."

"Yes, ma'am." The water turned straw colored. Garreth discarded the tea bag.

Lien pushed hash browns around the plate with her fork. "I threw a hexagram for you this morning. It was number sixty-four, Before Completion."

His gut tightened. Her tone indicated a less than favorable hexagram. Leaning against the cabinet, he sipped the tea. "Which is?"

"The text says there is success, but if the little fox gets his tail wet before completing a crossing of the river, nothing furthers. Which means that deliberation and caution are necessary for success."

He gave her a thin smile. "A good reminder for a cop. What did *I Ching* say about Harry?"

Her eyes danced. "Number twenty-three, Splitting Apart."

Despite the drag of daylight and the knots in his gut, Garreth had to bite his lip to keep from laughing aloud.

Then Lien went sober. "It does not further one to go anywhere. I wish you'd call in sick, Harry."

Harry sighed. "Half the squad will be feeling as bad or worse than I am this morning."

"Then at least be very careful."

He reached out for her hand and kissed it. "I always am."

Maybe now was the time to slip in a question. Garreth said casually, "Earl Faye is one who'll definitely be worse off than you are." He sipped his tea. "He was reaching a point last night when I didn't know whether to believe him or not. He tried to tell me that Maruska's roommate is Count Dracula."

Lien giggled. "Oh really?"

"Really," Harry said. "That's what the guy calls himself. When Faye and Centrello came back from the murder scene, they said there was even a coffin in his bedroom that he sleeps in."

162

Maybe living with this dude was a clever move on Ricky's part, Garreth mused. Next to the hamming of the counterfeit vampire, the hustler would have seemed normal. "I wonder if we ought to talk to him again, now that it looks like Lane is connected to the killing. It might give what he has to say a different slant."

Harry started to frown in thought, then abandoned the gesture with another wince of pain. "Maybe."

"Is he still at the apartment?"

"No. There's a temporary address for him in Centrello's notes. We'll look it up when we get to Bryant Street."

7

From the doorway of his office, Serruto eyed his inspectors sardonically. "Ah, the cast from *Dawn of the Dead,* I see. It must have been quite a bash, Takananda. Not without benefits, either. I see our hotshot author hasn't managed to make it in. Let's wish him a long, undisturbed rest while we grab our cups of strong black coffee and go to work." He strolled out to sit down on a desk in the middle of the room and read the list of cases that had come in overnight. In the middle of facts about a cab driver's knifing, he glanced up and broke off with a solicitous, "I'm not keeping you awake, am I, Bennigan?"

The offending detective opened his eyes with a start and dragged himself upright in his chair. "I was just concentrating on what you're saying, sir."

"Good. Then you and Roth can handle this knifing."

After reviewing and assigning the rest of the overnights, Serruto had each team give a brief update on their current cases.

A bright-eyed, rested-looking Girimonte reported for Harry and her. "No breaks on the liquor store shooting yet, and no ID on the woman in Stow Lake. Which now looks like an accidental drowning. The autopsy found water in her lungs and a high level of alcohol in her blood. The autopsy on our hustler wasn't done until late yesterday afternoon so there's no official report yet, but I stopped by the morgue on my way up this morning and got some preliminary findings from the assistant M.E. who did the post."

Cold shot through Garreth. He had not thought about autopsies on vampires before. What internal differences were there? Any that might generate dangerous curiosity?

He waited tensely while the black woman pulled a notebook from the pocket of her suit jacket and flipped it open. "The victim died of a severed spinal cord. No surprises there. And the reason there wasn't much blood from the slashed throat was because it was cut after death."

"Which fits Barber's MO," Harry said.

Serruto raised a brow. "Not quite. Mossman and Adair died of blood loss, remember? *Both* the broken necks and cutting their throats and wrists came after death."

"Maruska wasn't bled out like the other victims, either," Girimonte said.

"She had a different reason for killing Maruska . . . self-preservation."

Girimonte sent a glance at Garreth. "We don't know that. There's no evidence definitely linking Barber to the murder."

Harry scowled. "We—"

"This is a briefing, not a debate," Serruto said shortly. "Go on, Inspector."

She glanced back at her notes. "There isn't much else. The doc is excited about some internal anomalies, but he says they're unrelated to the cause of death. He found severe pulmonary edema and edema of the throat and nasal passages, which also doesn't appear connected to the cause of death but which he can't account for. That's it."

What anomalies? Garreth bit his lip. An unanswerable question at the moment. He had enough to worry about anyway with Girimonte sending suspicious glances at him and Harry frowning at her.

When Serruto dismissed them and returned to his office, Harry turned on Girimonte. "We have evidence that implicates Barber. And if we ask the roommate about red-haired women—"

"Excuse me," a hesitant voice interrupted. "A detective by the door said two of you are the detectives in charge of the case of a woman found in Stow Lake Sunday night?"

They all turned. A young brunette woman in a ski sweater and blue jeans stood twisting the strap of her shoulder bag.

"I'm Sergeant Takananda," Harry said. "This is Inspector Girimonte. Do you know something about the case?"

The young woman drew a deep breath. "I think I know who she is."

Girimonte pulled a chair over by Harry's desk. "Please sit down."

Across the room, the door from the hall opened and Julian Fowler came in. He looked as impeccably dressed and groomed as ever but the writer walked, Garreth noted, like a man carrying a bomb. Or wearing one?

Garreth left Harry and Girimonte with the brunette to meet the writer. "Good morning, Mr. Fowler."

Fowler leaned against a handy desk and closed his eyes. "I think not. Lord. Do American coppers really party like that all the time?"

"Oh, no," Garreth said solemnly. "Sometimes we get wild."

The pale eyes opened to glare at him. "Don't be cheeky. I wonder if your lieutenant would mind if I helped myself to a spot of coffee?"

"He isn't my lieutenant, so go ahead."

Fowler almost dropped the cup, though. Garreth took it away and poured the coffee for him. Harry and Girimonte left the squad room with the brunette, probably taking her to the morgue to identify the body.

They came back a short time later. The brunette had gone pale. Shaking, she sat down again. While Harry fed a report form into his typewriter, Girimonte stalked over to the coffee pot.

"Sometimes I wonder why we bother to protect the public. We ought to just sit back and let natural selection weed the stupidity from the population."

"What happened?" Garreth asked.

She grimaced. "A bunch of grad students from the U of San Francisco drinking Sunday night. They thought it would be fun to go swimming. No one counted heads before or after, and it took until today, when the professor she works for started bitching because she wasn't there to teach a lab for him and grade some papers, for them to start wondering where she was and remember that there'd been 'something in the paper Monday about a dead woman in a lake.' Christ."

"Yes, but well, it does clear the case, as you say, doesn't it?"

"Yeah. It clears the case." She carried the coffee back to the brunette.

In another ten minutes the statement was finished and the shaken citizen gone. Harry said, "Let's visit Count Dracula."

Fowler perked up. "I beg your pardon?"

Girimonte smiled thinly. "Our dead hustler's roommate. A weirdo. Perfect for your book."

Harry dug the case folder out of his desk and flipped through the reports in it. "Here's his temporary address: the Bay Vista Hotel."

Girimonte grimaced. "That fleabag."

"I dare say it isn't easy for a vampire to find accommodations," Fowler said.

Snickering, they headed for the door.

They had not been out of the parking lot five minutes, however, when a message came over the radio for Harry to phone Serruto. They stopped at the first public phone.

A grim-faced Harry came back to the car. "Van, forget Count Dracula and head for Holle's place."

A cold trickle of foreboding moved down Garreth's spine. "What's up, Harry?"

"It's what's gone down." Harry slammed the car door close. "Holle's housekeeper just found him dead in bed . . . his throat slashed and his neck broken."

8

From the doorway, Holle appeared to be merely asleep, lying on his back in bed, the blankets pulled up to his chin. To Garreth, however, the reek of blood, stagnant and clotting in death, pervaded the room, and on second glance, peering over Harry's shoulder, the pillow showed red stains.

Fowler craned his neck to see over Girimonte. "That isn't much blood for a slashed throat. It ought to be everywhere."

"Not if the killer drained Holle dry first, or used the knife after the victim was dead," Harry said. He turned toward the housekeeper hovering tearfully in the hall where she could not see into the bedroom. "Ms. Edlitza, I can understand you coming up to check on him when he slept so much later than usual, and going in and realizing he wasn't breathing, but why are you so sure his neck is broken and throat cut?"

She choked out, "I saw the bloodstain, and—" Her voice broke. "And I looked under the covers."

Harry exchanged quick glances with Girimonte. "Only one of us better go in. I'll do it. Ms. Edlitza," he suggested gently, "why don't you join the others in the library now?" When she had gone, he crossed to the bed and lifted one side of the blankets.

"Good God," Fowler whispered.

Garreth swallowed.

Under the blankets, Holle's body lay chest down. A wound gaped in the throat, pulled into a spiral by the near one-eighty twist of the neck.

"Arguing with you is becoming fatal, Mikaelian," Girimonte said. "You didn't happen to be restless and out driving after the party last night, did you?"

Anger flared at the acid edge in her voice. "I was home sleeping it off like everyone." Beneath the anger, however, consternation churned in him. Irina. It had to be Irina doing this, logic said, though why she could be so desperate to cover her tracks he still had no idea. *Lane,* his gut insisted. *She has the motive, Mikaelian.* But how could it possibly be Lane?

His only answer was her laughter echoing in his head.

Harry dropped the blankets back into place. "Van—" he began sharply, only to glance at Fowler and break off. Torn between loyalty to his old partner and the desire to avoid arguing with the new one in front of an outsider?

That, too, Garreth reflected, but something else also showed in the almond eyes, something new that tightened his throat . . . uncertainty. In his head he watched the fires on the bridge blaze higher.

The doorbell rang downstairs. Over the hall railing, Garreth saw one of the uniformed officers from the black-and-white responding to the initial call open the door. The team from the crime lab trooped in with its equipment.

"Up here, Yoshino," Harry called down. "If you

need us, send a uniform to the library. Where we'll be listening to what our witnesses have to say before we make accusations, right, partner?" he said to Girimonte, then headed up the hall toward the front of the house.

Today the library looked incongruously cheerful. Someone had opened the drapes and light flooded the room. Three guests waited with the housekeeper: an attractive dark-haired woman and a young couple who looked pasty-pale under their tans and sun-streaked hair.

Garreth moved around the wall to stand by the fireplace, as far from the windows as possible.

Harry slid the doors closed. "Thank you for waiting. I'm Sergeant Takananda. This is Inspector Girimonte, Officer Mikaelian, and Mr. Fowler. Mr. Fowler is a writer riding along with us to do research for a book. Does anyone have objections to talking with him present?"

After a quick glance at each other, the guests and housekeeper shook their heads.

Harry smiled. "Then shall we begin? You are?" He pointed at first the dark-haired woman, then the couple.

"Susan McCaul. That's spelled M-C-C-A-*U*-L."

"Alan and Heather Osner," the man said.

"You're all guests and were sleeping in the house last night?"

They nodded.

"When did you last see Mr. Holle?"

"As everyone was leaving for the ballet," the housekeeper said. She fished a sodden tissue out of her dress pocket and mopped at a new flood of tears.

McCaul bit her lip. "We all got back about one-thirty. He bolted the front door and was headed in the direction of the kitchen when I went upstairs to my room."

Mr. Osner nodded. "He said he was going to check the rear door and turn on the security system."

"I heard him coming up the back stairs a little later," Osner's wife said.

"Did anyone see or talk to him after that?" Girimonte asked.

They shook their heads.

Harry said, "What sounds did you hear later on in the night? We need to know all of them, even something you might think is insignificant."

"I didn't hear anything," McCaul said. "I went to bed and d—" She broke off, her throat working, then a breath or two later, stumbled on in a strained voice: "I went straight to sleep. The next thing I heard was . . . was Ms. Edlitza screaming."

"Me, too," Mrs. Osner said.

Her husband nodded. "I slept straight through."

The hair raised on Garreth's neck. "None of you woke up? Not for any reason? No one made a middle-of-the-night trip to the bathroom?"

"No." They shook their heads.

Then unless one of them was lying or walked in his sleep, the footsteps Garreth heard had to belong to the killer. They sounded again in his head, a stealthy whisper on the stairs from the third floor. God. He had fled from them and left Holle alone to die.

"Ms. Edlitza," Girimonte asked the housekeeper, "were all the doors still bolted this morning?"

The housekeeper nodded.

"What about the security system?"

"On and functioning."

"But someone got in past everything." Garreth raised a brow at Harry. "Maybe we ought to find out how."

Girimonte snapped her notebook shut. "I'll check the ground floor."

"And I'll take this one," Harry said. He recorded the home addresses of the three guests, then smiled politely at them and the housekeeper. "Thank you all very much for your cooperation. That should be it for now, except I do ask that you please keep out of the areas our officers and crime lab have marked off until we've finished examining them for evidence."

Garreth caught the housekeeper's eye. "I'll check the upper floors, if Ms. Edlitza will be kind enough to guide me."

Girimonte stopped in midstride heading for the library door and turned, frowning. Harry hesitated visibly, too, but said, "All right."

The housekeeper followed them into the hall. As they reached the stairs, however, Fowler started up after her and Garreth.

Garreth waved him away. *Go with the others,* he mouthed.

Fowler's brows rose, but after a moment he turned and trotted downstairs after Girimonte.

Garreth and the housekeeper continued on to the attic alone, where he began checking windows, starting with those in the rear bedroom. He pulled aside the heavy drapes. The window was firmly latched.

Outside, the sun no longer shone so brightly, he noted with relief. Clouds had begun rolling in from the west to darken the sky. It would be raining by noon.

He dropped the drapes back in place. "Where did Irina go?"

The housekeeper started. "Who?"

Garreth sighed. "Don't you play that game with me, too. This was her room. It still smells of her perfume." He pulled off his glasses. "When did she leave and where's she gone?"

She hissed and spun away. "Don't you try that with me! The agreement is that your kind will respect the rules of hospitality in this house. You take no advantage and touch no one."

So she, too, recognized him for what he was and knew how to resist his power. "Then talk to me."

She kept her back to him. "What do you want with Miss Rudenko?"

Rudenko! Was that the name Irina used now? He put back on the glasses. "I couldn't very well mention it in front of the other officers, but we know she can easily come in and leave without disturbing either the alarms or door bolts."

The housekeeper turned on him scornfully. "That's ridiculous! Mr. Holle and Miss Rudenko are—" Her eyes filled. She groped in her pocket for another tissue and wiped her eyes. "They were friends."

Friends? With a vampire? Knowingly? Garreth wished he had time to pursue the question. "Friends fight and fall out. Irina left very suddenly, didn't she?"

The lady did not shake easily. Give her that. "It had nothing to do with any disagreement." She blew her nose. "Shouldn't you be checking the other windows in case you're wrong about who came in last night?"

Exasperation hissed through Garreth. What hold did Irina have that kept these people so close-mouthed? Promises of immortality, like Dracula gave the wretched Renfield? He smiled thinly. "Maybe you should start thinking up explanations to give Sergeant Takananda about why you keep bottles of human blood in your refrigerator and where it comes from." Where *did* it come from?

Not even that rattled her. She just sniffed. "Blackmail? You're wasting the effort. I really don't know where Miss Rudenko is."

Her voice carried a ring of truth. Garreth sighed and headed for the door. "Let's check the other windows."

Those in the bedrooms were all secure with no signs of tampering. As expected.

174

"There are two storage rooms," the housekeeper said. "Shall I unlock them?"

A quick vision of finding footprints in the dust and having the crime lab identify them as his flashed through Garreth's head. He eyed the dead bolt on each door. "Do they unlock from the inside?"

"No."

"Then I think we can skip those windows. No one could get out into the rest of the house except . . . someone like me."

Not quite true, but if he mentioned someone could open the doors from the inside by pulling the hinge pins, she might insist on examining the storerooms. He headed down the stairs to the third floor.

The windows on that floor were all locked, too, including those in the housekeeper's rooms. Ms. Edlitza kept a cross above her bed, the Eastern Orthodox type with a double crossbar.

Garreth raised his brows. "Insurance?"

Her mouth thinned. "No, religion. Insurance would be an atomizer full of garlic juice."

Vampire-style mace. Just the thought of the scent left Garreth feeling suffocated.

A whoop went up in the hall. He and the housekeeper raced out to find Fowler at a window by the back stairs. "It's unlocked!"

Harry and Girimonte came pounding up from the second floor.

Fowler used a pen to push open the window and leaned out without touching anything. "There's nothing but wall below, though. You'd need bloody wings to reach it."

Girimonte looked out the window, too. "No, I'd say he let himself down from the roof. Standard technique. Isn't that what you learned in burglary, Mikaelian?"

If anyone had actually come in the window. Garreth was willing to bet that Irina opened it from the inside to satisfy human investigators with an obvious entry point for an intruder.

Harry said, "We'd better get someone up here to dust for prints."

The housekeeper squeezed past them down the back stairs. "How reassuring to know we're not dealing with someone who walks through bolted doors. I think I'll make myself some tea."

The rest of them headed down the front stairs.

In Holle's room, Bill Yoshino nodded at Harry's request for a technician. "Sure thing. Linda," he called to one of the team brushing fingerprint powder on the faucet handles in the adjacent bathroom, "you go when you're finished there. Glad you've come, Harry. I was about to send a uniform for you. We have a couple of things that ought to interest you."

The smells of living blood overlaid that of death, though not enough to mask it completely. The combination sent a small wave of nausea through Garreth.

An assistant M.E., an hispanic woman, leaned over the body on the bed. She looked around as everyone trooped in. "Good morning, Sergeant Takananda. Gruesome. Is this one tied to that midnight cowboy Mitch Welton posted yesterday? The injuries look alike."

"The two could be related."

"Then maybe this one is a Martian, too. That will—"

Harry started. "Martian?"

The assistant M.E. grinned. "That's Dr. Thurlow's name for people with certain anomalies. Mitch was all excited about the ones he found in his stiff. He was going to write it up for journal publication. Then Dr. Thurlow said there've been three others like him in the past ten years."

"What anomalies?" Fowler asked.

Head them off at the pass, man. "Harry, look,"

Garreth said. He touched a vertical cut above Holle's left eye. "Did he do it or did the killer hit him?"

"I'm more curious about the time of death," Girimonte said.

The assistant M.E. shrugged. "He hasn't been dead more than a few hours. The body's still warm and there's no rigor except in his jaw and neck."

"It happened after the party folded, then." Girimonte raised a brow at Garreth.

Harry's forehead furrowed. He turned toward Yoshino. "You wanted to show me something?"

"Yeah." Yoshino pointed at Holle's arms. "Look at his wrists, first off."

A narrow, abraided groove circled each. Garreth bit his lip. At some point Holle had been tied tightly with something thin, like drapery cord, and struggled desperately against his bonds.

"Look at this, too." Yoshino pointed at the hair coming down over Holle's forehead. It lay in clumped points. "It's been wet. The pillow under him is still damp."

Harry felt the pillow. "What else?"

"In the bathroom." Yoshino led the way through the connecting door into a bathroom the size of a small ballroom, lushly carpeted in blue shag that covered even the steps around two sides of the sunken tub. "We've got more water in here, a soggy rug in front of the washbowl, and marks where splashes on the counter and mirror have dried."

Harry knelt down to feel the carpet. "He didn't do this brushing his teeth."

"Uh-uh. We also collected skin and blood off the edge of the faucet. I'd say that's where your dead man cut his forehead."

"Christ," Fowler whispered down at Garreth. "*Shadow Games.*"

Harry snapped around. "What?"

Fowler grimaced sheepishly. "One of my books.

There's a point in it where the protagonist, Charlie Quayle, needs information from one of the villain's henchmen who he's captured. He gets it by filling up the washbowl in his hotel room and dunking the henchman until he's almost drowned."

And that had happened to Holle. Anger flared in Garreth. It was so pointless. Why resort to torture when a little hypnotic persuasion would make Holle answer any question Irina asked? Or did she have to use force because Holle, like the housekeeper, knew how to resist? Garreth felt sick. If he had only thought of using his own hypnotic powers on the person on the stairs this morning, and stayed long enough for a confrontation. He would have met Irina instead of a curious guest, of course, and they might have clashed as he had with Lane. Irina being even older and more experienced than Lane, this time he would probably have lost the duel, but Holle might still be alive.

"The killer wanted information?" Girimonte asked. She frowned at Harry. "That doesn't fit Barber. Why should she have to torture information out of a man who's been her friend and caretaker? What kind of information could she want anyway?" Her gaze slid toward Garreth. "It doesn't fit Barber."

Harry stiffened.

Did she ever let up? Garreth wondered angrily. "Why don't you can it, Girimonte."

Harry sighed. "Both of you can it." He frowned. "The killer tortured Holle and Holle struggled, but the only signs of it are in here. Because he knew and trusted the person, and didn't realize his danger until he was in here and it was too late? *That* would fit Barber."

The assistant M.E. appeared in the bathroom doorway. "If you're finished with the body, we'll take it now, Sergeant."

"Fine." Harry watched from the door while they zipped Holle into a body bag and wheeled out the stretcher, then turned away, grimacing. "So much for the fun part. It's time to talk to the neighbors, partner. One of us needs to stay here until Yoshino and his people are finished, though, so how do you want to handle it? Flip a coin?"

She stretched with a cat's grace. "You're the sergeant. You stay. I'll hit the bricks. Want to come along, Mr. Fowler?"

"Too right!" The writer grinned. "Just let's stop at the car first long enough to pick up my mac. The heavens look ready to let open any moment."

Harry and Garreth followed the other two out into the hall, where Harry leaned on the railing watching them trot down the staircase and across the hall out the front door. "She's a good cop, Mik-san."

"She certainly has her ideas about who the killer is."

It came out with more acid than Garreth intended. Harry straightened abruptly. "You have to admit you've been in some wrong places at the wrong time. She's raised good points, too. Why *would* Lane torture Holle for information? *What* information?"

The same questions applied to Irina, unfortunately. Could some other vampire be involved, one with other interests here, someone he did not know?

"As computers say, Harry-san: *Insufficient data. Will not compute.* The housekeeper said she was making tea. Shall I see if I can talk her into some for us?"

Harry shook his head. "None for me, but you go ahead. You didn't have breakfast and I expect it's going to be a long time to lunch."

Garreth found the housekeeper at a table in the kitchen with tea, but crying over it, not drinking it. He touched her shoulder. "I'm sorry to bother—"

She started violently. Jumping up, she snapped, "Why don't you people ever walk so someone can hear you!"

He sighed. "I'm sorry. Ms. Edlitza, do you meet many of my kind?"

"What's many? I meet some." She bustled away toward the sink with her teacup. "Mostly they're the same ones over and over, like Miss Rudenko. She's been visiting since I was a child and my parents were part of a full staff here." A fat raindrop hit the window over the sink, followed by another, and another, until it streamed down the window in a sheet.

"Irina and who else?"

Water blasted into the sink. Rain hammered on the window. "Are you trying to involve others in this, too?"

He hissed in exasperation. "What I'm trying to do is find out who killed Mr. Holle!"

Her head bent suddenly. Her shoulders heaved in a soundless sob.

The anger leaked out of Garreth. He sighed. "Ms. Edlitza, I need to meet some of the others, and I don't know how or where."

Her fingers twined together. She studied them as if searching for something there. After a minute she looked up. "I'm sorry, I can't help you. I'm not one of their circle, just a servant."

Instinct told him that she was lying . . . but since she appeared experienced at resisting vampire powers, what could he do short of using force to get the truth? God knew there had been enough of that in this house already. "All right. Thank you."

He left the kitchen. As the door closed behind him, he heard her move quickly across the kitchen in his direction and he halted. She was not coming after him, however. Her steps stopped on the other side of the door, followed by the sound of a phone receiver lifting.

Garreth plastered himself against the door. Closing his eyes, he strained to hear. There. He could just hear the dial tones, four of one digit, one of another, two of a third. He listened for the voice answering on the other end, but that came through too faintly to make out more than a murmur, though the voice said something longer than hello, and a rising tone indicated a question. May I help you, perhaps?

All he could really hear was the housekeeper's end of the conversation, "This is Mr. Holle's housekeeper. I'd like to leave a message for Miss Rudenko. Ask her to call me, please. . . . Yes . . . it's very important. Thank you."

As he heard her hang up, Garreth hurried away from the door. It would not help to have her catch him listening. He headed for the hall extension to try working out the number while the tones remained fresh in his head.

But Holle's guests sat in the living room in full view of the phone. He sighed in regret. Better not play with the phone now. It would arouse their curiosity, and Harry's, if he happened to look over the railing. The directory on the shelf under the phone gave him an idea, however. Squatting down in front of the table, he checked the covers on all three sections of the directory. A number the housekeeper could dial without having to look up and expect the person answering to know Holle's name must be noted somewhere.

A sheet of paper taped inside the front cover of the white pages bore a typed list of phone numbers. Garreth scanned them quickly, only to grimace in disappointment. They were only those a visitor might be interested in: numbers for cab companies and airlines; for theater, ballet, and opera ticket offices; for museums and galleries.

He returned the white pages to the shelf and stood up. Holle must keep his personal numbers somewhere else. The library, maybe. A phone sat on the desk there.

Giving the guests a bland smile as he turned away

from the phone table, Garreth trotted up the stairs and along the hall to the library.

The massive old desk looked like two pushed back to back, with a tunnel of a knee hole and drawers on both sides. The five drawers facing into the room contained the standard clutter of paper, pens, and such. But no address book. The drawers on the back side would not open when he pulled on their handles.

Garreth slumped back in the big executive chair, frowning at the locked drawers and listening to the rain hammer the window behind him. Now what? The desk had been carefully built. The space along the top of the drawers looked too narrow for using either the paper knife or rulers from the front drawers to slip the locks. He needed X-ray vision, or the skill of TV's private eye/white knights of justice, who could pick locks like these with a bent paper clip in five seconds.

Harry's voice carried from downstairs, explaining that he wanted to fingerprint the guests and house-keeper as a way of eliminating their prints from those lifted in Holle's room.

Holle's room. Garreth sat up. Maybe breaking into the desk was unnecessary.

Pushing to his feet, he hurried down the hall to the bedroom. Technicians still at work glanced around as he came in. He gave them a nod and smile, then made a quick survey of the room. Keys.

There. On the bureau. Holle's keys lay in a brass tray amid a clutter of loose change, a cigarette lighter, card case, and billfold.

A film of white fingerprint powder smudged the bureau, but Garreth still asked, "Are you finished with those keys?"

A technician nodded without looking up from dusting the bedside table.

Garreth picked up the ring with its brass tag engraved LEONARD and strolled casually out of the bedroom.

Straight into Harry.

Harry's brows rose. "Looking for me, Mik-san?"

The evasions racing through Garreth's head choked off as he watched Harry's gaze drop to the keys. Holding them up, he said, "I'm hoping there's a key to the desk in the library. It's locked and I'm looking for Holle's address book. So we can check out his friends just in case Lane didn't do this."

"Address book? Good idea." Harry held out his hand.

No! But the protest remained unvoiced. He, the unofficial cop here, the ride-along, had no grounds for protest. Reluctantly Garreth handed over the keys. He could only ride along some more, dogging Harry's heels to the library, watching while his ex-partner unlocked the desk and found a slim, leather-bound address book in the center drawer.

Harry picked it up and flipped through it. "He certainly has a lot of friends."

Garreth ached with the effort of not snatching the book away. "Any corporate or institutional affiliations?"

Harry shrugged. "I expect. A man like him is bound to be on the board of museums and service organizations. I'll have a close look later."

Garreth could only swear silently, helplessly, as the book disappeared into the pocket of Harry's suit coat.

9

After the lab finished at the house, Harry and Garreth joined Girimonte and Fowler in the legwork, trudging through the rain to talk to Holle's neighbors around the block and across the street.

"Just like old times," Harry said with a grin.

Not quite, Garreth reflected unhappily. Harry asked all the questions and kept watching Garreth from the corner of his eye.

By the time everyone had been reached, either at home or by phone at their various offices, midday was ancient history. The four of them headed for a Burger King on Fillmore to dry off and compare notes.

Harry frowned at Garreth's iced tea. "Is that all you're having?"

Garreth gave him a rueful smile. "The way I pigged out last night, I met my caloric requirements for an entire week, maybe the month."

Harry chuckled, but Girimonte's eyes narrowed. A moment later something stirred behind them and she sat back, smiling in satisfaction.

Fear washed through Garreth. She had the expression of someone who has finally found the answer to a nagging question. Had she, like Holle and the housekeeper, identified him for what he was?

Harry poured catsup over his french fries. "So what did you learn from the neighbors, Van?"

"Almost zilch." Girimonte put down her hamburger and opened her notebook. "There aren't many people looking out their windows from three to six in the morning. Except one." She flipped through the notebook. "A Mr. Charles Hanneman who lives directly across the street from Holle. He got up around five to check on his year-old son, who's been ill and was crying. He says he happened to glance out the window while he was carrying the boy around trying to soothe him back to sleep and saw someone on the sidewalk outside the Holle house."

Garreth's heart lurched. Carefully he sipped his tea. "Then we got lucky for a change."

"Not really, sad to say." Fowler sighed.

"He couldn't say the person came out of the house." Girimonte frowned at her notes. "He couldn't give us much of a description, either, not even the sex. The person was either a tall, lean woman or a slender man . . . shortish hair . . . wearing a warmup suit."

"Color?" Harry asked.

She grimaced. "Something dark . . . green or blue, maybe even red. Hanneman couldn't tell in that light. He didn't really pay much attention. He thought it was just someone out for early exercise, and he's probably right. The person jogged off south, out in the open and making no attempt to hide, according to Hanneman."

Garreth let out his breath.

"We didn't get even that much," Harry said. "There's this, though." He pulled out the address book. "In the interest of completeness, we ought to check Holle's friends."

"In case he includes second-story men in his circle?" Girimonte asked through a mouthful of hamburger.

"Why does there have to be a burglar?" Fowler asked. He munched a french fry. "Perhaps Holle himself admitted the killer."

Everyone blinked, and Garreth cheered silently. That idea should certainly distract anyone from wondering how a killer could enter a locked door.

"Go on," Harry said.

Fowler took a bite of hamburger. "It's just a theory, mind, but it does explain the apparent lack of forced entry or struggle. What if Barber rang Holle up yesterday afternoon after he left us, pleading innocent to everything and begging him to help her, and also asking that he not tell anyone about her call? Holle arranged to have her come to the house that night. When he ostensibly went to check the rear door and set the alarm, she was waiting outside. He let her in and sent her up the back stairs to one of the rooms on the top floor."

Harry pursed his lips. "Then she came down later, maybe pleading a need to talk to him. He didn't realize how ugly things were going to get until too late."

"Quite." Fowler finished off his french fries. "Of course, you realize the scenario could fit almost anyone Holle considered a friend. I imagine there are a score of excuses for someone to use to warrant a clandestine entrance—abusive husband, a misunderstanding with creditors, a virago of a wife or girlfriend."

Garreth eyed the address book, his mind racing. How could he manage a look through it without appearing to care? Maybe . . . Casually he said, "In the interest of completeness, I wonder if any of the names in that book will also check out as acquaintances of Ricky Maruska, either social or . . . professional."

"Now there's a thought," Fowler said. "We could ask his roommate."

Harry traced initials LEH tooled on the cover. "I'd also like to ask Count Dracula about Lane Barber, now that we suspect she's involved in the murder."

Girimonte washed down the last of her hamburger with her soft drink. "So let's go roust the count out of his coffin."

10

The only vista the Bay Vista Hotel enjoyed was a slantwise glimpse of the Embarcadero, a frontal view of the warehouse across the street, and the traffic of I-80 north beyond that. In the lobby, sagging easy chairs held down a threadbare carpet. A blowsy woman behind the desk divided her attention between a paperback romance and the histrionics of game show contestants on a small TV at one end of the counter.

Harry flipped open his badge case. "What's Count Dracula's room number?"

"Cute," the woman said without looking up. She turned a page. "I suppose you want Frankenstein's room number, too?"

Harry frowned. "There *is* a man registered here who calls himself Count Dracula. Thin, pale, fake Balkan accent. Wears a black cape."

"Oh, sure."

Fowler asked, "Do you have a guest named Alucard?"

Of course. *You should have thought of that, Mikaelian.* Especially after taping and watching every vampire movie that showed on the channels Baumen received.

The desk clerk rolled her eyes. "*That* weirdo. Three-oh-six, and if he complains about his room not being made up today, tell him the maid only goes through once and he opens up then or the room don't get done."

With a wink at Harry, Girimonte said in a flat, *Dragnet*-style voice, "Yes, ma'am; we'll tell him."

The narrow stairs creaked at every step. Ribbed rubber glued to the treads flapped loose on several, threatening to trip the unwary climber.

"Fowler," Harry said back over his shoulder, "where did he come up with the name Alucard, and how did you know about it?"

From behind Garreth the writer said, "Elementary, my dear Sergeant, at least to a fan of old horror movies. Alucard—Dracula spelled backward—is an alias used by Lon Chaney's Dracula, so I thought it likely our count would copy him."

"As he says: elementary, old chap," Girimonte murmured.

They reached the third floor. Harry rapped on the door of 306. "Count, it's the police. Sorry to disturb you but we need to talk to you."

No one came to the door.

After a minute Harry knocked again, harder. "Count?"

No one moved in the room as far as Garreth could tell.

"Count Dracula!" Harry shouted. He pounded on the door with a doubled fist. "Open this door!"

"I doubt he'll answer," Fowler said. "Vampires don't move around by daylight, after all."

Girimonte said grimly, "This one will. I'm not coming back at night just to satisfy a fag's idiosyncrasies." She hammered on the door hard enough that the numbers shivered. "You! Cupcake! We don't have time to play games. Now open the fucking door!"

Still no response.

"Let me try," Garreth said. He moved up to the door. "Count, it is possible for you to move around in daylight. Dracula does sometimes in Bram Stoker's book, and Louis Jourdan did in the PBS production of *Dracula*. It's a beautiful day out, too . . . raining. There's no sun shining at all."

Harry and Girimonte leaned on each other, choking with laughter. The corners of Fowler's mouth twitched.

The count, however, remained silent.

Garreth leaned his forehead against the door. "Count, will you please—"

The plea died abruptly in his throat, strangled by a terrible realization: a hotel room, though just a room, became a dwelling for the person in it, yet he felt nothing touching this door, not a flicker of barrier flames. A distinctive odor seeped through the door, too, the same one that had filled Holle's room. "Shit. Harry, get the pass key."

They gaped at him. "What?"

"The pass key! He's dead in there!"

Still they stared. "Dead? How . . ."

"I can smell him!"

Girimonte took off for the stairs like a deer.

Garreth slammed the wall with the side of his fist. Another one. He tried to tell himself that this death might have nothing to do with the others. Considering the Bay Vista's usual clientel, he could have been killed by someone ripping off the room. Maybe.

When Girimonte came pounding back up the stairs with the key a few minutes later to unlock the door, all possibility of that scenario evaporated. The count lay stretched on his back on the bed as if in state, dressed in a tuxedo, hands folded across his chest, but blood dried to dirty brown covered the pleated shirt and out of the middle of it protruded a shaft of wood.

"Good Lord," Fowler said hoarsely.

The dead man's head twisted grotesquely to the side, but his expression of terror and pain—eyes popping, mouth stretched open in a soundless shriek, hands frozen into claws—testified that his neck had not been broken until after he had suffered the agony of the stake being pounded into his chest. Like Holle, his hair lay clumped in points on his forehead. The crossed wrists bore braided grooves where he had fought bonds, grooves like those on Holle's wrists. More abrasions from mouth to ears indicated he had been gagged, too.

Dried blood also covered a pillow on the floor, especially around a hole in the middle of the pillow.

Fury boiled up through Garreth. The dead man's final screams had sunk unheard into his gag, but they must have echoed and re-echoed endlessly in his head as the killer laid the pillow over the victim's chest to absorb any splattering blood and pounded in the stake through it. Garreth's head rang with those screams. Lane and Irina, blood mother and daughter indeed. They shared the same taste for inflicting wanton pain. This little man had harmed no one with his fantasy. He certainly did not deserve a death like this. *I'm going to find her, Count, just as I found Lane. That I promise you.*

"The stake's been made from a chair rung," Harry said.

He pointed to a wooden desk chair with a rung missing from between its front legs. Curls of wood from sharpening the rung to a point littered the desk top.

Girimonte disappeared into the bathroom. "The washbowl has the plug in and there's a little water still standing in it. Looks like he got the same treatment Holle did."

"But much earlier." Harry sniffed. "Maybe yesterday."

Girimonte eyed Garreth from the bathroom doorway. "Where were you yesterday, Mikaelian?"

Garreth's breath caught.

"You know where he was!" Harry snapped. "I found him at home in bed asleep."

"At three o'clock in the afternoon, yes. What about before then?" She raised her brows. "We have hours unaccounted for between the time you left for work and went home after Mikaelian. Maybe he didn't answer the phone, not because he sleeps so sound, but because he wasn't there."

"Van, don't start that again!"

"Harry, why don't you stop burying your head?" Girimonte ticked off points on her fingers. "He fights with a hustler he claims had information about a killer he has very personal reasons for wanting to find, and the hustler dies. Later that day the hustler's roommate is killed, too, with signs of having been tortured, possibly in an effort to gain information. That afternoon someone else connected to our lady killer has words with him and today *he* turns up dead. Also tortured. And this bloodbath started the day after he arrived in town."

"Oh, come now," Fowler began.

"This is ridiculous," Garreth said. He intended the statement to be calmly firm, but it emerged with the sharp edges of fear and disbelief he felt. How could anyone seriously think he— "I want to collar Lane so desperately that I commit murder myself? Three innocent civilians? Come *on!*"

Girimonte pulled one of her elegant cigars from her breast pocket and lit it. "You come on, Mikaelian. You're dirty. You know a lot more about this case than you're telling anyone. I can smell it."

She was the kind who, believing something, would dig until she got what she was after. He could not afford to have her digging; it would turn up more than she counted on, more than he wanted anyone to know. "Harry, you know me. Straighten her out."

Harry sighed heavily. "A year and a half ago I'd have said I knew you. Now—you've changed, Mik-san. I can't guess what you're thinking or feeling anymore. And I can't help feeling that Van's right about one thing—killer or not, you do know more than you're telling." The almond eyes slid away from Garreth, dark with unhappiness and profound un-ease.

Hare and Hound

1

God, he hated daylight! Today even late afternoon dragged on him with as much force as high noon. Garreth splashed water on his face and pushed himself upright.

The mirrors above the sinks in the men's room at Bryant Street reflected a face thinner and paler than ever, with eyes smudged by weariness. The eyes he saw, though, were violet, dancing amid the flames of a blazing bridge. Since they had come back from the hotel, his former colleagues in homicide had been watching him sideways, and when they spoke to him it was in the flat voice usually reserved for outsiders. Lane's laughter whispered in his ears.

Fowler came out of a stall behind him. "What bloody fools those coppers are!"

Garreth snatched for his glasses. He had almost forgotten about the writer following him into the men's room. "They're just doing their job. As luck would have it, I've been in the wrong places at the wrong times."

"I wonder if luck has had much to do with it." Fowler turned on the water in one basin. The heat of it carried his blood scent toward Garreth. Garreth's stomach cramped with hunger. "Have you considered that for purposes of hanging a frame on you, you've been exactly in the right places at the right times?"

Hunger vanished in dismay. "Frame!"

Fowler rinsed his hands and reached for a paper towel. "Of course. I've been thinking about this a good deal and a frame makes sense of everything. I admit I'm no policeman, only a writer, but that's to my favor. I can recognize a plot when I see one. Don't you see? The torture wasn't to gain information at all, only to make it *appear* that someone wanted information . . . a role your Miss Barber has carefully tailored to you."

"Why? It doesn't gain her anything." Even if Lane were alive.

Fowler smiled thinly. "Except revenge, old son. You've seriously inconvenienced her, after all, haven't you? Making her give up her job and go into hiding, forcing her to move twice, turning friends against her. So now she's returning the favor. It's much nastier than killing you outright. This way she destroys you. Even if you aren't prosecuted or convicted, you'll become a pariah."

But Lane was dead. The same motive fit Irina, though. Since leaving that note at the apartment, she might have found out he killed Lane. He sucked in his breath. "Maybe you're right."

"In which case you'd best find her quickly, before she kills again."

Before another innocent person died. Garreth's mouth thinned. Find her how? The hexagram Lien had thrown for him that morning—only that morning —ran through his head: If the little fox wets his tail crossing the river, nothing furthers. Thought and caution are necessary for success.

He sighed. "I think I'd be playing into her hands going after her on my own. It's better to lay your theory on Harry and let him check it while I keep low and out of trouble."

"Hang about now!" Fowler snapped. "You're already *in* trouble, up to your bloody eyebrows. And you'll get no help from that lot in the squad room, either. They're already half convinced by the frame."

"But you're not?" Garreth asked sardonically.

Fowler leaned against a sink. "No, and I want to help you prove your innocence."

"So you can have a happy ending for the book?"

Fowler jerked upright. "*To hell with the bloody book!*"

A uniformed officer coming in the door stopped short and stared at them.

Taking a deep breath, Fowler lowered his voice to a whisper. "You are a bloody fool! There's a woman out there trying to put you in the dock and she's got to be stopped! That's all that matters at the moment. Look here; I *can* help you. I'm a famous writer. People will talk to me who'd never open their mouths to a copper. And as long as I'm with you, you've got an alibi, haven't you, whatever Barber tries."

Garreth reached up under his glasses to rub his eyes. They burned. But then everything else in him ached, too. He sighed. "I'll think about it."

"You do that, old son." Fowler headed for the door. "But don't take long or it may be too late."

2

Garreth explained Fowler's theory to Harry on the drive home.

Harry bit his lower lip. "It's a possibility. I'd like it to be the case. It'd mean your only involvement is as a fall guy. Van won't go for it, though. Too complicated. She'll have a point, too. Most people in Barber's position would just kill *you*. Plots like Fowler's suggesting only happen in books and the movies." He paused. "Mik-san, what is it you know you haven't told me about? It might help if you did."

He wished . . . but even if he could feel confident that the resources of the police department would find Irina, not only was there too much risk that they might learn what she was, but Harry could become her next victim. Once before, his carelessness had nearly killed Harry. That must not happen again.

In the interest of appearing cooperative, though, maybe he could risk a partial truth.

He shrugged. "It's nothing, just one of Grandma Doyle's feelings. I'm not even sure how you'd act on it. She warned me to beware of a violet-eyed woman. I . . . asked Holle if the woman asking for Lane had violet eyes."

"And?"

"He claimed he never noticed their color. When I asked him if he was sure, he acted like I'd accused him of lying."

"That was the hassle?" Harry shook his head. "Why didn't you say so before?"

"I'm not about to drag my grandmother out in front of your partner and Fowler to be ridiculed or turned into a character in a book."

Did Harry believe that? Garreth could not tell. Harry smiled, but said nothing more, only drove the rest of the way home in silence.

They pulled into the drive. Then as they climbed out, he looked at Garreth across the top of the car. "There's no point upsetting Lien with the . . . problems in this case, so—"

"I don't want to distress her with the fact that I'm a suspect, either, Harry," Garreth interrupted.

"Thanks."

Lien met them at the door, shaking her head in mock exasperation. "I don't know why I bother cooking for you two. Everything is mummified by the time you finally come home. It would make more sense to wait until I see you, then send out for pizza or make a quick run to the Colonel for fried chicken."

Harry kissed her soundly. "Think how dull life would be if you always knew where I'd be and when."

"You might start taking him for granted," Garreth teased.

For a moment the laughter died out of her eyes. She reached out to touch Harry's cheek. "Never."

In that one word Garreth heard her morning ritual with *I Ching*—"Will my husband be safe today?"—and the memory of that terrible wait in the emergency room to learn if Harry would live or die.

A moment later she laughed again. "Come along, honorable husband, honored guest; your tea is waiting."

She served it in the family room as always, but instead of sitting down to enjoy it, they followed her into the dining room and kitchen, joking with each other and her. Garreth pretended to sip from his cup, then set it down and "forgot" it as he helped her set the table. Without actually talking shop, Harry filled dinner with a string of anecdotes about people seen or interviewed during the day, mimicking some like Fowler and the clerk at the Bay Vista Hotel with wicked accuracy.

"It was great being partners with Garreth again, right, Mik-san?"

"Right." Garreth wished his tea had no brandy in it so he could drink it. As the kitchen and dining room filled with blood scents, his stomach cramped in a savage hunger that burned all the way up his throat. "Like old times." He gulped down his glass of water. It eased the pangs a little. "How was your day?"

"I had my children's art class this afternoon." She launched into stories about teaching drawing and painting.

As she talked, however, she kept glancing from Harry to him with a searching gaze that sent his stomach toward his feet. Did she suspect something?

His answer came at the end of dinner. He picked up his plate and started to stand and carry it into the kitchen.

She reached across to catch his arm. "That can wait, Garreth. All right, you two; tell me what's wrong."

Harry regarded her innocently. "Wrong? What do you mean?"

She stared at him. "I mean you've come home running a relentless two-man comedy routine, but you're just picking over your beef stroganoff and

Garreth hasn't eaten any at all. Every time you do that, something has happened that you don't want me to find out about because you think it will upset me. Once it was a knife wound on your arm. Another time the two of you had fought over whether to release a suspect you felt sure was guilty but didn't have the evidence to hold. What is it this time?"

"There's nothing—" Harry began.

Garreth interrupted, "Girimonte and I mix like gasoline and matches." He should have remembered. Lien always knew when they dragged home psychological baggage. So give her something to chew over.

Lien eyed them both for a minute, then nodded. "Yes, I can imagine, and my poor Harry is caught in the middle, not sure which to side with, old partner or new partner."

After reaching over to pat Harry's arm, she appeared satisfied and let the subject drop. They washed dishes and adjourned to the TV to watch the news, then to groan and hoot at police procedure as portrayed on the late-night rerun of a cop show.

Garreth slipped out to the refrigerator in the kitchen during the show. He drank straight from the thermos, but even as he gulped down the blood, his appetite continued to snarl in frustration at every maddeningly unsatisfying swallow. The memory of Holle's refrigerator taunted him.

A sound in the dining room warned him that he was about to have company. Blood scent drifting around him told him who. Moving casually, he crossed to the sink and rinsed out the thermos. Hunting time again tonight. "Hi, Lien."

From behind him, she said, "You're still using that liquid protein diet you were on when you left San Francisco? Do you ever eat anything else?"

He glanced over his shoulder. "Of course." Water rinsed the last traces of blood down the drain. "I just wasn't hungry tonight."

She leaned against the kitchen door. "Harry's gone up to get ready for bed. I don't suppose you'll tell me what the real problem between the two of you is."

He set the thermos upside down on the drain board to dry and turned to face her. "I can't."

Her forehead furrowed. "Or what the problem eating you up inside is? Before you left San Francisco, remember, I told you I wished I could help you. I still want to."

"I wish you could, but . . . no one can. It's something I have to work out for myself."

"That's what you said last time, but you obviously haven't worked it out yet. *Why* can't you tell me? You let me help when Marti died, and you came here when you ran away from the hospital after that Barber girl tried to kill you." She paused. "I dream about you, Garreth. I reach out to touch you and I can't. You're so far away . . . farther and farther each time."

All her dream lacked was the burning bridge. Longing gnawed at him to tell her everything.

But he could visualize her reaction—disbelief at first, then concern as she decided he had gone bonkers. He imagined proving himself by showing her how his fangs extended, and how he could move through shut doors. Then disbelief would turn to horror and revulsion, and worst of all, to fear of him. He could not bear that.

He made himself smile. "Don't let a stupid nightmare upset you. I'll be fine."

She ran a hand through her hair. "While I waited for you two to come home tonight, I threw tomorrow's hexagrams. Yours was number twenty-nine, The Abysmal. If you are sincere, you have success in your heart and whatever you do succeeds."

He eyed her, his stomach knotting. "So why aren't you smiling?"

She bit her lip. "A change line in the third place means that every step, forward or backward, leads into danger. There is no escape. You must wait for the way out."

Cold ran down his spine. "No escape? The change line makes a second hexagram. Does it offer a solution?"

She shook her head. "Number forty-eight, The Well, is a bit esoteric, but in this context, I think it reinforces the first hexagram."

Cold ate deeper. Every step leads into inescapable danger. But he could not afford to wait it out. He had to find Irina before more people died and what remained of his bridge collapsed in ashes.

3

That thought echoed in Garreth's head all night. Even in the brash light of morning, sitting on Harry's desk with the squad room's stew of tobacco smoke, coffee, after-shave, and blood scents washing around him and Centrello droning through an update of his and Faye's cases, urgency drummed at Garreth. Find the violet-eyed vampire.

His gut knotted. Of course, if he did he courted disaster, according to *I Ching* and his grandmother's feeling. But retreat meant danger, too, and surely it was better to meet danger head-on than in retreat.

The question still remained of how to find her, and no matter how often he asked it, now or last night while slipping out of the house to Golden Gate Park to fill his thermos from a horse in the police stable—a closer source of blood than the rats on the waterfront —one answer came up: the number the housekeeper phoned. A number somewhere in the address book Harry had locked in his desk last night.

The reporting voice became Harry's. ". . . call from

a pawnshop owner last night. He left a message. A watch like the one taken from the liquor store clerk during the robbery has turned up at his shop. Van and I will check it out this morning once she's back from prying the autopsy report on Maruska out of the coroner's office. Holle and Count Dracula—whose name we're still trying to learn—should be posted today or tomorrow. That open window at Holle's isn't going to help us make a case against anyone. The lab found no evidence of forcible entry and the only prints belong to the housekeeper and another woman who cleans part time. It looks like the killer spotted and took advantage of a window someone left open."

"Let's hope he left traces in the bedroom," Serruto said. "Your turn, Kolb."

The front of the top desk drawer felt slick and cool under the sliding exploration of Garreth's fingers. He touched the handle and tried it tentatively. Locked. His hand itched with the desire to wrench open the drawer. A glance around, though, found Fowler eyeing him and he pulled the hand back to shove it into the pocket of his coat.

Kolb finished her report. Serruto nodded. "That's it then. Carry on, as our esteemed author-in-residence might say." He poured himself a cup of coffee and vanished into his office.

Fowler raised a brow at Garreth. *Have you thought about our discussion?* the expression asked.

Harry came over to sit down at his desk. Garreth moved off it.

He had thought about the discussion, yes . . . all last night while he filled his thermos and wondered how to find Irina. As much as he appreciated the offer and the support it represented, the idea of a partnership did not appeal to him. How could he effectively hunt Irina when he had to appear to be hunting Lane? On the other hand, Fowler had a point about his fame opening doors, not to mention his presence providing an alibi. All things considered . . . Garreth dipped his chin. *You're on.*

Fowler smiled.

Occupied with unlocking his desk and taking out the address book, Harry missed the exchange.

Girimonte swept in from the corridor waving a sheaf of papers. "Got it." She dropped the autopsy report on Harry's desk and lit a cigar. "I gave it a quick read on the way up in the elevator. No surprises."

"You mean he wasn't a Martian after all?" Fowler asked.

Did he have to bring that up? Garreth glanced sidelong at Girimonte, but if she connected the other dead men the assistant M.E. mentioned with whatever she had decided about Garreth, she showed no sign of it.

She shrugged. "I don't know what anomalies Welton was so excited about. So Maruska was obviously healthy and athletic when the total lack of body fat and minimal intestinal contents should indicate severe starvation. There's something about the color of the liver indicating a high iron intake and tarry feces being present without a site for upper G.I. bleeding, but all I see that's really different is his teeth."

Garreth's stomach lurched. He peered over Harry's shoulder at the report. ". . . unusually sharp upper canines, grooved on the posterior side." His tongue traced the grooves down his own fangs. At least the pathologist had missed the fact that the teeth extended and retracted.

"How disappointing," Fowler murmured. "I had hoped for green blood at the very least."

Girimonte blew cigar smoke at him. "Vulcans, not Martians, have green blood."

Garreth smoothed his mustache. Martians. Maybe there was another lead after all. If those bodies *were* vampires, too, then someone they knew must be a link to others of the blood in the city, others who might point the way to Irina.

"This is very interesting, I'm sure, but," Harry said and pushed to his feet, "we have a pawnshop owner to talk to, and after we've followed that lead as far as it'll go, we need to look up Holle's friends to talk about possible enemies." He waved the address book. "Shall we hit the bricks?"

Garreth debated hurriedly. Following one lead meant abandoning the other for a while. Which way to try first? *No contest, man. The one without Girimonte.* He smiled at Harry. "While you're working on the liquor store shooting, I think I'll go over the files on the Mossman and Adair murders with Mr. Fowler. We can catch up with you later."

Fowler blinked, then grinned. "Capital."

"Go over the old files." Girimonte's eyes narrowed. She tapped the ash off her cigar.

"Yes, of course." Fowler's brows rose. "What do you think, that we'd go haring off on our own?"

"The thought crossed my mind."

"Well, you're wrong . . . again," Garreth snapped. "After going over the case files, at most we might visit the Barbary Now and the alley where Lane attacked me, to let Mr. Fowler soak up local color. Nothing more." He focused on her as he said it, though, not looking at Harry.

Harry eyed him and Fowler.

"Cross our hearts and hope to die," the writer said cheerfully.

Harry shook his head and started for the door. "Come on, Van. Contact dispatch for our twenty when you two want to catch up, Mik-san."

Fowler waited until the door had closed before turning to Garreth. "Right. Now, old son, suppose you tell me what you really have in mind."

4

"The morgue?" Fowler's brows rose as they walked into the reception area of the coroner's office. "Are we interrogating the dead men?"

Garreth gave him a thin smile. "Something like that. This won't take long. Wait for me here." He turned the smile on the receiving clerk. "Morning, Barbara. Where's Dr. Thurlow?"

The clerk stared. "Inspector Mikaelian? I heard you were back. Lord, I hardly recognize you. You got serious about dieting. The old man's in the autopsy room."

The effort needed to walk down the corridor had nothing to do with the drag of daylight. Garreth hated coming here. He always had, even before having to identify Marti's body. Waking up in one of its drawers himself had not endeared it to him, either. The place served the living, but it was a world of death, of tile and stainless steel . . . shining, cold, hard.

Pushing through the door of the autopsy room, though, he realized that oddly enough, he disliked this room the least. Perhaps because here corpses ceased to be people. Lying with bellies and chests spread open, scalps pulled inside out and down over their faces, they no longer looked quite human.

Down the long line of tables the light shone on a stylish mane of silver hair. Garreth made his way toward it through the flood of smells: disinfectants, dead blood, diseased blood, putrifying flesh, the acrid stench of intestinal contents, and in sparse, tantalizing whiffs almost lost among the other odors, the warm saltiness of living blood.

The murmur of voices filled the room, pathologists talking to assistants and dictating into microphones dangling overhead, sentences punctuated by occasional laughter and the sharp whine of a bone saw slicing through a skull. Light gleamed on instruments and clay-gray flesh. Water hissed, running down the tables to carry away the blood. More water swirled rosy in sinks at the end of the tables, where floating organs waited to be sliced open for further examination.

"Dr. Thurlow?"

The chief medical examiner looked up from studying lungs as red as the liver lying on the table beside them. He peered at Garreth over the top of half glasses. "Morning, Mikaelian."

Garreth blinked. "You recognize me?"

"I remember all my patients who get well and go home." Thurlow's knife sliced through the lung in quick, sure strokes, sectioning it like a loaf of bread, then scraped across several of the exposed internal surfaces. "What can I do for you, Mikaelian?"

"I'm interested in your Martians."

Gray eyes peered keenly at him over the half glasses. "You, too? This is the most attention the poor bastards have had in ten years. Mitch Welton has all the autopsy reports in his office."

Where going to ask for them would make the entire

staff of the coroner's office aware he had asked about the Martians? No. "If you know the names offhand, that's all I need." Garreth kept his voice casual.

Thurlow snorted. "After the recent chance to refresh my memory, the facts are graven in my offhand, Inspector." He sliced off several pieces of lung and dropped them into a specimen jar an assistant held out, then picked up the liver. "December 15, 1975, Christopher Parke Stroda, suicide. A jumper. Number whatever from the bridge."

In the middle of grabbing for his notebook, Garreth caught his breath. Suicide! "The fall broke his neck?"

"It broke almost everything," Thurlow replied dryly. His knife sliced expertly through the liver. "Thomas Washington Bodenhausen, October 11, 1979, construction accident. Decapitation."

Garreth stared. "Construction? He had a *day* job?" The words were out before he thought.

He could only curse himself silently as Thurlow's brows went up. "What's so strange about that? But this happened at night, if I remember right. Last Martian: Corinne Lucasta Barlow, July 20, 1981. Traffic fatality. Another broken neck. Multiple fractured vertebrae, in fact. Also fractures of assorted long bones, plus ruptures of liver, spleen, and kidneys. Heart impaled by a broken rib." He paused. "Corinne Lucasta. Unusual name. Old-fashioned."

Maybe not when Corinne Lucasta had been born. "Thanks, doc." Garreth headed for the door.

Back in the reception area he found Fowler leaning on the receiving desk flirting with the clerk. The writer abandoned his conquest abruptly as Garreth appeared. "Have a nice chat?"

"We'll see. Come on."

"Ta," Fowler called back to the clerk.

In the breezeway outside, Garreth sucked in a deep breath of relief and laughed inwardly at himself. Even open daylight was preferable to the morgue? Hierarchies.

"Where now?" Fowler asked.

"Records."

He picked a clerk there he knew, but she just looked at him across the counter. "Do you have authorization to pull these files?"

Garreth frowned. She was not going to be as accommodating as Thurlow. "Authorization?"

"Of course. We can't hand records over to just anyone."

Cursing inwardly, he put on a mask of indignation. "What? Belflower, that's a crock. You know me."

"I know you don't work here anymore." Then she smiled. "I'll tell you what, though. You're riding along with Harry Takananda, right? I'll call him or Lieutenant Serruto for the authorization." She reached for the phone on the counter.

Self-control kept him from grabbing her wrist. That would only attract attention. "Belflower." Garreth pushed his glasses up on his head and caught her gaze. "That isn't—" He broke off. Was this a stupid thing to do with Fowler watching?

In the moment of inattention, she broke away from him, but before her hand touched the phone, Fowler finished, ". . . going to help. The lieutenant doesn't know anything about the lead and Sergeant Takananda is out of the building. I'm sure he would have given us a note or something, but he didn't think there would be this flap." He leaned on the counter and smiled at the clerk. "Look, love, we're just helping out the sergeant, Mikaelian as a favor to an ex-partner, and me tagging along gathering material for my book."

Her eyes widened. "*You're* Graham Fowler!"

He grinned. "Guilty, I'm afraid. Now . . . what do you say?"

She frowned. "Well . . ."

"I don't need to take the files *out*," Garreth said hastily. "A quick look here will give me everything necessary."

"I'd be most grateful," Fowler said.

Belflower smiled at him. "All right."

She hurried off.

Pulling his glasses back in place, Garreth breathed in relief. "Good show."

Fowler smiled dryly. "Well, we can't have the investigation bogging down in red tape, can we?"

Belflower reappeared shortly with three folders. Garreth scanned the reports in each, looking for names, addresses, and telephone numbers of people connected to the victims. It did not surprise him to find very few.

Discovering Bodenhausen was black raised his brows, though on consideration he wondered why it should any more than finding the names of parents and siblings for Christopher Stroda. The Stroda file also included a transcript of a tape recording left on the Golden Gate Bridge with his coat, shoes, and sunglasses. The text whispered its despair in Garreth's head long after he went on to the next file.

"Anything I can do to help?" Fowler asked.

"Thanks, no."

"Do you mind if I have a look anyway?"

Was there more harm in letting him, or in piquing the writer's curiosity by refusing? "Go ahead."

Fowler paged through the folders. "I wonder if I might ask who these people are? They're all old cases, none of them murders. What's their relevance to our murderous Miss Barber?"

The inevitable question. Could he bluff his way out of answering? "Maybe none. It's just a hunch. Don't ask me to explain right now."

Fowler's brows skipped but he did not press the subject.

Garreth grinned inwardly in satisfaction. Moments later, though, satisfaction exploded into a shriek of alarm. The report on Corinne Barlow's accident gave the Philos Foundation as her employer.

Holle had driven a car with personalized plates: PHILOS.

The Philos Foundation! The name reverberated in Garreth's head. He could kick himself for not thinking of it when he first saw Holle's tags. The nonprofit organization kept a low profile, but its storefront blood collection centers dotted the city, and every hospital kept its two numbers handy, 555-LIFE for the blood bank and 1-800-555-STAT to reach the organ transplant hotline at the central offices in Chicago. He had seen the card numerous times at the receiving desk in San Francisco General's trauma center when he dropped by to visit Marti at work. And 555-LIFE, he confirmed by taking a peek at the telephone on the counter, translated into 555-5433, the same pattern of numbers Holle's housekeeper called.

"Find something interesting?" Fowler asked.

Garreth thought fast. "I was thinking about transportation. My car's in Harry's driveway. Do you have one?"

Fowler arched a brow. "Yes, of course. One is crippled in America without one. I take it you intend visiting the people on your list there?"

"Give the man a cookie." Garreth shoved the files back across the counter. "Thanks, Belflower. I'm through. I owe you one."

5

Stroda's parents still lived in Marin County. Garreth almost wished they did not, that he had been unable to find them.

The mention of her son brought raw pain to Sarah Stroda's face. "You want to talk about Christopher?"

Only moments earlier, Garreth had been admiring her youthfulness and the humor glinting in her eyes as she handed back Garreth's identification, accepting his story of being temporarily attached to the San Francisco Police through a continuing-education program for small-town officers. Now the humor had gone, while years etched themselves into her face.

"No." She shook her head. "Let's not talk about him. I've read your books, Mr. Fowler, and except for the way your protagonists treat people as disposable tools, enjoyed them, but I don't want my son in one of your books."

"He won't be," Garreth said. "This doesn't have anything to do with your son himself, just people he might have known."

Mrs. Stroda bit her lip. "Come in." She stepped back inside the neo-Spanish house, opening the carved door wide, though her expression said she longed to close it in their faces. "I think I'd like fresh air." She led the way to a deck overlooking the bay, where she stood at the railing with her back to them, her fingers white on the wrought iron.

Garreth sat down in a redwood chair. "I'm sorry to be bothering you. I wouldn't if it weren't important."

Without looking at him, she said, "It's been ten years. You'd think I'd have gotten over it by now, or at least come to terms with it. Instead, it's like it happened yesterday, and I still don't understand why! He was twenty-four, with everything to live for, and he—" She turned abruptly. "What do you want to know?"

He hated himself for opening old wounds. "I need the names of people he saw regularly before he died."

She groped for a chair and sat down. "I don't know who his friends were. The last two years Christopher became a total stranger."

Protest rose in his throat. She had to know something more, anything, even a single name! He forced his voice to remain soothing and patient. "Think very carefully."

He doubted she heard him. Her fingers twined tightly together. "I wish I could find that woman and ask her what she did to him."

The hair rose on Garreth's neck. From the corner of his eye he watched Fowler's eyes narrow. "Which woman?"

She shook her head. "Someone he met in Europe the summer between college graduation and medical school. That's when he changed."

"Do you know her name?"

"No. He never talked about her. We just happened to learn from friends of friends that he'd been in a serious car accident in Italy and would have died except that this woman he was traveling with gave blood for him and saved his life. We asked him about it but he kept saying it was nothing and he didn't want to talk about it." She drew in a shaking breath. "Over the months he had less and less to say to us. He dropped out of medical school, and stopped seeing his friends . . . withdrawing, slipping farther away each day, until—" She turned away abruptly.

Garreth fought to keep his face expressionless. Until the widening gulf between Stroda and humanity became unbearable. Going off the bridge was certainly one solution to the pain.

"We thought it was drugs," Mrs. Stroda said, "though he always denied it. I guess it wasn't. The autopsy didn't find any." She turned back: "Who are these people you're looking for? Could they be responsible for what happened to him?"

If only he could tell her. Except that could cause far more anguish than it cured. "I can't tell you much about them, but no, they didn't cause your son's death."

She let out her breath. "Good. So I don't have to feel guilty about not being able to help you."

"Perhaps one of your daughters knew something," Fowler suggested.

Mrs. Stroda stiffened. "No! I won't have them hurt again! Allison was only fifteen at the time. How could she know his friends?"

"Mrs. Stroda, it's very important that we find these people," Garreth said.

Fowler nodded. "Lives depend on it . . . sons and daughters of other mothers."

Mrs. Stroda flung up her head, catching her breath.

"Fowler!" Garreth snapped.

But Mrs. Stroda shook her head. "No, he's right. I'll give you the girls' addresses and phone numbers." She stood and disappeared into the house.

Garreth turned on Fowler. "That was a cheap shot!"

The writer smiled. "But effective."

"The end justifies the means?" Garreth asked acidly.

The smile thinned. "Don't go casting stones, old son. I've noticed you're not above deceit and manipulation when it suits your purposes."

Garreth opened his mouth, then closed it again. What did he think he was going to say, that he acted for a righteous cause, that he tried not to hurt anyone in the process? Rationalizations. No matter how reasonable, they did not change the fact of deceit.

Mrs. Stroda reappeared with a sheet from a memo pad. She held it out to Garreth. "This time of day Janice will be at work. I've included that address, too."

Fowler glanced over Garreth's shoulder at the sheet. "Your daughter Allison is at the Stanford Medical School. Following in her brother's footsteps?"

"Tracking him might be a better description." Years and grief looked out of Mrs. Stroda's eyes. "Allison is studying to become a psychiatrist. Good day, gentlemen."

6

Good was not quite how Garreth could describe the day, not when he opened painful old wounds in three people in vain. Neither Allison Stroda nor Janice Stroda Meers, who worked in a crisis center near the University of San Francisco campus, could tell them any more than their mother had. Maybe the situation would be better with Thomas Bodenhausen. The police report had listed no next of kin for him.

Bodenhausen had lived comfortably for a night watchman. The apartment building, a solid Victorian structure, offered its tenants a beautiful view of the marina and the Palace of Fine Arts. The apartment manager, however, offered little. Frowning at Garreth from the open doorway of his apartment, he said skeptically, "Bodenhausen? Six years ago? Officer, you can't expect me to remember a tenant who left that long ago." He eyed the badge case still in Garreth's hands. "Are police interns paid?"

The question caught Garreth off guard. He had never expected anyone to ask for details of his cover story. His mind raced. "Yes . . . living expenses anyway. I think you'll remember this tenant, Mr. Catao. He—"

"Who pays you?"

Impatience stung him. He had no time for this; he had to find Irina! Damn! If only Fowler were not along, he could use his powers on the manager. "My department, of course. About Mr. Bodenhausen—"

The manager's brows went up. "So the city gets extra officers like you two for free?"

Who *was* this bastard, a member of the budget council? Garreth fought the itch to pull off his glasses and trap Catao's gaze. "No. They profit. My department pays a fee to send me here. Now, may we *please* talk about Thomas Bodenhausen?"

Catao spread his hands. "I told you, I don't remember him."

Garreth sighed in exasperation. "He died, Mr. Catao. You must remember that . . . a fire and explosion at a construction site? A flying piece of metal decapitated the night watchman?"

"Oh." Recognition bloomed in the manager's face. "*Him.* Yes, I remember that guy, but I still can't tell you much. I didn't know him. He'd been here since before I took over as manager fifteen years ago and he was a good tenant—quiet, always paid his rent on time, kept his apartment in good shape. What's this about? I heard that fire and explosion was an accident."

Garreth opened his mouth to reply. Fowler cut in first. "I'm considering making it sabotage for the purpose of my book."

Catao focused on Fowler for the first time, eyes narrowing. "Your book? Aren't you an exchange from Scotland Yard?"

Despite the urgent situation, Garreth had to bite back a grin. Fowler's expression was the epitome of innocent surprise. "Did we give you that impression?

I'm terribly sorry. No, I'm a writer. Officer Mikaelian introduced me as Julian Fowler but my full name is Julian *Graham* Fowler. The San Francisco Police are very kindly cooperating in some research I'm doing and they lent me Officer Mikaelian to—"

The manager's eyes opened wide. "*The* Graham Fowler? Who wrote *Midnight Brigade* and *Winter Gambit?*"

Fowler rubbed his nose. "Well, at the risk of learning you consider them trash, those are two of my efforts, yes."

"Are you kidding?" The manager grinned. "That Dane Winter is great. Have you read the books?" he asked Garreth.

"Not those two." The evasion avoided an admission he had not read any of Fowler's books.

The manager shook his head. "You ought to. He's this guy who's past fifty and the hotshot kids in British Intelligence keep trying to claim he's over the hill but he can still spy rings around them all. He doesn't go getting himself beat up all the time, either. When you're our age you'll appreciate seeing a hero like that for a change. Hey, why are we standing out here in the hall? Come in, Mr. Fowler." He led the way into his living room. It smelled of a sweetly fragrant pipe tobacco.

"It's gratifying to hear my heroes are appreciated." Fowler strolled over to the bay window. "What a magnificent view of the bay. Are you sure you can't help us with Bodenhausen?"

The manager's forehead furrowed. "Damn, I wish I could. But I just never knew him."

"You said he took good care of his apartment," Garreth said. "That sounds like you were in it."

"Yeah, from time to time, when something needed fixing."

"Was anyone else ever there? Or do you know if he was particular friends with any of the other tenants."

The furrows deepened. "Keith Manziaro, I think. Once when I was up in his apartment he was telling his wife about fighting the Battle of Bull Run against Bodenhausen."

"Bodenhausen was a war games buff?" Fowler asked.

"More than that." Catao grinned. "His spare bedroom where he spread those battlefield maps on the floor looked like a museum. I mean, he had muskets and swords and Civil War rifles all over the walls. He even had some military uniforms from the Revolutionary and Civil Wars, handed down from ancestors who'd worn them, he told me."

Possibly Bodenhausen himself had worn them, Garreth mused.

"And he also had this letter he claimed was signed by George Washington, freeing another ancestor who'd been a slave at Mount Vernon. I don't know if I can believe that, but it makes a good story."

A letter signed by George Washington! Garreth caught his breath. That letter and the other relics would be priceless heirlooms to most families. Who had Bodenhausen's belongings gone to? A friend who could appreciate them, perhaps a fellow vampire? "Mr. Catao, what happened to Bodenhausen's property after he died?"

Catao blinked at Garreth. "His executors took it all away, of course."

"Executors? Who were they?"

"Hell, I don't remember." He rolled his eyes as Garreth frowned. "Christ, what do you think, I have a photographic memory? I saw the name once six years ago when this guy shows up with a key to the apartment and papers signed by Bodenhausen making some museum or something his executor."

"Museum?" Garreth frowned. "A local one?"

"I don't know. Probably not. I didn't recognize the name. Hey, I didn't pay much attention, okay? The papers looked legal so I let them have Bodenhausen's things and forgot about it."

A throb started behind Garreth's forehead. "Naturally," he said wearily. Did not know. Did not remember. Had paid no attention. Had forgotten. The same damned roadblocks over and over again. "Isn't there *anything* you remember? What the man looked like maybe? The markings on the moving van?"

"I remember the guy's car."

That was a start. "What about his car?"

Catao grinned. "The name of the museum was on the plates. I remember thinking museum work must pay pretty well for him to be driving a BMW."

The hair rose all over Garreth's body. *Lady Luck, you bitch, I love you!* "This guy, was he in his fifties, average height and weight, graying hair, mustache, glasses?"

"I'm not sure about a mustache and glasses." The manager's forehead creased with the effort of remembering. "But the rest sounds right. How——"

"Thank you very much, Mr. Catao." Garreth hurried for the building door. "Sorry to have bothered you. Have a nice day."

At the car he waited impatiently for Fowler to catch up. The man who came for Bodenhausen's belongings had to be Holle. How many men in San Francisco drove BMW's with personalized plates carrying the name of an organization that might be mistaken for a museum name? The Philos Foundation. This made four people with links to that organization: Irina, Holle, Bodenhausen, and Corinne Barlow . . . two of them part of the murder case, three of them vampires. Too many people for pure coincidence. Philos bore looking into.

Fowler unlocked the car. "Hello, hello. Something he said put a piece in the puzzle, did it?"

Sooner or later the writer would have to be given some answers, but not yet. "Maybe." Garreth climbed into the car and lay back in the seat, giving up the fight against daylight's drag for a few minutes.

"Maybe?" Fowler said. "You know it bloody *did*. That was Holle you described. Now what's the connection?"

Maybe he needed to confide in Fowler a little at least. "It was Holle. The connection is the Philos Foundation. But since Harry and company will end up there sooner or later, too, on their way through Holle's address book, we can't afford a straightforward visit." Garreth closed his eyes. "Head for Union Street. We'll think up something devious on the way."

7

All that distinguished the yellow-with-brown-trim foundation headquarters from the other shop-filled Victorian houses around it was drapes instead of some commercial display inside the bay window and a discrete brass plate on the door at the top of steep brick steps. PHILOS FOUNDATION, was the script engraving. PLEASE RING FOR ADMITTANCE.

Fowler pushed the bell.

A minute later the door was opened by a slim young woman whose modish dress and frizzy mane of hair made her look like a fashion model. A spicy scent that smelled equal parts cinnamon and clove wafted out of the house past her. "Good afternoon. May I help—" She broke off, staring past the writer at Garreth.

His gut knotted. She recognized him for what he was! If she said anything in front of Fowler . . .

But she only said, "Please come in."

Garreth followed her and Fowler inside, feeling as if he were walking into a mine field.

Judging by the house's interior, the Philos Foundation suffered from no shortage of money despite its nonprofit status. Garreth could not help but compare the bargain furnishings and poster-decorated walls at Janice Stroda's crisis center with this thick carpeting and a front room furnished in chrome-and-leather chairs, modern sculpture, and signed-and-numbered prints. The spicy odor became more pronounced, drowning the blood scents in the room.

The young woman sat down at a desk made of chrome and glass. An engraved name plate said: MERESA RANNEY. "What may I do for you, Mr. . . .?"

Fowler smiled at her. "Warwick. Richard Warwick. A friend of mine came over here to work for your organization several years ago and as I'm in town for a bit, I thought I'd look her up. Corinne Barlow."

While Fowler occupied the receptionist Garreth strolled around the room, trying to look idle, peering out the bay window, touching sculpture, eyeing the prints, all the while studying the house covertly.

"Corinne Barlow?" The receptionist frowned. "I'm sorry but I don't know the name. What does she do?"

The rear wall had a large fireplace with a door to one side. Nothing identified what might be beyond it. Garreth remembered seeing double sliding doors in the hallway. They probably opened into the same room as this door. Which would be what, an administrative office?

"Corinne works with computers," Fowler said.

The accident report had mentioned that in vital statistics about the victim.

Garreth eyed the doorway to the hall. He could see the bottom of the stairs through it. Nothing indicated what lay up them, however.

The receptionist's frown deepened. She shook her head. "I'm sorry, I'm afraid—oh." Her breath caught. "Now I remember. There was an Englishwoman. I'd completely forgotten her, she was here so short a time."

"She got sacked? Damn." Fowler feigned disappointment beautifully. "I don't suppose you'd know where she went."

"She wasn't fired." The lovely model's face settled into lines of sympathy. "I'm sorry to be the one to tell you. She was killed in a car accident just a couple of weeks after she arrived."

Fowler also acted out shock and grief with the skill of a professional actor. "Damn." His throat worked, then he smiled faintly. "Well, thank you. Sorry to have troubled you." He headed for the hall.

Garreth moved up to the end of the desk so that the receptionist had to look away from the hall door to face him.

She regarded Garreth with surprise. "Aren't you with the other gentleman?"

"No, we just met on the steps outside. I'm Alan Osner."

The front door opened and closed. A moment later Fowler slipped past the doorway and down the hall toward the back of the house.

"I've been staying at Leonard Holle's—I'm sorry," he said contritely as her eyes filled. "I didn't mean to upset you." Inwardly he noted her reaction with satisfaction. They knew Holle here all right . . . very well.

"No, that's all right." She groped in a desk drawer. "I'm fine."

"I take it you knew Leonard?"

"He was our chapter president." The groping hand came up with a tissue. She carefully blotted her eyes and inspected the damage with a small mirror from the same drawer. "It's been a terrible—who are you looking for, Mr. Osner?"

Fowler reappeared in the hall and started up the stairs.

"Miss Irina Rudenko. Leonard's housekeeper said I might find her here."

On the bottom step, Fowler started, turning to stare at Garreth for a moment before continuing up the stairs.

"I'm sorry," the receptionist said. "Miss Rudenko isn't here right now. Would you care to leave a message?"

"I'd rather see her personally." He forced his voice to remain casual, to ignore the drumming urgency in him. "Do you have a home phone for her?"

"I can't give out that kind of information, sir."

Garreth casually took off his glasses.

Such improbably blue eyes had to be a product of tinted contact lenses. The depth and wideness of them was her own, though, and for an uneasy moment as he caught her gaze, Garreth wondered if a vampire could ever become trapped in his victim's eyes. He forced himself to widen his focus beyond the twin cobalt pools.

A mistake. A pulse pounded visibly in her long neck. The tantalizing warmth of her blood scent caressed him, perceptible despite the spicy odor filling the room. Hunger exploded in him. She stared into his eyes, her lips parted as though in anticipation. Anticipation seared him, too . . . the feel of her in his arms—pliant, yielding—the throb of that pulse against his lips and searching tongue . . . the exquisite salty fire of her blood in his mouth. He started around the desk toward her.

Laughter whispered in his head—eager, mocking. Lane's laughter.

Garreth caught himself in horror. Jumping back, he jammed on his glasses and shoved his hands into his coat pockets to hide their tremble. He fought to steady his voice. "Do you think Irina might be in later?"

The receptionist blinked up at him with the puzzled expression of a waking sleeper struggling to orient herself. "I . . . don't know. Mr. Holle gives—gave her the run of the place since her mother works for the foundation in Geneva, but since *she* doesn't work for us herself we never know when—" She hesitated a moment, then smiled. "I guess I can tell *you*, though."

The hair on his neck rippled. "Why me in particular?"

She gave him a brilliant smile. "Your aura, of course. People with black ones always seem to get preferential treatment around here. See, I have this gift for seeing auras. Mostly I don't tell people because they laugh or get nervous, like they're afraid I'll read their minds or something. The people here at the foundation don't mind, though. Mrs. Keith, who's Mr. Holle's secretary, even said it's one of the reasons they hired me. I usually see black just around dying people, but yours isn't the same kind of black. It's . . . bright, if that makes any sense, a very intense, fiery black. Very rare. Miss Rudenko has your kind of aura, though, and so does one of the blood bank techs who works nights. The Englishwoman the other gentleman was looking for had it, too."

Garreth breathed in slowly. This had to be the vampire connection Ricky the hustler and Holle's housekeeper hinted at. He remembered the blood in Holle's refrigerator. How much of the blood Philos collected ended up somewhere besides hospitals and the Red Cross?

"Do you suppose it's genetic?" the receptionist asked. "Maybe you're all related somehow."

Hunger still licked at him. He avoided looking at her throat. "We share a common bloodline, yes. You were going to tell me something about Irina?"

"Oh, yes. She mostly comes by in the evening, when she's bored with running around town probably. We're closed then, except for the blood bank staff, of course." She pointed at the ceiling. "So when you call back tell them Meresa said for you to."

In the hall, Fowler slipped down the stairs and past

the doorway. The front door opened and closed, and a moment later Fowler hurried into the front room. "I beg your pardon, but—"

The receptionist stiffened. "How did you get back in? The door is locked on the outside."

"Really? Perhaps it didn't close solidly behind me. Be that as it may, I came to inform this gentleman that his car has apparently slipped out of gear and is inching its way along the curb toward freedom. I do think you ought to get *out* there. Immediately."

Garreth caught the emphasis. "Shit!" He raced for the door. "Harry and company?" he muttered at Fowler.

"Just so. I spotted them from the hall window upstairs."

"How far?"

"Half a block."

Garreth's stomach dropped. That close? Step on the sidewalk and they would spot him. Yet where else was there to go? He looked around desperately as the outside door closed behind him.

The space between this and the adjoining building caught his eye.

Fowler followed his gaze in dismay. "You must be joking. Only a shadow will fit through there."

It did look narrow. However, he could see Harry and Girimonte coming closer every second. Their attention appeared to be on each other and the open notebooks in their hands, but the moment they looked up, they would see him.

Garreth vaulted over the side of the steps and dived between the buildings. It was a tight squeeze. It had to be even worse for Fowler. Somehow, though, the bigger man worked his way through the gap after Garreth.

"God bless adrenalin, which lowers every fence, lightens every weight, and widens even the eye of a needle for a desperate man," Fowler panted as they wormed their way free into the alley behind the foundation building. He brushed at cobwebs clinging to his suit coat. "I do hope all this is worth something. Am I wasting my breath asking who this Rudenko woman is?"

Garreth blinked. "From your reaction out there in the hall, I thought you knew her."

"Not her." Fowler shook his head. "Mada's stories mentioned a Polish woman named Irina Rodek, and I thought at first you were going to say her name." He lifted a questioning brow. "This is the fourth name now you've pulled out of the air."

"Not quite." *Careful, Mikaelian.* They headed down the alley toward the street. "She's the woman who asked Holle about Lane. The housekeeper mentioned the name."

The writer stared at him in disbelief. "Either you're around the twist or I am. If there's a chain of logic tying all of this together, it totally escapes me."

"No logic, I'm afraid, just the luck of the Irish." Garreth gave him a wry grin. "What did you find out about the rest of the house?"

"That it's quite true one can go anywhere so long as one appears to know what he's doing. No one questioned my story about checking the photocopiers. Fortunately I do know something about the contraptions from all the time I've spent tinkering with mine to keep it running. I chatted with a secretary in an office at the back of the house downstairs and some medical technologists and a computer operator on the first floor. None of them know the name Lane Barber; neither have they seen a tall, red-haired woman like Barber at the foundation. What did the receptionist have to say?"

"I just asked her about Rudenko. I can't risk her mentioning to Harry and Girimonte that they're the second people interested in Lane Barber today."

Fowler sighed. "Quite. Well, then, did she tell you where to find Rudenko?"

Garreth shook his head. "I think she knew, but she wouldn't say."

"Wouldn't say!" Fowler stopped short and spun around to scowl at him. "You didn't press her?"

Memory of what had nearly happened when he started to set him shaking again. "No."

"Christ! How the bloody hell do you expect to learn anything? That creature is out there killing people and blaming you and you're walking away from potential sources of information!"

Why was he so angry? "Hey. Easy. You sound like you're the one being framed."

"And you're bloody casual about it all!" Fowler snarled. His eyes narrowed. "Don't you *want* to find her? Don't you *care* she's going to put you in the dock and maybe make you swing?"

"We use lethal gas in this state." A correct hanging that broke his neck would be one way to kill him, though.

Fowler's hands came up as if to grab him by the throat, but before he actually touched Garreth, he stopped short, blinked, and backed away, grimacing sheepishly. "Good Lord. I am sorry. I don't know what the devil got into me. Identifying with you, I suppose . . . like I do with my characters. Forgive me."

Garreth eyed him. "No problem. The receptionist did tell me that Rudenko comes in evenings. I plan to call back then. For now, you must be starved. Let's get something to eat and head back to Bryant Street before Harry puts out an APB on us."

8

Harry and Girimonte dragged into the squad room after five. Harry headed for the coffeepot. Girimonte flung herself in her chair, propped her feet on her desk, and lit a cigar. Puffing it, she eyed Garreth and Fowler, who sat at Harry's desk with cups of tea and the Mossman and Adair files. "Well, don't you two look comfortable and satisfied with yourselves. Where've you been all day?"

"Retracing my nightmares," Garreth replied. True enough considering the incident with the receptionist.

"You mean visiting the Barbary Now and places like that?"

Garreth sipped his tea. When she and Harry played Bad Cop/Good Cop she must do one hell of a job in the tough role. Her question smoldered with accusation. "Was someone killed there this afternoon?"

She blew out smoke. "Cagey, Mikaelian, but it doesn't answer the question."

"Oh? Is this an interrogation?"

Fowler slapped the Adair file closed. "What this is,

is juvenile! *I'll* answer the bloody question. Yes, we visited that club, *and* the alley, and the Jack Tar, the Fairmont, and half a dozen other sites connected to the case. We also had coffee at Ghirardelli Square and visited a bookstore so I could buy a couple of little gifts." He picked up three books from a corner of the desk.

Fowler had spotted the Book Circus while they were working their way around the block back to the car and dragged Garreth inside. "Call it professional curiosity or vanity." He grinned at Garreth. "I want to see which of my books they carry."

Looking around as they entered, Garreth wondered if they would be able to tell. The store consisted of three houses joined by doors cut through the common walls. Book shelves covered every available inch of wall space, floor to ceiling, even along hallways, up staircases, and under windows. Tables of books and revolving racks also filled the center space in bigger rooms. The sheer abundance left Garreth dizzy.

A clerk drifted over while they stood staring around, wondering where to start. "Is there something in particular you were looking for?"

"Books by Graham Fowler," Fowler said.

The clerk had nodded briskly. "Those would be in mystery and suspense. That's up the stairs and the last door on your right. Paperbacks are in the same room. If you collect Fowler, you'll also want to see our British editions. His horror novels have never been published in this country. Go through that door on the left, clear through the room and the door on the far side, then up those stairs. The first door."

They visited both rooms. Looking over the British editions, Fowler grimaced. "Good God; they have everything. Doctors bury their mistakes, barristers argue about them, and politicians deny them, but the indiscretions of a writer's youth haunt him on bookshelves forever."

Garreth eyed the titles. Ones like *Shadow Games* and *Winter Gambit* sounded typical of spy thrillers, but others had a ring of horror: *Night Oaths. Wolf Moon. Bare Bones.* "Which are the indiscretions?"

"You don't really think I'm daft enough to say, do you?"

Garreth reached for one called *Blood Maze.*

Fowler blocked his hand. "Have you considered there might be sound reasons why American publishers don't buy my horror? If you want a book, let me choose something."

Now Girimonte reached out a long arm to take the books Fowler had picked out. "*The Man Who Traveled in Murder. A Safe Place to Die. A Wilderness of Thieves.* I've read the last one and some of your others. They aren't bad, though you do have a thing about tall, long-legged women." She pulled out the bookmark the clerk at the cash register had tucked into the book. "The Book Circus, Union Street." She tapped the ash off her cigar. "That's a bit off the path. City Lights is handier when you're running around North Beach."

Harry, Garreth noticed, had said nothing since coming in, had just poured himself coffee and without adding cream or sugar, moved over by a pillar and stood drinking the coffee, listening. Garreth's gut knotted. He could count on the fingers of one hand the times he remembered Harry drinking black coffee.

Garreth looked around at Harry.

His expression inscrutable, Harry said, "A Union Street bookstore is in the neighborhood of the Philos Foundation, though."

The knots tightened.

"The what foundation?" Fowler asked.

"The Philos Foundation, where you went this afternoon using aliases and asking for the daughter of a friend of Holle's and a staff member who died several years ago."

"Did we really?"

Garreth winced. *Shut up, Fowler; you're only making things worse.*

"Come off it!" Girimonte slammed the books down on the desk with a pistol-shot report that brought detectives whirling toward the sound and Serruto tearing to the door of his office. "While we were there a secretary came in to ask the receptionist if the copier serviceman was still in the building. The receptionist knew nothing about any serviceman. So the secretary described him—'a tall, good-looking Englishman,' she said—and the receptionist said, 'I remember *him*, but he wasn't here about copy machines. Where did you see him? After I told him Corinne Barlow was dead he left . . . until he came back to tell the skinny little blond guy in the sunglasses that his car was slipping downhill.' Skinny little blond guy in sunglasses running around with a tall Englishman." Girimonte stared at Garreth. The scent of her cigar circled him.

"Takananda!" Serruto's voice cracked like a whip. "I want all four of you in my office."

They trailed in under the stares of the entire squad room. Garreth held his back straight and his chin up.

With the door closed behind them, Serruto motioned them to chairs, sat on the edge of his desk, and looked them each over, his eyes narrow. "All right, Takananda, tell me about this."

Harry finished his coffee and set the cup on the desk. In a flat voice he said, "We were going through Holle's address book in a routine check of his acquaintances for quarrels and enemies. The Philos Foundation was one of the entries. It turns out he served as chapter president."

"I heard the part about the secretary and the copier serviceman. Then what?"

"As the situation appeared suspicious, Inspector Girimonte and I proceeded to interview all Philos staff members in the building. According to them, while the 'serviceman' was locating the photocopiers, he made idle conversation, asking the various staff members if they knew a 'friend' of his that he thought 'used to work there,' a tall, striking red-haired woman named Barber."

"What was the other man doing?"

"Keeping the receptionist busy talking about this daughter of a Philos VIP in Geneva so she wouldn't realize the Englishman hadn't left the building," Girimonte said. "We figure the Englishman asked the questions because given a choice between those two," she said, tipping her head toward Garreth and Fowler, "who would *you* talk to most readily?"

Garreth bit his lip. With luck, they would never consider that Fowler had been given the task because questions about Lane did not matter while those concerning Irina did.

Serruto stood and moved around his desk to his chair. Sitting down, he leaned back. "Did you enjoy playing detective, Mr. Fowler?"

Fowler met his gaze coolly. "Suppose I deny being there?"

"We'll just invite the receptionist to have a look at you."

Fowler frowned. "Lieutenant, I fail to see what we've done that's so reprehensible. We just lent assistance to—"

"Lent assistance." Serruto leaned forward in his chair. "When did your status here change from observer to investigator?"

Fowler stiffened.

"And how is it you see nothing wrong in assisting a man, who may be involved in three murders, with a line of investigation he has conducted without informing official investigators, an investigation he has conducted with all possible secrecy, in fact?"

Fowler stared at the wall behind Serruto.

The lieutenant sat back again. "So . . . I hope you learned everything you needed for your book because . . ."—his voice went glacial—"this little stunt has just cost you all your privileges in this department."

Fowler's mouth thinned. "I doubt you speak for your entire department, Lieutenant. We'll see what your superiors have to say about this."

"Fine. Talk to them." Serruto smiled thinly. "Then I'll tell them how you've gone about researching your book and abusing our hospitality."

The anger died in Fowler's eyes. "No. That . . . won't be necessary." Glancing at Garreth, he grimaced. "Sorry. We did have a good go at it, though, didn't we? There are no hard feelings, I hope, lieutenant." He extended a hand across the desk.

Serruto ignored it. "Good-bye, Mr. Fowler."

Fowler shrugged. "Good-bye, Lieutenant."

When the door had closed behind the writer, Serruto swiveled toward Garreth, his mouth set in a grim line.

He already sat stiff as a board in his chair. Now Garreth fought to breathe. The air had suddenly become suffocatingly thick with the smells of blood and cigar smoke. At least fear kept him from feeling hunger—fear less of what Serruto might say and do than of having Harry here to see and hear it. Even now his old partner's face did not manage to be quite inscrutable enough to hide the anger and pain behind it. And there was nothing to say in defense. He had broken promises to limit himself to riding along. He had lied this morning about what he intended to do with the day. Had lied by evasion minutes ago about where he and Fowler had been. Worse, he had lied to Harry.

I Ching missed the point today. The danger in floundering ahead was not personal but what his actions did to other people he cared about: shattering trust, destroying the last vestiges of friendship. He heard Lane's chuckle in his head. *That precious bridge of yours may not go down in flames after all, lover. I think you've just dynamited it.*

"I warned you, Mikaelian," Serruto said.

Garreth looked down. "Yes, sir."

"But you wouldn't—take off those damn glasses! I'm sick of looking at my own reflection when I talk to you."

Slowly Garreth pulled them off. Light slapped at him. He winced. Logic said that exposing his eyes could not increase the pressure of daylight on him, but it felt that way. He gritted his teeth against the drag.

"And look at me. I want to see your eyes."

Garreth focused on a point past the lieutenant's ear. It would not do to inadvertently hypnotize Serruto to a friendlier attitude with two witnesses to wonder at the sudden change.

Serruto leaned forward, his elbows on the desk. Steel rang in his voice. "Now talk to me, mister. Explain yourself. Tell me why I shouldn't consider you a prime suspect in these murders and arrest you."

The tightness in Garreth's throat made talking difficult, especially maintaining a calm tone. "Because you don't have any hard evidence, no witnesses, no associative evidence that can put me at the scene of any of the murders. More than that, they're clumsy murders. If I can break into Holle's house so slickly, do you see me being careless enough to leave obvious evidence of torture and to kill those men under circumstances that implicate me?"

Not even Girimonte rebutted that.

Serruto pursed his lips. "So . . . the question becomes, what do we do with you then? This Lone Wolf

Mikaelian crap is *over!* Terminated. Finished." He punctuated the words with a stabbing finger. "But I can't just pack you back to Kansas—even if I could be sure you'd go—because if there's no hard evidence, there's also too much circumstantial evidence to ignore."

"I wouldn't go, no. Not until this thing is settled." Garreth folded and unfolded the temples of his glasses.

Girimonte ground out her cigar in the big glass ash tray on the lieutenant's desk. "If you really wanted this case solved, you'd be working with us, sharing your information instead of hiding it from us."

How did he answer that without more lies? He put back on the glasses. "There's nothing I can tell you." *Not without giving away too much about myself in the process.*

She snorted. "Nothing you *will* tell us, you mean. Evasions and half truths are nice strategies . . . not-quite lies that still avoid the truth. You use them expertly, but then, you've had lots of practice from using them in the rest of your life, haven't you? Just like my sister."

His chest tightened. "Your sister?"

"She was like you. That's how I recognize what you are. I've seen all the little tricks before, especially the ones for dealing with meals."

The air petrified in Garreth's chest. She *had* figured it out.

"What do you mean, recognize what he is?" Serruto snapped.

There was no way to run, nowhere to run to. *No escape*, I Ching had said. Garreth braced himself.

Girimonte shook her head. "It's personal, nothing to do with the case. But one day soon you and I will talk, Mikaelian. The problem has to be dealt with."

All the relief he felt with the first part of her reply to Serruto vanished beneath a flood of cold. She had spoken of her sister in the past tense. Could Grandma Doyle have mistaken the eye color of the woman deadly to him?

She lit another cigar. "Sorry for the digression, Lieutenant. You were wondering what to do with Mikaelian. Why not call him a material witness?" She drew on the cigar and blew smoke toward Garreth. "That gives us the perfect excuse to keep him under surveillance and on a short leash . . . without some lawyer screaming that we're violating his civil rights."

Serruto's brows hopped. "Thinking truly worthy of a future chief." He leaned back, lacing his fingers together behind his head. "All right, you're a material witness, Mikaelian. Any objections?"

"Does it matter if I have?" Garreth asked bitterly.

"Of course. If you'd prefer I find a charge to book you on, I'll accommodate you." When Garreth said nothing to that, he turned toward Harry. "He's already your guest, Takananda. Will you hold the leash? I want it short. I don't want him out of your sight."

Harry sucked in his lower lip. Garreth wondered if he were going to say he would just as soon have nothing more to do with his ex-partner. Right now he must be angrily regretting ever having invited Garreth out from Kansas. After a moment, however, Harry said in a flat voice, "Count on it, sir. Until this is over, it'll be like we're handcuffed together."

9

By unspoken agreement, Garreth and Harry banged
into the house tossing one-liners at each other . . .
despite a ride home in strained silence. The effort was
wasted, though. The tightness of Lien's face told
Garreth that she already suspected something had
gone terribly wrong between them.

She made no attempt at light conversation, either,
just gave each a fierce hug and said, "Your tea is in the
family room. Don't bother to help me set the table. Sit
down and relax."

They sat down and reached for the teacups in
silence. Lien must have had a bad day, too, Garreth
reflected. She had forgotten to put rum in his tea,
though he smelled it in the steam of Harry's tea. Not
that he minded. Now he could actually drink the tea.
The warm liquid eased the edge on his hunger, if not
the knots of misery in his stomach.

True to her word, Lien reappeared in less than five
minutes. "Dinner's ready. But Garreth, dear, I hope

you won't mind that I've put yours in the kitchen. I need to talk to my husband alone."

That was fine, except for the scent of shrimp fried rice filling the kitchen, making him simultaneously ache with longing for some and nauseated at the thought of it lying in his stomach. But both longing and nausea vanished abruptly when he saw what Lien had set out on the counter for him. Nothing but his thermos and a tall pewter tankard. And a note:

THERE'S NO POINT GIVING YOU A REGULAR SERVING
THAT YOU'LL JUST LEAVE UNTOUCHED ON THE PLATE.
GO AHEAD AND HAVE WHAT YOU WILL EAT.

He sat down hard on a stool. Lien had written him many notes over the years, but never one that brusque.

He filled the tankard from the thermos and sat sipping the blood, but it tasted sour and dead. Lien had tired of him snubbing her cooking. Harry no longer trusted him and, along with Serruto, thought he had killed Holle, Maruska, and the count. His bridge had blown up indeed. Nothing remained of it.

There were other bridges, though. The text of Christopher Stroda's suicide tape played back in his head:

I'M ABOUT TO JUMP OFF THE GOLDEN GATE BRIDGE.
IF MY BODY IS FOUND, PLEASE CREMATE IT AND
SCATTER THE ASHES. I WANT NOTHING LEFT OF ME.
MOM, DAD, PLEASE FORGIVE ME FOR DOING THIS TO
YOU. I KNOW IT'S GOING TO HURT YOU AND SPOIL
CHRISTMAS ... BUT I CAN'T FACE ANOTHER FAMILY
MOB SCENE ... ALL THAT GAIETY AND TOGETHERNESS
... AND FOOD. WHAT I'M DOING ISN'T YOUR FAULT.
IT'S NO ONE'S FAULT, NOT EVEN MELINA'S. ALL SHE
WANTED WAS TO SAVE MY LIFE. BUT IT'S TRAPPED ME

ON THE OTHER SIDE OF A CHASM FROM EVERYONE I
LOVE, WITH NO WAY TO EVER REJOIN YOU, AND I
CAN'T BEAR THE LONELINESS. GOOD-BYE.

Garreth swirled the blood in the tankard. Maybe
Stroda was right. Even Lane dreaded the loneliness.
How many vampires secretly welcomed the stake even
as they screamed at the pain? How many, like Stroda,
committed suicide? Nothing about Bodenhausen's
death suggested anything except an accident. However, had Corinne Barlow accidentally swerved into the
oncoming traffic, controlled by reflexes schooled to
driving on the left-hand side of the road, or was it a
deliberate act of self-destruction?

Lien banged through the swinging door from the
dining room and dumped a load of dishes in the sink.
"That man! He's obviously in anguish, but he won't
talk to me and he won't hear anything I have to say."

Garreth tensed. Would she ask *him* what was going
on?

"No, I won't try to pry out of you what's wrong.
That would only aggravate things, I'm sure."

He started, staring at her.

She smiled and reached out to pat his arm. "Don't
look so panic-stricken. I'm not reading minds, just the
expression on your face." She turned back to the sink,
reaching for the faucets. "Of course, if you want
someone to talk to, I'm always here."

"I know. Thank you." She wanted so much to help,
never realizing that the problem lay beyond even her
compassionate understanding. He changed the subject. "Did Harry show you the book Fowler gave
him?"

"Yes. *That* he would talk about. You have one,
too?"

He nodded, then faked a yawn. "I'm bushed. I think
I'll go to bed. Say good night to Harry for me."

In his room he locked the door and stretched out on the bed with Fowler's book. It would pass the time until Harry and Lien went to bed.

It would have, that is, if he had been able to concentrate. He could not. Stroda's words echoed in his head over and over. No matter how many times he read the print before him, all Garreth saw was a tortured figure arcing off the Golden Gate Bridge in a parody of a swan dive. After an hour all he could really say about the book was that Fowler had written a very accurate description of a second-story burglary. The man obviously did his research.

Then a new character appeared, a woman . . . tall, red-haired, fascinating. Goose bumps rose on Garreth's neck and arms. Maybe Fowler had another image in mind, but Garreth could only think: *Lane*.

From Lane his thoughts jumped to Irina. Where was she? Planning another murder?

A rap sounded on the door. "Garreth?"

Harry's voice. Slowly Garreth went over to the door and opened it. His stomach dropped. What was wrong now? He had never seen Harry look so acutely embarrassed before. "What's—" he began, but stopped abruptly.

One glance at Harry's hand answered the question. He carried a key. Holding it up, he said, "I—I just wondered if you needed to use the bathroom anymore because—damn it, Garreth, I'm sorry, but I'm going to have to lock you in."

That was how thoroughly trust had been destroyed. Numb, Garreth spoke across the bottomless, bridgeless gulf between them and marveled at how casual he managed to sound. "I understand. Go ahead. See you in the morning."

He closed the door.

The lock clicked.

The sound cut like a knife through his control. Garreth hurled the book across the room and smashed a fist down on the bureau. The wallet/pocket/change caddy on top hopped with the force of the blow. *Irina, you bitch, damn you! Damn you!*

If he had had any doubts about what he planned to do tonight, they had vanished. To hell with the warnings from *I Ching* and his grandmother. He had to find Irina, for his own satisfaction as well as to prevent another murder. Even if it meant dying. Better him than a fourth innocent person, and tonight death seemed less something to be feared than welcomed.

10

Union Street still had enough traffic that Garreth quickly decided using Philos' front door was too risky. Someone might see him. But in the alley behind the foundation that afternoon he had noticed a back door opening onto the alley. He found it again now and after pulling on the gloves he had carried with him in the pocket of his warmup jacket, moved through into the building.

This entrance apparently did not see much traffic. He caught little trace of human scent in the strong musty odor of the basement. File cabinets and open shelving stacked with boxes of office supplies lined the outer wall of the long, narrow room that ended with stairs. An open door in the opposite direction revealed the furnace room.

A second door beyond it was closed . . . and locked, as Garreth discovered when he tried the handle. Moving through, he found himself in a darkness so total not even his vampire vision could see anything. He felt space around him, however, and the air smelled dry and stale. Exploring along the edge of the door, he located a light switch and flipped it on. His brows rose. The large room, occupying nearly half the floor area of the building, was a bomb shelter, equipped with not only a dozen bunks and supplies enough to feed twelve or so people for months but a shortwave radio and refrigeration equipment with a gas motor clearly intended to store a massive amount of blood. The unit held several plastic bags of blood even now.

Philos was prepared for the desperate need that would exist if there ever were a nuclear attack, Garreth reflected. Presuming they did not sit on ground zero. But was this just for the future? Eyeing the room, it occurred to him that the shelter would make an ideal place for someone to hide.

A quick examination of the bunks and careful sniffing of the air quickly told him no one had done so recently. The stale air carried no trace of sweat or perfume, certainly not the spicy-musky perfume he had smelled in the attic bedroom of Holle's house.

With a grimace of disappointment, he switched off the light and moved back through the door.

The basement stairs came out under the stairs in the hallway. After opening the door a crack to make sure no one would see him, he slipped out into the hall and stood pressed against the wall, listening and sniffing. Voices and a laugh floated down the stairs to him. At least two people were upstairs then, but he smelled no blood scent strong enough to suggest that anyone might be on this floor.

Still, he was careful to move soundlessly as he explored. A large, comfortably appointed office sat behind the reception area. Holle's. Garreth only glanced around it before moving on down the hall. Since Holle never had the chance to come back here after Irina moved out of his house, he could not have a new address for her. At the back of the house was a kitchen slightly remodeled into an employee lounge. A utilitarian office with files and several desks adjoined it and connected to another office next to Holle's, smaller but carpeted and furnished more stylishly. A framed photograph of a woman with two teenaged children was on the tidy desk between a vase of tulips and a Rolodex file and appointment book. Holle's secretary? He hoped so. If Irina had told anyone where she could be reached, it would have been Holle's secretary.

Sitting down, Garreth reached for the Rolodex. This was probably a slim chance. Still . . . he might get lucky.

He spun the side knob to bring the R's around. RE . . . RI . . . RU . . . RUDENKO. But the card was for a Natalya Rudenko at the Philos Foundation in Geneva, Switzerland. Irina's "mother," no doubt. He eyed the appointment book. Perhaps a local number had been written down there.

He pulled the book over close and turned the page back to Wednesday. Was it only the day before yesterday they had found Holle's body? It seemed an eternity ago.

The page had little writing: a few appointments written in precise, square printing, crossed out by a shakier hand. But there was one telephone number, scribbled in the margin near the bottom of the page, with a note under it in that same unsteady hand: something heavily crossed out followed by a legible word, "Rieger."

Garreth stared at it, sucking on his lower lip. Was it what he was looking for? He squinted at the crossed-out word but could not decipher it through the scribble over it. He turned the page to study the back side and the preceding page, then grimaced. Only the impressions of the cross-out strokes had come through, not those of the word itself.

Or two words, maybe, he decided, turning to Wednesday again and studying it more. It started with "SH," but something looking vaguely like a capital P appeared halfway along the word, and a lower-case L shortly after that. Garreth frowned in concentration. Sh . . . P.l . . .

A click sounded in his head. He grinned. Sheraton-Palace?

The longer he studied the notation, the more logical that seemed. The name fit the space, and the Sheraton-Palace was an old hotel that had survived the 1906 quake. If Irina had been visiting San Francisco for a very long time, it would be one place she remembered from the past. Rieger could be the name she registered under.

He glanced around the office for a phone book. One look at the classified pages should verify if the telephone number was for the hotel.

"I believe the directory is locked in the lower right drawer," a female voice said behind him.

Garreth whipped around in disbelief and panic, adrenalin flushing icy hot through him. How could anyone sneak up on him? He had not heard or smelled anything!

But now a scent reached him . . . sweetly spicy-musky, wafting from a slight figure standing against the still-closed door from the hall.

He stared, his breath frozen in his chest. Meeting her anywhere else, he would have taken her for just another sixteen- or seventeen-year-old, especially in her designer jeans, ankle-high fashion boots, and oversized shirt. Lane had described Irina as exquisite, like a Dresden figurine, but at five-foot-nothing, flat-chested, and dark hair cropped boyishly short above a face with slavic cheekbones, pixyish described her better. Except there was nothing pixyish in her faintly slanting eyes . . . nothing childlike, either. Darkness robbed them of color but not expression; they watched him coldly, appraising, noting his every move.

Nor was there anything remotely pixyish about the Beretta she pointed at him.

"You are Garreth Mikaelian, I think?"

Garreth could not identify her accent. Eastern European originally, perhaps; now very diluted. "And you're Irina Rudenko."

"But of course. I see you're staring at my toy." She hefted the Beretta. It looked gigantic in her small hand. "Do you like it?"

"I'm wondering what you think you're going to do with it." She must know bullets could not hurt him.

"Shoot you perhaps," Irina replied. "The clip has ebony bullets."

Adrenalin spurted in him again. Ebony! Little pieces of wooden stake tearing through him propelled by exploding powder! "You'd kill one of your own kind?"

Stupid question, man, an inner voice snarled. *Of course she would. She already has.*

"Why not? *You* do."

The adrenalin turned to ice. She knew about Lane! He covertly eyed the distance between his chair and the far corner of the desk.

The gun waggled fractionally side to side, like a head gesturing *no.* "It would be foolish. I learned to shoot before pistols had bullets or rifling in the barrel and I could knock the flies off a horse even then."

The matter-of-fact statement sunk the ice into his bones. Garreth fought rising panic, fought to think of a defense, or escape.

"But I prefer not to shoot. It's best this seem like an accident and not another murder." She stepped away from the door. "Shall we go?"

His mind raced. Could he jump her as he passed

her? No, she had moved well to one side. So he remained seated. "If you want me dead, you'll have to kill me here."

"As you wish," she said calmly. "It just means I must be sure your body is never found." Her finger tightened on the trigger.

Desperation acted where logic had failed. He hurled the appointment book at her, then flung himself after it, grabbing for the gun. But she ducked sideways before he was halfway there. His hands found only empty air.

Movement blurred across his peripheral vision. He had just time to identify it as the gun barrel slicing at him before pain exploded in the side of his head.

The floor smashed up into him.

From a great echoing distance, Irina said mockingly, "Thank you."

Dimly he felt her bend over him. A hand caught the back of his head, another his chin. Terror exploded in Garreth. She intended to break his neck!

He tried to roll, to catch her wrists and break her grip, but his body obeyed weakly, sluggishly. Her foot pinned his left wrist to the floor.

"I've always wondered about the afterlife," Irina said. Her grip tightened. "Usually I have hoped none exists. There are too many souls I would not care to meet again. But for you, I hope there is, so your victims may confront you."

One word penetrated the storm of terror and dizzying pain. Victims? Who else besides Lane? He struggled to force his tongue into cooperation before she started the fatal jerk. "What . . . victims?"

"Leonard Holle and that male prostitute, of course."

Confusion thundered through the fog in his head. She had not learned about Lane after all! Then why had she killed those three men? But she accused *him* of the murders. Except she was one victim short. Because she wanted to confuse him or because she knew nothing about the count?

He wrenched at the wrist trapped under the instep of her boot. "I didn't kill either of them, or Count Dracula, either!"

The grip on his head tightened still more. "Dracula! What are you talking about?"

Too late he realized how ridiculous the remark must have sounded. He said hastily through his teeth because of her grip, "The hustler's roommate. We found his body later the same day Holle died. He called himself Count Dracula and acted like a movie vampire. Someone drove a stake through his heart."

Above him, her breath caught. "Holy Mother. And you claim that someone wasn't you?"

"It *wasn't* me."

She released his head, but only to grab him by the shoulders and slam him backward into the desk. "Then why are you here, Garreth?" she asked softly. Glowing ruby red, her eyes stared into his. "Why, if not hunting me to kill, too?"

He squeezed his eyes shut in a chilly rush of fear. He did not dare yield to her. What if she asked about Lane?

She whispered, "Garreth, look at me."

No! he thought.

"You say you didn't kill Leonard and the others, but how can I know that?" Her voice purred. "Look at me, Garreth. There is only one way to be sure. Only one way. You must know that. Look at me."

Her voice pulled at him. Lane had been able to do that, he remembered. While he lay on his driveway with her arrow through his shoulder, her voice alone had almost made him turn where she could take a second, fatal shot at him. Irina had even more of that kind of power, he sensed.

"Look at me."

The whisper slid through the pain and fog in his head.

"Look at me."

It snagged him. Slowly, inexorably, his chin lifted. His eyes opened.

Irina's eyes filled his vision, pulling him in until nothing else existed but their glowing ruby depths. He barely heard her voice, distant and warmly approving. "That's better. Now, did you kill Leonard and the other men?"

"No."

She spun away and paced across the room, hands clasped together at her chin, as if in prayer.

Freed, Garreth slumped back dazed against the desk. "I—I thought you killed them. Only another vampire could have overpowered Maruska that way at night."

Irina looked around. "Go. Leave the city and go home to the prairie where you'll be safe."

He blinked at her and sat up straighter. The action set his head throbbing. He ignored it. "No way. There's a murderer loose, killing people and trying to frame me. I have to find who it is."

Irina's mouth thinned. "What a foolish child you are! You have no idea what you're dealing with. Go home and leave this to those with the experience to handle it."

He eyed her. "Could it have anything to do with the reason you wanted to find Lane so urgently?"

She hesitated, and before answering, came back and leaned down to catch his arm. Pulling him to his feet, she said, "Be sensible and go. You are a child of Mada's excesses. Do not become a victim of them also."

A part of him bristled at being shooed away like a bothersome child, especially by someone who looked like a child herself, but the irritation dissipated before a chilling thought. Back at Holle's house he had wondered if another vampire might be involved. What if that were the case? An old, powerful, perhaps crazed one might explain Irina's concern. But only one vampire would explain those last two statements. Lane. He fought to breathe.

"Irina, it is possible—"

Belatedly he realized he was talking to the air. In the few moments he was lost in thought, Irina had left, moving so silently, not even he heard.

He sat down at the desk again, shaking. Lane. Death waited for him in this city, Grandma Doyle said. Could that mean Lane, not Irina? Could she really be here after all, in spite of everything? But if that were true, if all his precautions had still not kept Lane in her grave, what was it going to *take* to finish her once and for all?

Bloodlinks

1

For once, it was a relief to be awake and moving around in the daylight. The pounding on his door had rescued him from dreams of finding Lane's grave blown open as if by dynamite and Christopher Stroda sitting at the bottom of the gaping hole, gestering for Garreth to join him. Lien's *I Ching* reading for the day gave him something else to think about. Number three, Difficulty at the Beginning.

"It leads to supreme success, which comes through perseverance," Lien had said at breakfast. "But no move should be made prematurely and one should not go alone; one should appoint helpers. A change line at the beginning reinforces the need to have helpers, that change line producing hexagram number eight, Holding Together. For good fortune, we must unite with others who complement and aid one another."

Garreth followed Harry into the Hall of Justice elevator. Helpers. Sure. He grimaced. Who? It would be difficult to team up with Fowler again, even if he wanted to, and telling Harry everything would only make the case against him worse.

Girimonte already sat at her desk when they walked into homicide. She looked up with a grin. "Good news. We finally ID'd Count Dracula. Clarence Parmley, formerly of Columbia, Missouri. His prints came in from the FBI this morning, on file from an arrest in 1971 for civil disobedience—protesting U.S. involvement in Vietnam." She puffed her cigar. "I gather that was in the halcyon days of youth, before he became a vampire."

Serruto appeared in the doorway of his office. "Briefing. Let's get to it, troops. Bad news, Harry. Lieutenant Fogelsong in burglary just called me. There was a break-in at the Philos Foundation last night. A blood bank technician is in the hospital with a concussion and the file cabinets were all jimmied open. Another tech in the building who caught a glimpse of the intruder describes him as a man with light-colored hair and a stocking over his face."

Garreth's stomach dropped in dismay.

"It couldn't have been Garreth," Harry protested. "I had his door locked from the outside."

"Did you have the window barred?" Girimonte asked.

Serruto said, "We ought to know something one way or the other before too long. The tech said she'd come downtown sometime this morning to look at mug shots. You won't mind sticking around here for a lineup instead of going out with Takananda and Girimonte, will you, Mikaelian?"

Harry's mouth tightened.

But Garreth made himself shrug. "Of course not."

He slumped in a chair, closing his eyes. A break-in. It had to have happened after he left. But who? Lane? She had passed as a man before. Last night's dream came back to him. Cold ran down his spine. The hair color could be from dye, or a wig.

Had she followed him there? She must have. She must have been watching him all along. It was too much for coincidence that Maruska's killer intercepted him before Garreth arrived and that Holle's killer and the Philos burglar went to work just after Garreth left them.

After the briefing ended, Harry and Girimonte picked up their coats and headed for the door. "Oh, if you need something to do, Mikaelian, you can read the book Fowler gave me," Girimonte called back. "It's in the upper left-hand drawer of my desk."

You know what you can do with your book, honey, Garreth thought.

Fifteen minutes later he found himself reaching for the book anyway. It was the only thing to do. Everyone else remaining in the squad room avoided him as if he had caught AIDS. Concentration proved as difficult as it had been the night before, though. His mind kept slipping back to the break-in and Lane, a distraction not helped by a tall, charming brunette in the book who reminded Garreth of Lane. He gripped the book with white knuckles. How could she still be alive? *How?*

Serruto tapped his shoulder. "Let's go. That witness from the Philos Foundation is in burglary."

Garreth had filled in for several lineups before. Since he had not been the man the technician saw, this should be no different, he told himself. Then while shuffling into the well-lit box with four other lean, blondish officers, it occurred to him that the technician might have described not someone she saw at all but someone Lane, using hypnotic powers, told her she saw. He bit his lip. This could be the evidence Lane intended to incriminate him once and for all.

"Face the front," a voice said from the speaker overhead.

Garreth put his back against the height-graduated wall.

"Number three, take off your glasses."

Slowly he complied, then stood squinting into the lights that kept him from seeing who sat on the darkened side of the glass wall facing him.

An eternity dragged by while the hair prickled all over Garreth's body and cold ate into his bones. Smells of blood and after-shave and cigarette smoke pressed around him, strengthened by confinement in the lineup box.

"That's all," said the voice from the speaker.

He put back on his glasses and they all shuffled out.

To Garreth's surprise, only Serruto waited for him. Grinning, the lieutenant slapped his back. "Congratulations; you're too short."

He could not feel much relief. That might lift suspicion from him, but a taller burglar did not rule out Lane.

2

Being cleared of suspicion in the break-in changed nothing back in homicide, either. The activity in the squad room continued to flow around him as if he were invisible. He went back to his book and speculation. If Lane broke into the foundation, why had she bypassed the perfect opportunity to finish the frame? Maybe, he decided hopefully, she was not responsible after all. The burglary did not have to be connected with this case at all. It could have been just some junkie aware of a medical facility there and hoping to find drugs.

In the file cabinets? That thought mocked him.

Questions without answers. Garreth tried to forget them for the time being and concentrate on the book.

He still had trouble enjoying it. Mrs. Stroda's comment on how Fowler's characters treated other people as disposable tools came back to him. The protagonist callously used and discarded several colleagues and supposed friends. Garreth found himself almost regretting that the tall brunette, who proved to be working for the other side, failed in her attempt to kill the hero.

A feeling of danger jerked him away from the book. Looking around swiftly, he saw nothing new or threatening in the squad room, only Faye and Centrello marching in with their lunch in takeout boxes.

Lunch! He lurched to his feet. From one of the boxes came the scent of garlic! Panic exploded in him as air turned to concrete in his lungs. Suffocation! Clawing at the turtleneck of his shirt, fighting for breath, he bolted for the door and the untainted air of the corridor. Someone shouted behind him but he kept going.

The odor of garlic hung in the corridor, too. The movement of air was dispersing it, though. That made the air seem like syrup instead of concrete. He sagged against the wall, head thrown back, eyes closed, and concentrated on forcing the syrup in and out of his lungs.

Footsteps pounded toward him. He opened his eyes to find Serruto, Faye, and Centrello piling out through homicide's door and screeching to a halt in the middle of the corridor, staring at him. Other people in the corridor stared, too.

"Mikaelian, what the hell are you doing?" Serruto demanded.

How did he answer without giving himself away? Why not the same excuse he gave Maggie for his tenseness in movie theaters. "Sorry. I get . . . claustrophobic sometimes."

Serruto raised a skeptical brow. "Claustrophobic? That looked more like a panic attack to me. How long have you had them? Is that what happened in the restaurant the day Harry got shot?"

Faye and Centrello exchanged grimaces. Garreth groaned inwardly. Terrific. Now they thought he was psycho. "No, this is something different," he snapped. "It's a reaction to being a murder suspect."

Serruto scowled. "Don't get cute. Are you over whatever it is now?"

The undertone of genuine concern dissolved Garreth's anger. He signed and nodded. "I will be if I can stand out here a minute longer."

"Faye, Centrello, stay with him."

Serruto turned and went back into the squad room.

Mischief glinted in Faye's eyes and tweaked a corner of his mouth. "Panic attack. Partner, I know we're ugly, but this is the first time it's sent someone screaming from the room."

Garreth managed a weak smile. "Not you, your garlic rolls. Garlic has some bad associations for me."

Faye grinned. "It does, huh. A-ha! Another vampire."

Only the detective's grin prevented a surge of panic. "*Another* vampire?"

"Sure. You and Clarence 'Count Dracula' Parmley. When we answered that call the other morning, he met us in the hall outside the apartment and wouldn't go back in." Faye's voice went high and mincing. "'The place positively reeks. I almost didn't find him because of it. I only went storming in because I was so furious at Ricky for fixing Italian food when he *knows* I can't tolerate garlic.'"

Shock jolted Garreth, followed by a rush of relief. Garlic! Then Lane could not possibly be involved.

Centrello's long face distorted in a grimace and rolling eyes. "I didn't smell anything, but he swore garlic was there, and he refused to stay at the apartment even after the body was removed. He insisted on going to a hotel, only then he started carrying on about how he was going to reach the hotel when it was daylight outside." Centrello shook his head.

Faye chuckled. "Fortunately Fowler knew how to handle him."

Garreth started. "Fowler?"

"Yeah. He was in the squad room when the call

came and asked to ride along. You should have seen him. It was a class act, man. With a perfectly straight face he tells the count that in Stoker's book, Dracula moved around in daylight, so another vampire should be all right, too, as long as he wears a hat to shade him from direct sunlight. Then he takes the count downstairs and puts him in a cab for the Bay Vista Hotel."

Fowler? Garreth frowned. Later when Harry and Girimonte started talking about visiting the count, Fowler gave the impression of never—

"Ready to go back inside?" Centrello asked.

With the garlic rolls? Garreth shuddered inwardly, forgetting Fowler. Garlic rolls or not, though, he could not stand out here all day. "Maybe if we leave the hall door open and I sit near it." Where air currents from the corridor would carry the deadly scent away from him.

He eased into a chair by Kevin Chezik's desk, the closest to the door, and took a cautious breath. Yes, this might work. The air smelled mostly clear of garlic. "Centrello, toss my book over, will you?"

Centrello skimmed it across the room like a Frisbee, nodding approval when Garreth plucked it from the air.

Instead of opening the book, however, Garreth ran a finger across a puddle of blood pictured on the dust jacket. Garlic in the apartment. If there really were, and he had only the count's word on it, that ruled out not only Lane as Maruska's killer but any other vampire as well. It also explained how someone other than a vampire could overpower Maruska.

So he needed to confirm or disprove the presence of garlic.

Garlic was insurance against vampires, Holle's housekeeper had said, implying all vampires. So it had to be a physiological, not just psychological, reaction, which meant someone affected must show physical changes. The autopsy on Maruska found severe pulmonary edema. Thinking about it, that was how the garlic reaction felt, like his lungs swelling shut.

Chezik was not at his desk, and no one appeared to be paying much attention to Garreth. He picked up the phone and dialed the coroner's office. "This is Garreth Mikaelian in homicide. May I speak to any available pathologist?"

A minute later a female voice came on the line. "This is Dr. Alvarez. How may I help you, Inspector?"

"What causes severe pulmonary edema?"

The voice on the other end paused before answering. "There are several possibilities. Cardiac failure is one, also electric shock or allergic reaction—"

"Allergic reaction?" *Bingo!* "Thank you very much, Doctor."

He hung up, thinking. So chances were good that Maruska's killer was human after all. But who? The killer had tailed Garreth around the city night after night. He had seen no one following him, however, not ever. It was understandable, acceptable, that another vampire could do that, but a *human?*

Holle's housekeeper had talked about keeping an atomizer of garlic juice. Her guilt would also explain why there was no evidence of anyone breaking into Holle's house, but how could she possibly have followed him? The killer had to be someone else, someone who knew Garreth before the first murder, someone athletic and skilled in the art of surveillance.

Fowler's name stared up at him from the cover of the book's dust jacket. Garreth traced the letters with his finger. Strange how the writer had not mentioned riding along with Faye and Centrello on the original call about Maruska's death. More than strange. Suspicious. He had, in fact, acted surprised at the name

Maruska's roommate used. Why should he pretend he had never heard it before unless he wanted to hide his previous contact?

Garreth leaned back in his chair. Could Fowler be tied to the other killings? The writer had been in North Beach the night of the scuffle with Ricky Maruska. He could have seen it, and heard the remark Maruska made climbing into the john's car. Fowler appreciated the difference between theoretical and applied knowledge and went for the latter when doing research. So he had probably practiced burglary techniques. Look at his demonstrated wizardry with handcuff locks. So he could have gotten into both the foundation and Holle's house. Surveillance had to be part of his research, too. Could he actually follow someone, though, and how could he tail a vampire without being seen?

On top of that, Fowler lacked one vital qualification for a suspect—motive. What reason would he have for killing three men and torturing two of them?

Did Irina know about the garlic? Garreth wondered. He picked up the phone again. If so, maybe she could be persuaded to tell him what she knew about the killer. If not, she ought to be told, warned that an unfriendly human knew vampires existed.

"I'm sorry, Miss Rudenko isn't here," the Philos receptionist said when Garreth asked for Irina.

He had not really expected her to be. "Will you please give her a message? It's very urgent. This is Garreth Mikaelian. Tell her there was garlic in Ricky Maruska's apartment at the time of his death and we need to talk about it. I should be here in the homicide section at the Hall of Justice the rest of the day. This evening I can be reached at 555-1099."

"I'll tell her."

He hung up. Now all he could do was hope she showed up there this evening, and that she bothered to call back.

3

Girimonte showed up alone about four o'clock. She dropped into her chair and lit a cigar. "Harry had to make a pit stop. Did you have an exciting day, Mikaelian?"

He gave her a thin smile. "Rewarding. I'm too short to be the Philos burglar."

"Too bad." She dragged at the cigar. "Everyone we talked to says about the same thing about Holle. He was a quiet, friendly man who always had room to put up someone for the night, was always a gracious host, and never too busy to lend a hand if someone needed it. He didn't make enemies. And no one has ever heard of a Lane Barber." She blew out smoke. "Face it, Mikaelian; you're still our best suspect. Why not just save us all trouble by confessing? You can probably beat the rap with an insanity plea. Just say your condition has unbalanced you . . . vitamin deficiencies due to your diet. The Twinkie defense revisited."

Garreth clenched his fists in his jacket pockets. Her blood scent curled around him with the sweet smell of her cigar. A pulse throbbed visibly in her long mahogany throat. He watched it, malicious hunger licking at him. Perhaps there was a human or two after all he would not mind not drinking from. *Better not wander into any alleys with me, Girimonte.*

The squad room door, shut now that the smell of garlic had dissipated, opened. Harry came in, not alone. "Look who I stumbled over at the elevator."

Lien followed Harry, but it was the woman behind her who brought Garreth jumping to his feet. "Grandma Doyle! What are you doing here?"

His grandmother gave him a broad smile. "Why else but to visit me own dear grandson?"

Lien said, "I know you want to spend time with Harry, Garreth, but today would you be willing to leave early with Grania and me?"

The name puzzled him for a moment. After a lifetime of calling her just Grandma Doyle, it was hard to remember that she had a regular name: Grania Megan Mary O'Hare Doyle.

Girimonte straightened in her chair, frowning. Garreth caught Harry's eye questioningly.

Harry glanced in the direction of Serruto's office. Garreth did not turn around to see the lieutenant's reaction, but when Harry's eyes shifted back to Garreth, Harry dipped his chin in assent. As Garreth moved past him toward the door, he warned, "Stay with them. If I hear you've taken off on your own, we'll be after you with a warrant."

Garreth gave him a thin smile. "I don't throw away an alibi, Harry."

Riding down in the elevator, he said, "Grandma, do Mom and Dad know you're here?" He had uneasy visions of Phil Mikaelian calling his old buddies and setting every law-enforcement agency in the state looking for her.

She sniffed. "Am I a child who needs permission to go where I wish? I've been looking after meself quite well, thank you, since I was seventeen." She paused. "I left them a note."

Maybe only the San Francisco Police would be asked to check on her. "Why did you really come?"

This time she did not smile. "I saw you last night, dying, and someone laughing like the devil's own above you." Her eyes flashed. "I'll not sit home knitting when me flesh and blood is in mortal danger."

Despite the wash of fear in him, he wanted to hug her. And despite the fear, he could not resist pointing out an error in her feeling. "Not from a violet-eyed woman."

She gave him the same withering stare she used to in church just before thumping him on the head with a knuckle. "There's a violet-eyed woman involved, isn't there?"

He wilted under the stare as he always had. "Irina Rudenko."

She smiled in satisfaction. "I went to Lien's studio from the bus station. I see why you like her. She's a fine, intelligent woman. We've been discussing you."

His stomach took a sickening plunge. "Grandma—" The elevator opened. Catching her arm, he hurried her out, down the corridor and into the parking lot. "Grandma, please, you didn't tell her—"

"What you've become?" Lien said from behind him. "She didn't have to; I already knew. After our talk last night, I opened your thermos."

His stomach dropped. He turned slowly. "And from that you figured out the rest." Exactly what he had feared.

She smiled. "After all, I am Chinese, and we understand that reality is not as simple as it appears. Once we made gods out of characters in novels. If fiction can be considered real, then it follows that some of what we consider fiction may *be* real. It's a relief to finally understand your behavior."

Belatedly he realized she was not shrinking from him, nor regarding him with revulsion. "And . . . you don't mind?"

Her chin snapped up. "Of course I mind! Look how unhappy it's made you. I'd like to kill that woman for what she's done to you! But I accept what you are, of course. What else can I do?"

He could hardly believe what he heard. "You . . . aren't afraid of me?"

"Afraid of someone I love?" she asked indignantly.

He stared at her in wonder. Knowing about him had not changed her feeling toward him? Could it be Irina's "hold" on Holle and the housekeeper was not one of fear after all, that humans and vampires could actually be friends?

"I did wonder where you collected a thermos of blood," Lien went on. "It was . . . reassuring to realize that the lip and lid of the thermos smelled of horse." She peered anxiously at him. "Is this change in you why there's trouble between you and Harry?"

"Partly." As long as she knew about him, he might as well give her some of the rest. "I thought at first a vampire was responsible for these murders, but since I couldn't tell anyone that, I investigated on my own. Harry suspects I know more about the case than I'll admit. Since he doesn't know why I'm keeping the information to myself, he—" No, he could not tell her about being a suspect! "He assumes I'm shutting him out to grab the glory of the collar for myself."

"You're a terrible liar," Grandma Doyle said. "Why don't you admit he's afraid you're the killer?"

Her feelings were just too damn accurate!

Lien caught her breath. "Oh, God. Poor Harry. Poor Garreth. I wish you'd trusted our friendship enough to confide in us."

Guilt stabbed him. If only he had.

His grandmother poked him. "There's no point feeling sorry about that now. What's done is done."

Lien nodded. "Now we have to clear up this ridiculous mess. Tell us what to do."

Warmth spread through him. What super ladies, both of them. He shook his head. "You do nothing. I don't want you involved. It's dangerous."

"*I Ching* says you must appoint helpers in order to reach success," Lien reminded him.

Grandma Doyle pushed him toward the car. "Tell us everything on the way home."

Now he understood why he had always felt so close to Lien. She and his grandmother were spiritual twins. Caught between them, though, he felt like someone on a runaway train. He sighed. Lack of sleep and the drag of daylight left him too tired to try stopping it. "Yes, ma'am, but, Lien . . . head for Pacific Heights while I talk."

4

Holle's housekeeper admitted Garreth with obvious reluctance. "This can't be an official visit, or are these undercover officers?" She eyed the two women.

He gave her a thin smile. "Call it semi-official. Mrs. Doyle and Mrs. Takananda are assisting me with a private line of investigation into Mr. Holle's death. May I see the top floor again?"

The housekeeper frowned. "Why?"

"To check the storerooms for forcible entry. It appears now that a human, not Irina, killed Mr. Holle, and he or she had to come in somewhere."

The housekeeper's tight smile said: *I told you Miss Rudenko couldn't have done it.*

She led the way up to the attic. Garreth kept track of Grandma Doyle behind him, but he quickly saw that worrying about her was wasted effort. The stairs had Lien and the housekeeper breathing harder than his grandmother.

In the attic the housekeeper unlocked the padlocked bolts on the storerooms. Nothing had been disturbed in the first. It lay silent, untouched, smelling of dust and sea air. The latch handle at one side of the window ran parallel to the sash in the locked position and all of the window's six panes proved firmly in place. To Garreth's relief, neither was there enough dust on the floor to show footprints from his previous visit.

From the doorway of the second storeroom, it looked as he remembered, too. Except, he realized a moment later, that the windowpane by the latch seemed slightly smaller than the others. Moving over for a closer look, he saw why. Black electrician's tape lapped the edges of the pane on the outside. Using his pen, he pushed on the middle of the glass. It started to give.

The housekeeper's eyes widened.

"It's been cut," Garreth said, "then taped back in place so a casual glance wouldn't spot the damage." A faint circle on the glass showed where a suction device had been attached, first to pull the cut pane loose in one unbroken piece and then to hold it while it was taped back.

"You think Mr. Holle's killer did it?" The housekeeper frowned. "But the door—"

A quick examination of the hinges found what he expected: scratches at the top where a screwdriver had been worked in to pry up the hinge pin. He pointed them out to the women.

"What do we do now?" the housekeeper asked.

"Pray we find this devil," Grandma Doyle said. She stared at the window, her eyes focused on something invisible. "If we don't catch him tomorrow, someone else will die."

5

Lien set him to grating carrots while she and Grandma Doyle worked on the rest of supper. Wrapped in the warm scents of food and the women's blood, sipping blood from a pewter tankard while he fed carrots into the food processor, Garreth's mind churned like the blade of the machine. A day to find the killer when he had no case against anyone. Evidence from the storeroom window might help, though. *I Ching* was right; he could not work alone. But he needed fellow professionals. However much they wanted to help, Lien and his grandmother had no experience with murderers and he would be irresponsible to risk their lives. It was time to trust friendship and confide in Harry.

He fed another carrot into the food processor. "Lien, Grandma, I'm telling Harry everything tonight."

Lien stopped stirring to glance at him. Instead of the smile of relief and approval he expected, she bit her lip.

He eyed her in surprise. "What's the matter?"

She sighed. "You're right; you need to tell him. I . . . just wish I could feel more confident that—"

"Feel more confident that what, honorable wife?"

All three of them whirled, startled. Harry stood in the kitchen doorway.

Lien ran to kiss him. "You're home almost on time for a change. What a lovely surprise. Garreth, I guess we can feel confident enough to set the table after all."

Harry held her off at arm's length to eye her skeptically. "That serious tone is about setting the table?"

She raised her brows. "Considering how often the dishes develop cobwebs before you show up—"

"It wasn't about setting the table," Garreth interrupted. "I'm sorry, Lien, but this has to be done." He emptied the tankard and set it in the sink.

"Garreth," his grandmother said in a warning voice.

He ignored her. "Harry, Lien is worried how well you'll take learning why I've been acting the way I have."

"Oh, I think I can handle it. You underestimate me, honorable wife." He gave Lien a hug and shoved her back toward the stove with a slap on the rump. Crossing to the work counter, he took one of the carrots waiting to be fed into the food processor and bit off a chunk. "I already know, in fact. Van told me this afternoon."

Garreth blinked in disbelief. Could Harry, too, really be accepting it so calmly?

Harry chewed the carrot. "I don't know why you didn't say anything before. There's no need to suffer alone, Van says. It's nothing to be ashamed of, though I can see why you might not want your father to know. He'd probably take it personally, as a reflection of some weakness in him."

Grandma Doyle sniffed. "Wouldn't he, though?"

"Can we leave Dad out of this?" Garreth asked irritably.

"He never needs to know," Harry said. "Van told me all about her sister. There's treatment. You can be cured."

Garreth blinked in astonishment. "Cured! Treatment?" In his peripheral vision, he saw the women staring, too. "*What* treatment?"

Harry glanced at each of them with a puzzled frown. "A combination of medical and psychiatric therapy."

Garreth realized in dismay that they could not possibly be talking about the same thing. "Harry, exactly what did Girimonte say my problem is?"

The almond eyes narrowed. "Anorexia, of course. What else?"

No wonder Harry reacted so calmly. Garreth sighed. "I'm afraid Girimonte doesn't have it quite right. I'm—"

"Before dinner is no time to be getting so serious," his grandmother interrupted. "It spoils the digestion." She smiled sweetly. "Sergeant, if you'll be good enough to take yourself out from underfoot, I'll bring you the tea your lovely wife tells me you like to have when you come home from work. Garreth, finish grating those carrots, if you please. We'll all talk later."

Whatever "later" meant. Not during dinner, Garreth discovered. Between them, Lien and Grandma Doyle, kept the conversation firmly on light subjects. Not after dinner, either. Then they insisted on watching television, though Garreth could not believe either had any real interest in *Miami Vice*.

"Grandma, Lien," he said during a commercial. "May I see you a minute?" In the kitchen, out of Harry's hearing, he demanded, "What are you two doing? We're under the gun for time, and we need Harry."

Her forehead furrowed. "Yes, but . . ." She sighed. "He won't believe you if you just come out and say you're a vampire. He has to be eased into it."

The phone rang.

"I'll get it!" Harry called from the other room.

Garreth ran a hand through his hair. "We don't have *time* to ease him into it. Tomorrow this turkey will kill again, Grandma's feelings say. Tomorrow! Maybe you underestimate him, Lien. *You* accepted—"

"It's for you, Garreth!" Harry called. "An Irina Rudenko."

Garreth snatched up the kitchen extension, but he said nothing to Irina just yet. Harry's breathing came over the line from the family room extension. "I've got it, Harry."

"I'd like to speak to Miss Rudenko, too," Harry said. "Miss Rudenko, I'm Sergeant Takananda of the San Francisco Police. We're trying to find who killed Leonard Holle. I wonder if you can answer a couple of questions."

"About Mr. Holle?" the voice on the far end of the wire said in a tone of disappointment. "Is that what this is for? What a bummer."

Garreth blinked in astonishment. Only the accent remained Irina's.

The tone went petulant. "Meresa said there was this cute blond guy looking for me. Takananda doesn't sound like a name that belongs to anyone blond."

"I'm the blond one," Garreth said. "Garreth Mikaelian."

"Mikaelian. Mikaelian." She rolled the name around as if tasting it. "Are you the guy who kept trying to catch my eye at the performance of *Beach Blanket Babylon* last Saturday?"

Harry said patiently, "Miss Rudenko, this is important. How well did you know Mr. Holle?"

She sighed. "Jesus. I didn't know him. I mean, I

knew him, but I didn't *know* him, if you know what I mean. He's a friend of my mother. They both work for the Philos Foundation. I don't know anything about who killed him. What a horror show. Do we have to talk about it? I'd rather talk to you, blondie. Where do I know you from?"

"You don't," Garreth said, swearing to himself. What a time to have to play games. *Hang up, Harry, please, so I can talk to her.* "A mutual friend suggested I look you up."

"Yeah? Who?"

This version of Let's Pretend could have been fun under other circumstances. Irina played it very well. "Does it matter?"

She giggled. "Nope. Hey, let's get together, say the Japanese Tea Garden, twelve or so our time? See you then, blondie."

She hung up before either Garreth or Harry could say anything more. But nothing else needed to be said. She wanted to see him and had made an appointment. Garreth grinned in admiration. Harry would interpret it in human terms, twelve noon. Our time, she said, though. Vampire time. Midnight.

From the other extension, Harry said, "Okay, meet her, but take along a tail, and steer the conversation around to Holle. She might tell you something she wouldn't say to me."

Garreth smiled grimly. "I certainly will find out what she knows about Holle's death." Until then he would go along with Lien and his grandmother and not confess to Harry. If Irina did know something, maybe they could clear up this case without official help. Then there would be nearly a week more to break the truth to Harry before his vacation ended.

6

Night robbed the Japanese Tea Garden of the color Garreth remembered from walks here with Marti. However, even reduced to the grays of his night vision, and a lining of silver from the setting half moon, the garden retained its elegance and serenity. Scents remained, too, an assault of floral, plant, and water odors filling the night. Slipping along a bamboo-railed path, Garreth realized this was the first time he had visited the garden since Marti died. Perhaps it was just as well he had come by night, when it looked so different from what he remembered.

He shifted the carrying strap on his thermos to the other shoulder, wondering if he should have taken time to fill it on the way here. Except there might still be people around the stables.

The last of the moonlight vanished, leaving only his night vision to see by.

"So," said a voice at his elbow. "There was garlic in that male prostitute's apartment. Why is that something we need to discuss?"

Garreth jumped. How did she keep sneaking up on him, especially since he had been watching for anyone following him since he left the house? Her dark slacks and sweater left her invisible to the human eye, but he should have seen or heard her. What if she had been the killer? Irritation at himself sharpened his voice. "Because it means some human, not a vampire, killed your friend Holle and the others."

She reached out to run her fingers across a great stone lantern. "Of course. That became obvious to me once I knew you weren't guilty."

"How?"

"It doesn't matter." She turned away, moving down the path ahead of him to an arched bridge, where she leaned on the rail and stared down at goldfish moving in gray flashes through the reflecting pool below. "It is not your concern."

He exploded. "The hell it isn't! Look, honey, you may know I didn't kill anyone but there are plenty of other people, some of them cops, who still think I did! And they're going to go on suspecting me until they find someone better. So if you know anything, I'd sure as hell appreciate being told what it is."

She hesitated, then still staring down into the water, sighed and shook her head. "I'm sorry. It's impossible. It is too dangerous."

He frowned. "I've dealt with dangerous killers before. This one can't be any worse. He's still only human. You point me in his direction. Harry and I will arrest him and the law will take care of him."

Irina turned, frowning, but a moment later, to Garreth's irritation and discomfort, the scowl dissolved in laughter. She swallowed the whoop almost immediately with an apology. "I'm sorry." Was she? Amusement still lingered in her voice and gleamed in her eyes. "Such innocence." She reached up to touch his cheek, then withdrew the hand as he backed away angrily. "Please, I'm sorry. I don't mean to offend. It is just that I never cease being astonished by this age's blind belief in law as an instrument of justice. For, of course, this matter is one beyond your 'law.' "

His gut knotted. Echoes of Lane rang in her words. "No," he said. "There's law or there's only anarchy. Everyone must be responsible for their actions and answerable to other people for them."

The experienced eyes looked up at him from the smooth, adolescent face. "Oh, I agree, but they cannot always answer in a court of law. The danger is not so much to you personally, Garreth, as to both of us. To all of the blood. Even as young as you are in this life, can't you see what we have? This killer knows we exist and is stalking us and our friends. He broke Leonard's neck, not only to prevent him rising again in case he carried the virus, but from hatred of one who would befriend us."

"So he's a vampire hunter," Garreth said. "He's still just a man."

She hissed. "Just? No. Holy Mother, no. In the past year three friends of the blood have been murdered in this same manner in Europe, and all three were intelligent, experienced, alert people who survived times when people actively believed in and hunted us. Dominic escaped the arena in Rome, the Spanish Inquisition, and innumerable witch hunts. Yet this hunter managed to destroy him. *Now* do you see why I want you away from here? You're too . . . naive to fight him. And what if you should succeed in capturing him? Punishing him through your legal system will only make public why and what he kills, and you will have helped him destroy us all. Garreth, leave the hunter to me."

Cold ran through him and sat in icy lumps in his gut. "I can't. The law you don't believe in won't let me leave. So you might as well use my help. Who knows?

My training might even come in handy. Tell me about the killings. Is there a clue at all as to who's doing them?"

She glanced around. "Let's walk. We've stood in one place too long."

They walked, following the paths winding through the garden. Irina said nothing more for nearly five minutes, then with a sigh: "I talked to people who knew my friends. They could tell me little, but they did say that shortly before each death, my friend had talked to a tall, fair-haired man. One had mentioned to a companion that the man asked for a red-haired woman who traveled with Irina Rodek in the years just before the Second World War. It was obviously Mada. That's why I came to San Francisco, to warn her, and to warn our friends against talking to anyone asking for Mada."

Garreth felt as if a fist sunk into his stomach. "Was the man an Englishman?"

She whirled to stare up at him. "I don't know. No one I talked to had spoken with him personally." Her eyes narrowed. "There is an Englishman who Leonard said was working with your police friends, the one who came with you to the foundation offices yesterday afternoon."

"Julian Fowler." Quickly he told her everything about the writer. "But I don't know that any of it means anything. There's no obvious motive for him killing anyone, and certainly no proof against him."

Irina pursed her lips. "If he were a hunter, hatred of us would be sufficient motive, but this man has a specific quarry."

"Madelaine Bieber," Garreth said. "He's very open about it. Would he be if he wanted her for more than the book he claims to be researching?"

Irina smiled thinly. "If he's clever. The hunter who killed my friends has shown himself to be very clever." She paused. "I think we must learn more about this Englishman."

Garreth nodded. "The library should have entrics on him in books like *Contemporary Authors*."

Irina pursed her lips. "I know an even better source that will not raise our killer's suspicions if he manages to follow us. Come. My car is parked by Stow Lake."

7

Irina headed her little Honda north.

"Do you have much trouble renting cars and hotel rooms?" Garreth asked.

She snorted. "Of course not. I refuse to suffer the inconvenience of being a minor. My papers identify me as twenty-one, and when necessary I can make up to look the age or older. I suppose I should be thankful that devil Viktor did not see me at thirteen or fourteen. Ah, here we are." She pulled over to the curb.

Garreth blinked dubiously at the building before them. "How do we find biographical information on Fowler at the Philos Foundation?"

"It is simple. Watch."

Irina swung out of the car, climbed the steps to the porch, and rang the bell.

"May I help you?" a voice asked.

Irina looked up. "I would like to come in."

Now Garreth noticed the small, round eye of a camera winking at them from the roof of the porch.

"Does your mother know you run around at this hour of the night?" the voice asked chidingly.

"Natalya Rudenko knows everything I do. Open the door, please."

The door buzzed. Irina pushed it open. Yelling a greeting to a face that appeared at the top of the stairs, she led the way to Holle's office and unlocked the door. "That is to make us look normal. This, too." She switched on the light.

For the first time he saw her in color. She had violet eyes indeed . . . deeply, richly purple as pansies. Except when they reflected ruby red.

She switched on the computer to one side of the desk and sat down at it. Her fingers raced across the keyboard, calling up a communications program, Garreth realized, reading the screen prompts.

He eyed her in surprise. "You know computers?"

Without looking up, Irina replied, "It is a matter of necessity, as is learning to drive an automobile and fly an airplane. Altering electronic records is becoming the only way to change identities. Hasn't Mada taught you—" She glanced up and sighed. "No, of course not. It is just like her to bring you into this life and abandon you without bothering to teach basic survival skills." She turned back to the keyboard and typed rapidly. "Mada avoids the use of advanced technology anyway, an attitude that will undo her eventually. One cannot cling to the age of one's birth. When this problem of the vampire hunter is solved, we must see that you're given proper—ah, there's what I want—a literary database." She typed some more, then turned away. "Searching out and transmitting the data will take a while. Several fresh units of whole blood have been 'discarded' in the shelter refrigerator. Shall I go after one?"

He stiffened. "I don't drink human blood."

She eyed him. "So I see." Irina paused, then added, "One can survive on animal blood to a point, but never well. We need human blood. That's why you're hungry all the time."

"A little hunger is better than treating people like cattle." As the words came out, Garreth winced. God, that sounded self-righteous.

Irina regarded him with amusement. "Is that what you believe we do . . . that we are all like Mada?" She sobered. "No. Think. How could we have survived all these centuries and faded into mythology if—" She broke off. "*Nichevo*. Never mind. I understand your feelings. Truly. Few of us entered this life by choice. When I realized what I had become, I despised Viktor with such passion that I, too, swore I would never treat people as he did and never drink human blood."

"You mentioned him before," Garreth said. "Is he the vampire who—"

"Yes. Prince Viktor Kharitonovich." She spat the name. "Some called him Viktor the Wolfeyed. I was sixteen, and much plumper, when he saw me in Prince Yevgeni Vasilievich's household. My mother was a kitchen servant there. She would never say who my father was, but I have always felt he must have been a boyar, quite possibly the prince's younger brother Peter. Sometimes I envied his legitimate daughters, but not usually. They had to live confined to the *terem* in the house and go veiled in the street."

Garreth blinked in astonishment. "Russian women lived like that?"

She smiled faintly. "Five hundred years ago, yes." Her eyes focused past him. "My freedom cost me, however, when it gave Viktor the chance to see me. He had his men abduct me one day on the way to market with my mother. I didn't know *he* was responsible, of course, not until three nights later, three terrible nights of abject terror, waiting for what I knew must appear sooner or later. For years peasant and servant girls had been vanishing, then reappearing days or weeks later as walking dead.

"I was almost relieved when Viktor came out of the dark with his fangs bared. I fought him, biting and scratching—my mother's father was a Mongol, after all—and though he still overpowered me and drank, it was not before I tasted his blood first. The second night he came, I was hiding behind the door. I hit him in the face with a stool and escaped." Irina smiled wryly. "Unfortunately it was winter. I froze to death before I reached home." The smile faded. "I woke in the snow. You can perhaps understand my feelings when I discovered cold no longer bothered me and realized why."

Garreth sucked in his breath. Oh yes, he knew.

Irina focused on him. "Only my hatred of that devil kept me from throwing myself on a stake. I swore to destroy him."

The words reverberated in Garreth. He thought of Lane's grave. "Did you?"

Her teeth bared in a wolfish grin. "I am a Mongol's granddaughter, remember. At home I resumed my life, claiming I couldn't remember where I had been. Pretending to be still human was difficult—agony when I went to church—but the thought of vengeance helped me endure the pain. At night I spied on Viktor studying his habits and his house until I knew when he was vulnerable and how to reach him. Then I pretended to recover my memory. I denounced him. Prince Yevgeni gathered a hunting party at Viktor's house. I led them to the cellar where he slept by day and persuaded the prince to let me drive in the stake."

"They didn't suspect you of having become a vampire?"

She smiled grimly. "I had sworn on an icon that I escaped before he fed on me: the most difficult thing I have ever done. It was like putting my hand in fire. That convinced them, but I took no chances anyway. While the prince was beheading Viktor and burning the body, I helped myself to as much gold and jewels as I could carry from that devil's treasure room and ran away to Moscow."

"Where you gave up your vow of not drinking human blood?"

He winced at the edge on his voice—he had not intended to sound judgmental—but she shrugged. "Where the rashness of youthful passion gave way to reality and necessity. Garreth, feeding does not have to be an act of—"

The computer beeped.

Irina spun her chair back toward it. "Finally. Several references, too. Very good." Before Garreth had time to read the list on the screen, she tapped a key.

The printing convulsed and vanished. The drive light flickered for several minutes. When it stopped, the computer beeped again. Irina tapped more keys.

CONNECTION BROKEN, the screen announced.

"Now let's see what we have."

At her tap on another key, the printer started. Paper spewed into the receiving basket. Irina ripped it off and after skimming the readout, handed it to him. "You will find this interesting."

The database had found and sent them three items: an entry from *Contemporary Authors*, an article on Fowler from *Writer's Digest* magazine, and an interview that had run in *Playboy* several years earlier.

According to the biographical data in *Contemporary Authors,* Fowler had been born in London in 1939 to Margaret Graham Fowler, the daughter of stage actor Charles Graham, and Richard "Dickon" Fowler. Fowler's father, who worked for British Intelligence with the French underground during World War II, died in France late in 1945 of a broken neck sustained in a fall.

A ripple ran across Garreth's neck hair. Fowler said his parents met Lane in France shortly after the war. That could not have been long before the father's death.

He went on reading.

Fowler's mother remarried and Fowler spent the rest of his childhood shuttling between boarding school and his actor grandfather. He enrolled at Cambridge, Trinity College, but instead of studying history, began writing horror novels. After selling one of those novels two years later, he quit the university to write full time. A few years later he switched from horror stories to thrillers. His first American publication came in 1972.

Garreth glanced back at the line about Fowler's father. His skin prickled again. "A broken neck."

Irina glanced up at him through thick, dark lashes. "Interesting, yes? Keep reading."

The *Writer's Digest* article talked only about writing discipline and how growing up around his grandfather had provided an atmosphere rich in imagination. Garreth went on to the *Playboy* interview. A few questions into the article, one leaped up at him.

PLAYBOY: IN A BBC INTERVIEW SEVERAL YEARS AGO, YOU STATED THAT YOU BEGAN WRITING AS AN ACT OF EXORCISM. THAT'S AN INTERESTING REASON TO WRITE. WOULD YOU CARE TO EXPLAIN FOR YOUR AMERICAN READERS?

FOWLER: YES, OF COURSE. WHEN I WAS SIX A SAVAGE DOG ATTACKED MY FATHER. HE FELL FROM A CLIFF TRYING TO ESCAPE FROM THE BEAST AND WAS KILLED. AS A CHILD I COULD NEVER ACCEPT THAT. HOW COULD A MERE DOG KILL MY FATHER THE SPY? IT HAD TO BE SOME MONSTER RESPONSIBLE. HIS DEATH HAUNTED ME FOR YEARS. I'M NOT SURE WHAT MADE ME TURN IT INTO A STORY AND WRITE IT DOWN, BUT EVENTUALLY IT BECAME MY NOVEL *BLOOD MAZE*. IN IT A BOY WITNESSES A WEREWOLF TEARING HIS FATHER'S THROAT OUT. NO ONE WILL BELIEVE HIM SO HE VOWS THAT WHEN HE GROWS UP, HE WILL FIND

AND DESTROY THE WEREWOLF. AS A GROWN MAN, HE
FULFILLS THAT VOW. IN A SENSE, THE SAME HAPPENED
TO ME. BY WRITING ABOUT DESTROYING THE INSTRU-
MENT OF MY FATHER'S DEATH, I LAID HIS GHOST TO
REST. I WENT ON WRITING HORROR NOVELS FOR A
WHILE, OF COURSE, BECAUSE I KNEW I COULD, BUT
EVENTUALLY I SWITCHED TO THRILLERS. THE HORROR
NOVELS WERE EXORCISM, THE THRILLERS A KIND OF
MEMORIAL. IN A SENSE, EACH SPY HERO IS MY FATHER.

Garreth felt for his own throat, tracing the scars
where Lane's teeth had ripped through the flesh.
"See this question also," Irina said, pointing.

PLAYBOY: IF YOUR CHARACTERS ARE SYMBOLS FOR
PEOPLE IN YOUR LIFE, WHO IS THE TALL WOMAN WHO
APPEARS AS CHATELAINE BARBOUR IN *BLOOD MAZE*,
TARA BRENNEIS IN *MIND'S EYE*, AND MAGDA EBER-
HARDT IN *OUR MAN IN HADES*, TO NAME A FEW OF HER
INCARNATIONS? WHEN SHE APPEARS, SHE IS ALWAYS
THE BEAUTIFUL SEDUCTRESS WHO TURNS TRAITOR.

FOWLER (WITH A RUEFUL LAUGH): I'M AFRAID I'LL
HAVE TO TAKE THE FIFTH ON THAT ONE, AS YOU
AMERICANS SAY. I DON'T FANCY BEING SUED FOR
SLANDER. SUFFICE IT TO SAY, SHE WAS AN OLDER
WOMAN I FELL MADLY IN LOVE WITH YEARS AGO AND
WHO SPURNED ME FOR THE CALLOW YOUTH I WAS. NO
DOUBT, IT'S UNSPORTING TO MAKE HER THE VILLAIN-
ESS, BUT . . . SHE KEEPS POPPING UP WHEN I NEED ONE.

"Lane," Garreth said. A beautiful seductress betraying the hero over and over . . . as she had turned
on Fowler's father? "I could have sworn he showed no
anger when Fowler talked about his childhood meeting with Lane. I didn't hear any bitterness or resent-
ment, absolutely no hint of hatred. Can someone hide
his feelings that well? He'd have to be one hell of an
actor." A hell of an actor, too, to come into the squad

room Wednesday morning looking like the most disturbing thing on his mind was a hangover, which had to be a pretense as well.

"He may be mad," Irina said. "Or both."

Fowler would have to be riding the edge of a crack-up carrying his obsession around buried that deep all these years.

Irina turned off the computer and stood. "So now we must catch this Englishman and deal with him."

Garreth stiffened. "Shoot him, you mean, like you were going to shoot me last night? No." Garreth shook his head. "I won't—" He broke off, but finished the sentence silently: *won't kill again*. The fact that taking Lane's life had, in the end, been a matter of self-defense made no difference in the wrongness of it. *What gives* you *the right to judge* me? Lane had flung at him that Thanksgiving night. He needed no second face haunting his dreams. "There's been enough killing."

The violet eyes reflected red. "How can I convince you how deadly and ruthless vampire hunters are? They are driven, blindly self-righteous, so positive we are evil that they see nothing but their cause. Like berserkers, nothing stops them but death."

"Criminals disregard the law, too, but we punish them through the system. How can you sneer at hunters for being self-righteous if we arbitrarily set ourselves up as *their* judges?"

She sighed. "Ah, your law again. What do you suggest?"

It furthers one to appoint helpers, *I Ching* had said. Garreth took a breath. "First we need proof Fowler is our killer, and since the killer has to be watching me, and now you, we can't be involved or he'll realize we're on to him. We need help, human help, official help . . . someone who can find probable cause and enter Fowler's hotel room to search it. We need my ex-partner, Harry."

8

Irina said, "You realize you are risking more lives than yours and mine."

Garreth nodded.

The two of them sat at the kitchen counter with pewter tankards of blood, his horse blood from his thermos, hers from a unit of human blood she had brought from the foundation. He buried his nose in his tankard in an effort to block out the tantalizing scent leaking toward him from hers. Thirst scorched his throat.

He distracted himself by thinking about Fowler. Where was the writer now? Watching the house, he had to assume. To keep Fowler from suspecting he was now the hunted, Garreth had come home from the Foundation on foot, with a stop at the police stables to fill the thermos. Irina had followed later, parking her car several blocks away and approaching the house through the backyards.

An anxious voice said, "Garreth, you shouldn't be out—who is this?"

He looked around at Lien in the kitchen doorway. "Meet Irina Rudenko." Then he noticed Grandma Doyle behind Lien. Introducing her, too, it occurred to him that Irina was also his grandmother of sorts.

A rap sounded upstairs. "Garreth!" Harry's voice called.

Lien glanced up. "I'll say I let you out."

Garreth shook his head. "I have to tell him everything anyway. We need him."

She studied his face for a moment, then sighed and nodded. Moving around the work island, she reached up into a cupboard for a bottle of brandy.

Grandma Doyle stayed near the door, fingering the Maltese cross around her neck as she eyed the girl.

Irina smiled. "Mrs. Doyle, you have nothing to fear from me." She held up the tankard. "As you see, I have my breakfast."

Grandma Doyle's expression became accusing. "You're the one responsible for the creature who did this to me grandson."

The smile faded. "To my regret, yes. Even one as experienced as I can be a fool."

Harry came thumping down the stairs and through the doorway from the hall. "Lien, see if you can —Garreth?" He plowed to a stop, staring in open-mouthed, almost comic disbelief. Garreth felt no desire to laugh, however. "Your door is bolted on the inside."

Here it came. Garreth's gut knotted. He took a deep breath. "Yes. I don't have to open doors to go through them."

Irina caught Garreth's wrist. "Gently, *tovarich*. I am Irina Rudenko, Mr. Takananda."

"Rudenko?" Harry's eyes narrowed. "You were going to meet him at noon today."

She smiled. "No. Twelve o'clock our time, I told him. That's midnight."

Harry blinked. "What?" Then he started, staring

back at Garreth. "What do you mean you don't have to open doors to go through them?"

That had taken long enough to sink in. "Harry, maybe you'd better sit down. I need to talk."

Harry groped for a stool. Garreth smelled an acid scent beneath his old partner's blood scent. Did he fear that Garreth was about to confess to the killings.

Garreth hurried to reassure him. "I didn't kill those men, Harry, I swear."

Harry let his breath out. "I didn't think you could, Mik-san."

"What I have to say is about me . . . why I act strangely sometimes, how I left the bedroom without unbolting the door."

The almond eyes narrowed. "You went out the window."

Garreth shook his head. "Harry—" *Shit. How do I say this?* Maybe he should take off his glasses and— He discarded the idea in mid-thought. No, this was something Harry had to understand and accept of his own volition.

Good luck, lover. Lane's voice laughed in his head.

He groped desperately for words. "Harry . . . if you were watching a movie and the detectives had some murders to solve where the bodies had two punctures in their necks and were all drained of blood, and then one of the detectives was found dead with his throat torn out by the killer, only he sat up in the morgue with his throat almost healed, and after that he stopped eating food and preferred night to daylight and he couldn't stand garlic . . . what would you say they were dealing with?"

Harry frowned. "I thought we were going to talk seriously."

"Harry, I'm dead serious."

A pulse jumped in Harry's throat. He stared at Garreth in silence for a long time, then, with face smoothed into a bland mask, said in a careful, flat voice, "This isn't a movie."

"No," Garreth agreed. "I wish it were. Then we could shut off the TV and go on with normal lives. But everything that happened to me is real. I wake up from sleeping and I'm still a—still changed."

The skin between Harry's brows rippled, as if he started to frown but thought better of it. He said slowly, "You know, Dr. Masethin sees private patients, too."

Garreth's gut twisted. Masethin. The department shrink. Harry thought he had gone bananas. *Well, what else did you expect, man?* He kept his voice even. "Harry, I'm not crazy."

"Of course not," Harry said hastily. "But maybe— you know, the mind plays funny tricks sometimes. Chemical imbalances from starvation might—"

Garreth slapped his hand down on the counter. "I'm not anorectic, either! I eat. This." He poured some of the blood from his tankard onto the counter top.

The pulse leaped visibly in Harry's throat again as he stared at the crimson puddle. After a minute he looked up with a friendly smile that sent Garreth's stomach plummeting. "All right. I'm convinced."

Like hell, Garreth reflected in disappointment. That was Harry's let's-humor-the-subject-until-he's-off-guard-and-we-can-jump-him smile.

From the faint shake of Irina's head, Garreth saw she read the situation as he did.

Grandma Doyle said, "I'd be thinking of a demonstration, Garreth."

Nothing less was going to convince him, it appeared. Hopping off the stool, Garreth strode over to the hall door and closed it. Then he leaned against it, his hands above his head. "Watch, Harry. I won't touch the knob."

Wrench. He stood in the hall. Turning, he pressed against the door again. *Wrench*. Would Harry be glaring in revulsion?

Not quite. Harry stared with white-rimmed eyes in disbelief, his mouth working soundlessly, face drained of blood.

Grandma Doyle eased him backward onto a stool.

Lien wrapped his fingers around a glass of brandy. "'There are more things in Heaven and Earth, Horatio, than you or I have dreamed,'" she said gently.

The brandy went down in a single gulp. Garreth doubted Harry even noticed the action, much less tasted the liquor. After Lien refilled the glass and he tossed that down, too, he stared at the glass in astonishment. Then he looked at Garreth and closed his eyes. "Tell me I didn't see that."

"You saw it," Irina said. "Speaking from experience, it is easier if you forget trying to understand what you saw; just accept it."

Lien put an arm around him. "Accept Garreth, too. Basically he's still the same person he always was."

Harry stiffened.

Garreth sucked in his breath.

But Harry turned to frown at Lien. "*You* knew about this, and you didn't tell me?"

He seemed almost relieved by the omission, Garreth noticed. Glad to have something comprehensible to think about?

Lien said, "I learned just yesterday. Garreth tried to tell you himself then, but you were too set on believing Vanessa's diagnosis of him." She poured more brandy.

He pushed it away. "I won't be able to drive if I have any more. Or maybe I'll call in sick. I can't handle anything more today." He picked up the glass.

Garreth caught his wrist. "Harry, you have to go in! We think we know who the killer is and we need you to prove it."

"The killer." The expression in Harry's eyes wiped the past five minutes out of existence to leap at Garreth's words. "A killer I can handle. Who is it?"

Garreth told him.

Harry listened with a concentration like a drowning man clinging to a life preserver. At the end of the recitation he jumped up. "Van hasn't been happy about that stair window as an entry point. I'll tell her that Garreth mentioned not checking the storerooms because they were locked. She'll jump at checking them. After the lab processes them, we'll bring Fowler in to compare prints and fibers."

"How can you do that without warning him that he's a suspect?" Irina asked.

Harry grinned. "Easy. I received an anonymous phone call from a woman saying she'd seen Fowler at Maruska's apartment. I'll say, of course, it's nonsense, probably some nut case looking for publicity by accusing a celebrity, but, of course, we have to check it out to clear him. In the course of it, we'll check him against associative evidence from Holle's attic, too." Harry kissed Lien and headed for the door. "I'll call you when I have something."

"Meanwhile," Irina said, draining her tankard, "we must keep our watcher occupied. Show yourself at the living room window and on the patio, then I think we should rest away from daylight."

9

A double thickness of blanket over the bedroom window hardly constituted blackout curtains, but it blocked a good deal of light, making the room at least comfortable. Irina knelt on the floor, unrolling an air mattress she had brought in from her car. Dried earth hissed inside as she smoothed it and arranged a sheet and pillow over it.

Watching her from where he sat on the edge of the bed, Garreth felt urgency throb in him. Time was running out. He ought to be doing more than sleeping. Fowler would kill again today if they did not stop him. How, though? He could hardly have Irina hunting Fowler her way.

Irina curled up, pulling the sheet around her, and closed her eyes.

He stretched out on his own pallet on the bed. "You don't approve of bringing in Harry, do you?"

Without opening her eyes, she replied, "I worry what we will do when he finds proof against Fowler. Arresting the Englishman will make public his motive for murder. Then either the sergeant will be ridiculed for believing such a thing and the hunter turned loose, or you, I, and all of our kind will be exposed." She opened her eyes and raised up on one elbow. "Destroying hunters is the only way to protect ourselves."

"There has to be way of stopping him without killing him or betraying ourselves."

Irina smiled. The warmth of it enveloped him like a thick, soft blanket. "You are a man of honor, Garreth Mikaelian, kinder toward your enemies than I. It's too bad you couldn't be with me when I lived near Yasnaya Polyana, Tolstoy's estate at Tula. I think you would have enjoyed listening to Tolstoy philosophize on law and justice."

Garreth started. "*The* Tolstoy? You knew him?"

"I attended many of his parties with a friend who posed as my guardian while waiting out some trouble in St. Petersburg. The talk and debate would last all night. Tolstoy's philosophies inspired the nonviolence embraced by Gandhi and your Dr. Martin Luther King, did you know that?" Mischief glinted in the violet eyes. "A Russian influenced them." Then the mischief faded. "It is too bad Mr. Fowler has not been influenced by Tolstoy also." Stretching out, she closed her eyes again. "At which thought I leave you to solve our problem with honor, and within your law, if you can. For myself, I am tired and wish only to sleep."

Garreth turned over. He would have liked to sleep, too; his body ached from exhaustion and daylight. But the clock ticked relentlessly in him, and his mind churned with doubt. Which was more important, law or finding Fowler? Following procedure took time. Was Irina right? Was he wrong to insist on applying human law to this situation? Would someone else die because of it? He might as well consider that he had killed those other three men. They died because he led the killer to them.

Garreth clenched his fists. *Why* had he not realized

he was being followed? Was Fowler really that good, or had Garreth just been so preoccupied with his own interests that he had committed the sin no good cop ever should, failing to pay attention to what was happening around him?

Irina sighed in her sleep.

He eyed her. There lay another problem. After being so insistent that the only way to deal with Fowler was kill him, Irina had given in far too readily to Garreth. Was she just humoring him until they had Fowler? In her place, he might do that, and then, having found the killer of his friends and bloodkind, he would brush aside the young vampire and his precious law to act as he felt necessary to protect himself.

Garreth bit his lip. He had to prevent that. Somehow. Restraining Irina was probably impossible, which meant he had to protect Fowler. He grimaced. As a cop he had often stood between a killer and those demanding vengeance, but never before had he been forced to side with one where the price of doing his job could be the destruction of a whole people . . . his own kind.

Grandma Doyle's voice echoed in his head: *I saw you dying, and someone laughing like the devil's own above you.* His pulse lurched. It could also mean his own destruction.

He sat up, hugging his knees. No, he refused to accept that either Fowler had to die or vampires did. There *must* be some way to protect everyone.

The clock on the night stand indicated ten o'clock. Sliding out of bed, Garreth put on his dark glasses, then picked up his boots, slipped over to the bureau, and eased his billfold, gun, and keys off it. Moving just as soundlessly to the door, he passed through without opening it, so it would not wake Irina.

His grandmother looked up in surprise from her

book as he came into the family room. "Why aren't you sleeping?"

He sat down in a chair to pull on and zip his boots. "I have an errand I have to run." He dared not look up at them for fear they would read the lie in his face. Enough lives were at risk already; he would not involve them further. "Have you heard anything from Harry?"

"He called about an hour and a half ago. They found the storeroom as we described it."

"Good." Standing, Garreth clipped his holster onto his belt.

His grandmother eyed him. "What kind of errand requires a gun?"

He made himself smile at her. "Cops feel naked without a weapon. You know that from Dad, Grandma." He pulled on his corduroy jacket. "I won't be using it." He hoped. But neither would he go near Fowler unarmed.

Lien frowned. "Should you go out alone? I mean, Harry knows you're innocent but others like Vanessa Girimonte don't yet. If something happens . . ."

They had to stay here safe. He forced his smile into a confident grin. "What can happen? It's just a short trip. I'll be back before you know it." Blowing them a kiss, he headed for the front door.

10

Being in the ZX again—the wheel in his hands, the engine snarling—felt wonderful. No matter it was daylight. Despite driving with half his attention on the rear-view mirror, the mere fact of being behind the wheel himself instead of riding along brought a sense of satisfaction and confidence, of finally being in charge again.

The question was where to let Fowler catch up. A public place would be safest, at least until he could make Fowler understand the situation with Irina, then they could find somewhere to hide the writer. The place to meet occurred to him almost immediately, a very public one he could expect to be crowded and one he knew every inch of from playing tag with officers from other black-and-whites at three and four o'clock in the morning on slow watches.

Garreth frowned at his rear-view mirror. Unfortunately the writer was not driving a car as conspicuous as the Continental he had in Baumen. The tan Colt he had rented here looked—deliberately, no doubt—like hundreds of others on the street. A tan subcompact had fallen in behind him a couple of blocks from Harry's house, but he no longer saw it. He had turned onto a busier street, though, and if he were being tailed, Fowler would be tucked out of sight several cars back.

His pulse jumped as tan appeared in his outside mirror. A moment later he let his breath out. The passing vehicle was a station wagon. Checking the traffic directly behind again, he decided there was indeed a tan car back there. Telling any more about it was impossible. The two intervening cars prevented him from seeing the tag and the driver showed as only a silhouette.

The matter shortly became academic because the car turned another direction midway across Golden Gate Park.

With the thickening of traffic on Fulton north of the park, more tan cars appeared, falling in behind, passing, weaving through traffic, turning off, which made it difficult keeping track of any particular one. That grew still more difficult as Fulton neared the Civic Center and traffic continued increasing. Garreth resisted the impulse to make a series of turns and see which cars stuck with him. He would know soon enough if Fowler were really following him.

To make it easy for any tail, both to follow and hide in traffic, he took a straight route on major thoroughfares: Fulton to the Civic Center, then north on Van Ness until he could turn east to the Cannery. But anyone following him was on his own finding a parking place. The best Garreth could do after locating one for himself was walk very slowly into the Cannery complex.

That was easy. The bright sunlight weighted and battered him. He felt like he moved through molasses.

He longed to be taking refuge in blissful darkness. Barring that luxury, a heavy rainstorm, or better yet, a pea-soup fog would have made today more pleasant.

Then abruptly the drag of daylight became a minor matter. Glancing over his shoulder, he spotted the face he had been looking for. His pulse jumped. Fowler wore a dark wig, mustache, and horn-rimmed glasses, but he was still unmistakably Julian Fowler.

Garreth sucked in a long breath. The chase was on in earnest now.

The red brick complex sprawled out like some vast Florentine palace. He kept moving through its court-yards and arcades and across its bridges, pausing to browse through a shop or take brief refuge in the shade of a tree, stopping to chat with an artist doing pastel portraits, then a musician playing her guitar in one of the courtyards. He asked directions to shops so Fowler would see the people pointing.

Covert checks over his shoulder via shop windows found Fowler sticking with him. The writer kept changing his appearance, putting on or removing the glasses, sometimes with or without a tweed roadster cap.

Garreth took another breath. Time for the fox to catch the hound.

He strode along an arcade and around a corner to a flight of stairs. There he quickly vaulted over the railing to drop down onto a bridge below, startling shoppers and tourists, then raced across the bridge into another arcade.

From the shadows he watched Fowler stop short at the top of the stairs, dismay spreading across the writer's face as he realized he had lost his quarry. Inaction lasted only seconds. His face tight with anger, Fowler plunged down the stairs and raced along the arcade, first in one direction, then the other, and finally across the bridge. By that time Garreth had retreated into a shop.

"May I help you?" a clerk asked.

Garreth glanced around at the display of women's sexy undergarments. "Just drooling."

Fowler hurried past the shop door. Garreth waited for several more people to pass before slipping out. He fell in behind two couples, using them to screen him from Fowler.

If Fowler still felt frantic, he did not show it. The grim set of his mouth had vanished. Except for turning every few seconds to scan the arcade or pausing to lean out over the balustrade and peer at arcades opposite and courtyards below, he might have been just another shopper.

Garreth waited until a turn in the arcade left a quiet corner, then quickly circled the two couples and closed on Fowler. "What are we going to do with you, Dr. Van Helsing?"

Fowler whipped around. As his face registered recognition, consternation evaporated, giving way to a watchful stillness in the pale eyes. Eyes like ice. "I beg your pardon?"

If Garreth had had any doubts about Fowler before, the question wiped them away. He knew that voice. He had heard it hundreds of times before, in a dozen accents in both sexes, across the table of an interview room and during field arrests, always the same, even and controlled, but not quite able to hide its mocking undertone, its catch-me-if-you-can arrogance. He eyed the writer with angry satisfaction. *You're dirty, Fowler, and now your ass is mine.*

He dropped his voice so only Fowler could hear it above the guitar music coming from the courtyard below. "My pardon is one thing you'll never have. Your appetite for blood is bigger than mine. Those men couldn't tell you where Lane was no matter what you did to them. They didn't know."

The ice-pale eyes focused on his glasses. "Why are you so sure? Because you do?"

Garreth felt suddenly very glad they stood with a crowd moving past them. He savored the eddying currents of perfumes, sweat, food odors, and blood scents. "Yes. You've seen her, too, though you didn't realize it. She was in Baumen, in the cemetery."

That startled him out of his complacency. "The cemetery!"

Garreth grimaced bitterly. "Ironic, isn't it? You followed me here and tortured and killed to find her . . . for nothing. She's already dead."

Fowler's face hardened. The pale eyes narrowed. "I don't believe you."

"You saw the grave. It had rosebushes on it."

Garreth waited for a sag of defeat as Fowler realized he had wasted those three lives and his. Instead, the writer's eyes narrowed still more. In a low, almost casual voice he said, "You're a bloody liar. You're just trying to protect that creature." He jammed his hands into his coat pockets.

You goofed, man, a voice murmured in Garreth's head. Screwed up royally. Fowler looked so rational that he had forgotten he was dealing with a loony tune. The man had spent most of his life hunting Lane, planning revenge, dreaming of it. Of course, he refused to accept that it might have been pointless.

Garreth reached for his glasses. This needed more persuasive methods.

At the same time Fowler's hand came out of his coat pocket.

Every alarm in Garreth kicked into action. Weapon! He lunged for the wrist.

The writer held not a gun, however, but a small bottle, the pump type used as a purse-size perfume container. Pushing Fowler's arm up made no difference. Fowler was already depressing the top. Mist caught Garreth full in the face.

Suddenly he could no longer breathe. The air congealed in his lungs. Garlic juice!

Backing against the arcade balustrade, he clawed for the turtleneck of his shirt. A part of him recognized the action as useless. It never did help, but he tried anyway, reflexively, in panic, struggling to suck in air.

Several passers-by stopped. One woman started toward him.

Fowler reached him first, catching him under the arm and groping for Garreth's coat pockets. "Christ, Sid; don't tell me you've come away without the bloody atomizer again." He looked around at the woman. "He has these asthma attacks when he's upset. He'll be right in no time once he's had his medication. You shouldn't be so touchy, though, Sid; it was just a joke. Come on. Let's get you back to the car and sorted out."

Fear spurted in Garreth. *No!* But, he had no breath to say it aloud, and no strength to do anything but struggle to breathe. Maybe he should just collapse.

The grip under his arm held him on his feet, though. Fowler half dragged, half carried him through the Cannery, chattering all the way. "Hang on, Sid; don't panic. We'll be back at the car before you know it. I do wish you'd remember to carry your atomizer all the time. Maybe Heather ought to hang the thing around your neck. Where's she got off to? Come on, come on; do I have to carry you all the way? Try to walk, can't you? Do you know how embarrassing this is? I daresay it looks like I'm abducting you or something. We'll be lucky if some copper doesn't stop us."

Fat chance. Through reddening vision, Garreth saw people turn to stare at them, but no one questioned or interfered.

His chest ached from the effort to expand it. His lungs felt as if they were about to burst. Unconsciousness could be only seconds away. It was incredible that he had not passed out already.

"Thank God, we're almost there," Fowler rattled on. Garreth could barely hear through the thunder of blood in his ears. "We'll have you set right straightaway. But one more of these attacks of yours, Sid, and I swear you can bloody well count me out of sightseeing with you and my sister again."

Near the street, Garreth's chest loosened. Air! He wanted to gasp in relief and gulp it in. Instead, he forced himself to breathe slowly. If Fowler did not notice he was recovering, he could jump the son of a bitch. He hoped. The hammer of sunlight on top of suffocation left him shaky and wrung out.

"Hey-ho, Sid, old son, here we are." Fowler propped Garreth against the car. "Let me just find the key and we're off."

Garreth tensed. Every breath came easier. A few more and he would be breathing normally. Then he would take the bastard.

"And here we are." Fowler held up the key. But he also had the perfume bottle palmed in the same hand, and before Garreth could move, squeezed a second round of garlic mist into Garreth's face.

Anger exploded in Garreth. Not again! Choking, he clawed for his gun.

Fowler caught his wrist and twisted the weapon away. "Naughty, naughty." He released the cylinder, flipped it out, and dumped the bullets in a smooth, one-handed motion. "We won't be needing these." The cylinder back in place, the gun went into Fowler's coat pocket. "Now shall we get on with it, with no more foolishness?"

Why did the incident give Garreth a feeling of déjà vu? Oh, yes. He had also tried to draw on Lane when she had him pinned in that North Beach alley, drinking his blood. With no better results, he remembered bitterly.

Unlocking the car, Fowler shoved him in. Garreth huddled in the seat, listening to his lungs creak and his heart slam against them with the strain of fighting to breathe.

Fowler climbed in the other side and started the car. "I'm sure you're uncomfortable. Suffocation is a terrifying sensation. At least in my personal experience it has always been a most effective method of persuading people to share information they might refuse to otherwise. You needn't worry about passing out or dying, however. Your kind doesn't. You only feel as if you're about to. Endlessly." He backed out of the parking space. "We'll finish our chat somewhere quiet. You still haven't told me where Mada is."

The words brought a terror totally apart from the panic caused by not being able to breathe. Déjà vu indeed. Fowler would never appreciate the irony of it, but he was an echo of the woman he wanted to destroy. Another victim of Lane's excesses. And as in the alley with Lane, Garreth was completely in his captor's power. Helpless.

11

Somewhere quiet indeed. Garreth bit his lip. No one would think of checking Lane's apartment when they started looking for Fowler and him.

The lock clicked open. Fowler dropped his lock picks back in the inside pocket of his coat. Picking Garreth up from where he had dropped him by the door, Fowler dragged him inside and deposited him in the wicker basket chair. Then in a quick circuit, Fowler opened the drapes several inches, closed the door, and came back to the wicker chair.

Sunlight streamed across the room in a beam that splashed over Garreth. He noticed it even in the midst of his other pain, and strained away from the slap of it toward the side of the chair still in shadow.

Fowler promptly dragged the chair so the beam fell directly across the middle, where no amount of leaning would avoid it. "We can't have you too comfortable, can we, old son?"

He reached into his coat pocket. Garreth stiffened,

expecting the perfume bottle again. Fowler had sprayed him twice more during the drive over, and with time between for only a few gulps of air, each renewed loss of breath had felt more terrifying than the last. Instead of the garlic, however, Fowler produced four thin plastic strips of the kind electricians used to secure a group of wires in one neat bundle.

He toyed with them. "Handy little gadgets, these cable ties. One can do all sorts of things with them where one needs a loop or a way to fasten something to something else."

Or tie up someone? The ties looked just the right width to make the marks on Holle's and the count's wrists.

Fowler wrapped a tie around one of Garreth's wrists, fed the pointed end through the lock loop on the other end, and pulled it snug. "I believe your law-enforcement agencies use a longer, wider version as handcuffs. It makes sense really. They're strong and there's no lock to pick." He pulled Garreth's arms behind him and wrapped the other wrist, this time looping the tie through the loop made by the first before closing it. Cable ties went around Garreth's ankles, too. "There now. You won't wander, even if I let you breathe for a while." He smiled. "Or should I say, if you earn the right to breathe."

Garreth tested his wrists. No good. The plastic strip cut in like wire with no feeling of give. At night and breathing normally, he might have the strength to break them, but not here, not now.

"The price isn't very high really. All you have to do is tell me where to find Mada."

The hell. How did Fowler expect him to talk when he could not breathe?

As if reading his mind, Fowler said, "You can whisper if you have a good go at it. I strongly advise you do so, old son."

Why bother when he would not believe the truth?

"Where *is* she!" A hand cracked across Garreth's face.

Through the pain came the thought that if only he could get out of this sunlight, he might find a way to fight Fowler. It would halve his handicap anyway.

Fowler slapped him again. The force whipped his neck and rocked the chair. But with the blow came an idea for getting out of the sun. Carefully Garreth mouthed: *fuck you*.

Fowler reacted instantly. Grabbing Garreth by the lapels, Fowler hauled him out of the chair and slung him halfway across the room against the bookshelves beside the fireplace. If Garreth had been breathing, it would have knocked the air out of him. "Tell me!"

Shadow brought no relief, though, no renewal of strength. He sagged to the floor. God, if only he could pass out. This was excruciating, swimming on the edge of consciousness like the half death of his transition phase, feeling and hearing everything but unable to move to roll over to relieve his aches or move to scratch his itches.

Above him, Fowler chuckled. Grabbing Garreth by the lapels once more, Fowler jerked him to his feet and slammed him backward again, into the brick of the fireplace itself this time, again and again, once for every word he spoke. Garreth's glasses shook loose and fell off. "You . . . will . . . tell . . . me. You'll tell me or learn just how much pain can be inflicted on one of your sort. It is a great deal, I promise you. I have seen. There's no refuge. You can't even faint. Until the central nervous system is disrupted, you must feel and endure every moment of agony, and you would be surprised how much of the body may be destroyed before damaging the spine or brain."

Garreth fought welling panic. Fowler had to be playing mind games. Not that he doubted what the writer said was true. There had probably been plenty of opportunity for observation of vampires in pain while killing Irina's friends in Europe. No wonder she hated and feared the man. But how much could Fowler do here? Whittle at him with a pocketknife?

Abruptly he wished he had not thought of that. He hated knives. The idea of being cut always bothered him far more than the possibility of being shot.

Fowler hissed through his teeth. "I don't know why you protect the vile creature. She condemned you to this life. One would expect you to hate her, to rejoice in seeing her destroyed." He brushed at dust on Garreth's lapels. "Perhaps what you need is the opportunity to reflect on it. Yes, that's it. I'll hang you up in the bedroom closet with a clove of garlic around your neck. I doubt very much that anyone will discover you there. In a couple of weeks or months then, I'll come back and resume our discussion. How does that strike your fancy?"

It struck pure terror—bone-melting, bowel-emptying, paralyzing dread. Visions spun behind Garreth's eyes of weeks or months without food or breath, also without unconsciousness or sleep, unable to die, only to hang there suffering ceaselessly. A living death.

"Or maybe we'll try a stake on you for size, not kill you, you understand, just give it a little tap so you know what it feels like."

Dumping Garreth back in a chair beside the fireplace, Fowler went out to the kitchen. A cracking noise came back to Garreth, then Fowler returned carrying a chair rung. With his pocketknife he sharpened one end into a long, thin point, carefully cutting so that all the shavings fell in the fireplace. "We don't want to be untidy, do we?"

Don't panic, Garreth thought desperately, watching him. That had been one of the first lessons in survival at the academy. Panic kills. He must stay calm and think rationally.

Or get mad, a voice whispered in his head. It sounded a little like Lane, but more like his father and the instructors at the academy. *Think survival. Fight. Even if your teeth are kicked in and you're shot full of holes, you never stop fighting. Never. Kick, claw, use any weapon you can find, but don't let the scum waste you.*

And this bastard in particular. He obviously enjoyed inflicting terror. He had probably hummed and smiled just like this at Count Dracula while preparing that other stake.

Anger boiled up as he thought about the savagery of the little man's death. Garreth let it come . . . welcomed it. Fowler had had enough fun. It was time to stop him. What was a little suffocation and daylight? Irina had made herself live a human rhythm without any aids like dark glasses, had forced herself even to go to church. He could surely bear some pain in the name of survival.

As anger grew, his mind started working again, planning. The first order had to be freeing himself. By twisting his wrists, he could reach around to slip a finger of one hand under the cable tie on the other. He pulled. The plastic bit into his finger and wrist. *Come on man,* he prodded himself. *Work at it. We're talking life and death here.*

Fowler whittled at the stake.

Garreth eyed the knife. That would have him free in a second. He could talk if he made an effort, Fowler had said. He would try. Straining, he managed to compress his aching chest, moving a fractional amount of air up his throat. "Fowler." It hardly counted as even a whisper, but it was a sound.

Fowler heard. He turned, smiling. "Hello, hello. Do you mean you have something to say to me after all?"

Garreth let the smile and arrogant tone feed his anger. He worked another bit of air out. "Closer."

Fowler came over and leaned down. "Now then, where's Mada?"

Garreth rammed his head into Fowler's nose as hard as he could. The writer reeled back with a howl, clutching at his face. Knife and stake clattered to the floor.

Garreth threw himself out of the chair on top of them. He could barely feel the knife. His fingers shook weakly as he tried to close them around the handle and the room spun beyond the red haze of his vision. Curses ran through his head. The garlic effect should have been wearing off, unless he was still being affected by some that had soaked into his coat. If only he could breath a little. *Well you can't, damn it*, he yelled at himself, *and you're not going to pass out, either, so forget about it.*

Biting his lip, he locked his fingers around the knife and turned the blade so he could saw at his bonds. It seemed to take forever to find the right position, then a sudden lance of pain in his wrist told him that he was also cutting his skin. He kept working anyway. Fowler would not remain blinded by pain forever.

Or even another minute. From the corner of his eye he could see the writer's hands coming down. He sawed desperately with the knife, cursing. How could a stupid damn piece of plastic take so long to cut?

A moment later he swore again. Fowler was stiffening; he had seen what Garreth was doing.

With a snarl, Fowler charged, swinging his foot.

The toe connected just behind Garreth's ear. Pain exploded in his head. A little more pain he might have ignored, but the force of the blow loosened his grip and the knife fell out of his fingers. He groped frantically for it.

At the edge of his vision, Fowler's foot swung a second time. Garreth rolled away, cursing. Dodging the kick meant abandoning the knife.

With a snort of triumph, Fowler kicked the knife into the fireplace and snatched up the chair rung. He came at Garreth, gripping it in both hands.

Garreth rolled again, not quite fast or far enough. The stake drove into his hip. A spasm of pain wracked him. He kept rolling. Maybe he could jerk the stake out of Fowler's hands, even if it meant landing on top of it and driving it in deeper.

No such luck. The point came free in a flood of wet warmth down Garreth's leg. Through the red fog clouding his vision, Garreth saw Fowler reset his grip on the stake and lunge again. Garreth flung himself sideways one more time and twisted his wrists desperately, straining at the cable ties.

With a sharp jerk, the cut tie broke. His hands came free. Just in time to reach up and deflect the stake. Instead of driving through the middle of his throat, it impaled the muscle where his neck and left shoulder joined.

This time Garreth pulled it out himself. Grabbing the shaft below Fowler's hands, he forced it back up toward the writer. A wordlessly snarling Fowler leaned on the stake to drive it down again. Garreth pushed up, resisting. Even as he held Fowler off, though, he knew he could not do so for long. The writer had gravity and daylight on his side and the strength was seeping out of Garreth's arm along with the warmth of blood spreading across his shoulder.

Garreth abruptly shoved sideways. As his arms went out from under him, Fowler came crashing down on Garreth. He rolled, taking the writer with him. Coming on top, he wrenched away the stake and hurled it across the room.

Fowler caught Garreth's belt and heaved him aside, then scrambling to his feet, dived to retrieve the stake.

Garreth rolled for the fireplace. He had to free his feet! His fingers closed around the knife as Fowler scooped up the stake and turned. Garreth picked up a log from the stack on the hearth and heaved it at the charging Fowler, then reached for the cable ties on his ankle with the knife.

The log struck Fowler's chest with no effect. To Garreth's dismay, the writer reeled back only a step before recovering and charging on. Sawing at a cable tie with one hand, Garreth picked up another log with the other.

Fowler deflected it with his arm as casually as if brushing off a fly.

Hunters were like berserkers, Irina had said. They had to be killed to be stopped.

The cable tie parted. Garreth tried to scramble to his feet. His body would not respond. The injured leg collapsed, spilling him backward. The knife popped out of his grip and skittered away across the floor.

Holding the stake two-handed like a dagger, Fowler dropped on him. Garreth caught Fowler's wrists with the point bare inches from his chest. With every ounce of his evaporating strength, he struggled to hold it there long enough to lash up with his good leg and sink the toes in Fowler's groin.

Fowler curled up into a squeaking ball of agony and toppled sideways. Garreth rolled one more time to throw an arm around Fowler's throat. The choke hold tightened. Fowler went limp.

Now, tit for tat, quid pro quo. Getting even. Garreth dug through Fowler's pockets. There was his gun. He shoved that back in its holster. And there was the perfume dispenser. He dropped that in his pocket, too. Then here was what he really wanted—more cable ties. Heaving Fowler over onto his stomach, Garreth secured both wrists and ankles with the ties.

If he could breathe, he would have sighed in relief. Now he could strip off this coat and— But the thought cut off there. He found he could not sit up.

His strength had all run out. Maybe his blood, too. It seemed to be everywhere, soaking his trousers, soaking his coat and turtleneck, streaking the hardwood floor.

He closed his eyes. Rest. That was what he needed. At sunset he would feel better. Surely by then the garlic would have dispersed enough for him to start breathing again.

Part of him prodded the rest sharply. *Sunset is hours away, you dumb flatfoot. What do you think Fowler will be doing in the meantime? Waiting politely for you to work up the strength to arrest him?*

No, of course not. Garreth forced his eyes open again. He could not lie here. He would only lose the war when he had fought so hard to win the battle. He needed help, though. *It furthers one to appoint helpers.*

Where was the phone? He peered around him, straining to see through red-hazed vision. There . . . on a table near the kitchen door.

He never asked himself if he could reach it. *Never stop fighting. Don't let the scum win.* He used his good arm to drag himself on his belly toward the phone, praying that Lane kept it hooked up while she was away.

Standing was impossible but a pull on the cord brought the phone crashing down from the table to the floor beside him. To his relief, the receiver buzzed at him. Carefully he punched Lien's number. Calling Harry would also bring Girimonte. Better to have Irina come with Lien.

"Hello?"

Would he be able to make her hear him? He struggled to breathe out just a little more. "Li . . . en," he whispered.

He heard her breath catch on the other end, then, quickly, anxiously: "Garreth? What's happened? Where are you?"

"Lane's . . . a . . . part . . . ment," he forced out.

Across the room, Fowler groaned and stirred.

"Hur . . . ry."

No time for more. No strength to waste hanging up, either. He left the receiver lying and dragged himself back to where he could keep choking Fowler into unconsciousness until help arrived.

12

It seemed like an eternity before Garreth heard the downstairs door open. From where he lay stretched on the floor with his hand on Fowler's throat, he listened to two sets of footsteps run up the stairs. Three sets. The third set was just a whisper of sound. They all echoed as if from a great distance through the thick fog enveloping him.

A rap sounded at the door. "Garreth?" Lien called. The knob rattled. "Damn! It's locked. What are we going to do?"

"Irina . . ." his grandmother's voice said.

"There is a difficulty. This is a dwelling and I have never before been invited—*Nichevo*. I will tend to it."

She had discovered the barrier gone. Garreth's pulse jumped. Now she knew Lane was dead. Would she guess how?

"Holy Mother!"

He twisted his head toward the door. Her voice came from this side of it now. She stood just inside. But stood only for a second, then she jerked open the door and ran for the bay window.

"Lien, Grania," she called in a voice turned to a

hoarse rasp. "Take him into the hall away from this garlic."

Footsteps raced into the room toward him, and halted in two gasps.

"Garreth!"

"Mother of God." Grandma Doyle dropped to her knees beside him. "The devil's killed you. I knew it. When you left I felt a wind between me skin and me blood."

Garreth shook his head. He was not dead yet.

Each of them grabbed an arm and began dragging him toward the door.

He pulled against them, shaking his head again. "Coat," he whispered. Being in the hall would not help a bit as long as he wore these clothes.

Irina had the drapes pulled wide and all three windows in the bay open. Coming back to them, she stopped short, too. "It's on him. Quickly remove his coat and shirt."

They sat him up and stripped him to the waist. Irina removed the two pieces of clothing, carrying them to the kitchen like someone with a bomb, held as far away from her as possible.

Gradually the unbearable pressure in Garreth's chest released. Air trickled in. Nothing had ever felt quite so good before. He leaned back against his grandmother and closed his eyes.

Her arms tightened around him. "He looks like a corpse, Lien."

"I'll call an ambulance." Her footsteps moved in the direction of the telephone.

"No," Irina's voice said firmly. "You cannot."

He opened his eyes to see her holding Lien's wrist with one hand and blocking the dial face with the other.

"But you can see he's seriously hurt. He needs a doctor."

Irina shook her head. "We're strong. We heal quickly. All he needs is blood." She turned to look at him. "Human blood."

Garreth stiffened. "No."

"Yes. This is the point at which animal blood fails us."

Fowler groaned.

Irina crossed swiftly to him. Rolling him over on his back, and removing her glasses, she sat down astride of him and stared hard into his opening, dazed eyes. "You are a statue. You cannot move or make a sound, nor can you see or hear anything unless I choose to talk to you again." Fowler went stiff. Irina put on her glasses again. Coming over to Garreth, she squatted beside him and took his face in her hands. "Listen to me, child. This is not a matter of choice but necessity. Only human blood will heal you."

He closed his eyes. "No."

She shook him. "You're being foolish. Taking blood doesn't have to be an act of rape."

He opened his eyes with a start to stare up at her in disbelief.

She smiled. "That *is* a choice. Ours is by nature a solitary existence, but not one in a vacuum. From humans we come, and we remain bound to them by our needs for food and companionship. Lack of either brings death of the mind, if not the body."

Like Christopher Stroda, Garreth thought suddenly.

"Does it not make sense, then, to treat people not as cattle but friends, and ask for what we need rather than take it?"

"Ask?" There he had her. She was crazy. "Who would say yes?"

"Me," Lien said. While he gaped at her, she unbuttoned the collar of her blouse. "You need blood; please take it."

"Or take mine," Grandma Doyle said. "Your life

comes from me already through your mother. Let me give it to you again."

He twisted his head to regard her with wonder. They meant it! But how could he sink his fangs into his own grandmother's neck, or Lien's?

Irina murmured, "There are vessels where punctures are less conspicuous than in the carotid artery —the brachial at the elbow, for example, and the popliteal behind the knee."

His grandmother stretched her arm out across his shoulder. It brushed his cheek, soft and freckled, smelling of lavender and warm, salty blood. "Take the blood. Don't let that devil destroy you."

Don't let the scum win. Think survival.

With the words reverberating in him, Garreth turned his head and kissed the inside of her elbow. A pulse fluttered against his lips. Blood. He could smell it, could almost taste it. Locating the strongest beat with the tip of his tongue, he sank his fangs into the arm. Blood welled up from the punctures . . . warm and sweetly salty as he remembered the girl's blood from the auto accident as being, everything he longed to drink, a delicious fire in his throat. He swallowed again and again. Slowly strength seeped back into him.

"Enough!" Irina's voice said. "Release her. Let . . . go."

A grandmotherly knuckle thumped him on the head. Reluctantly he drew out of her arm. "I haven't had enough," he protested.

"You have taken enough from her."

His grandmother smoothed hair back from his forehead. "I want to help you, but I've no desire to join you. The price of forever's too high."

Lien knelt beside him and held her arm out. "Take the rest from me."

He bent his head to her arm.

This time he drank less greedily, and found himself

feeling the rhythm of her blood, watching for signs he might be taking too much. But his hunger ended and he pulled back before she showed any weakening. He eyed her for some evidence of repugnance or regret.

Instead, she smiled. "Now you carry my blood, too. How do you feel?"

"Still shaky." Pain remained in his hip and shoulder. It had lessened noticeably, however, and the bleeding had stopped.

Irina handed him his glasses. "Do you feel strong enough to tell us what honorable, legal solution you have found to our problem?" She gestured toward Fowler.

Garreth bit his lip. If he admitted he had no solution, she might impose her own. Fowler's catatonic state gave him an idea. "We have the power to make people forget us. I think—"

Irina interrupted with a shake of her head. "Our powers are limited. We can edit his memories of the day, but not make him forget either us or his hatred of us. That stretches back through his entire life."

"What about making him one of you?" Grandma Doyle asked. "To tell anyone about you then would be to betray himself as well."

"I think that would make no difference to him," Irina said. "Would it, Garreth?"

He shook his head. "For a long time I hated what I'd become so much that if I could have brought Lane to justice by announcing to the world what she was, I would have, and not given a damn about the personal consequences. I would have welcomed true death."

"I, too," Irina said. "I planned to confess about myself to Prince Yevgeni as soon as I had my revenge on Viktor. I did not, obviously, but only because by the time I could, my instinct for self-preservation had reasserted itself. We have no time for that with the Englishman. He would run into the street screaming denounciations of us."

"Let him," Lien said. "There are more people like my husband than me in the world. Who will believe him?"

"Even a few is too many. We cannot afford scrutiny." Irina sighed. "It is a problem with only one solution. Grania, you and Lien take Garreth home. I will see to cleaning up here."

"There has to be an alternative," Garreth protested. He thought desperately. There *had* to be! Clearly people were much harder to convince about vampires than he had been afraid all along. He should be able to use that.

"I am sorry, Garreth."

Lien and Grandma Doyle each slipped an arm under his.

He shook them off. "No. Wait! What if—" What if what? An idea had raced past him just a moment ago. He struggled to find it again in the swirling chaos in his head. He snatched at it. Yes! It might work. "What if the people he denounces *can* bear scrutiny?"

Irina went still. He felt the hidden eyes staring at him. Finally she said, "Explain, please."

He explained.

Irina pursed her lips thoughtfully. "What if he attacks?"

"You and I will be close enough to intervene."

"This will prevent him from killing again?"

"That's the beauty of it. Once he's discredited, he's safe to run through the criminal justice system like any other murderer."

Grandma Doyle grinned. "You're the devil himself, boy. I'll do me best to make it work."

"Me, too," Lien said.

He knew he could count on them. "What super ladies the two of you are." He squeezed their hands. "Let's get cracking."

13

First they had to set Fowler up. While Irina prepared their prisoner to turn from a statue back into a man, Lien closed the windows and drapes. That left the room lighted by only a three-way table lamp beside the fireplace chair where Grandma Doyle sat, a lamp she turned off as soon as Lien sat down in the wicker chair they had positioned on the other side of the fireplace. She left her hand on the lamp switch.

The dark felt wonderful. Garreth savored it as he limped to the kitchen.

"Ready, Grania?" Irina asked from beside Fowler.

"Ready."

Curse of the Vampire. Act One. Garreth moved faster.

"Five . . . four . . ." Irina raced after him. "Three." They pulled back out of sight on each side of the kitchen archway. "Two. *One!*"

Fowler opened his eyes right on cue in the living room.

"Well now, I think he's rejoining us at last," Grandma Doyle said. "Good evening to you, Mr. Fowler."

Garreth peeked around the edge of the door. Fowler lay blinking in disorientation. After several moments, puzzlement became a frown. His head cocked in a listening attitude, obviously waiting for sounds to tell him about his surroundings.

"You're uncomfortable, I hope," Grandma Doyle went on.

Fowler craned his head in the direction of her voice. "Who are you?" he demanded.

"Your judge." She switched the lamp on its lowest setting. The shade had been adjusted to cast light across her lap, leaving her face shadowed. "It could be I'm your doom as well."

Lien said in an impatient voice, "Why do you bother talking to him?"

Fowler's head whipped around toward her. She sat beyond the direct light of the lamp. He could not be seeing more than a general form. "Who are *you?*"

She pretended to ignore him. "He's conscious again. He can feel pain." She picked up the stake lying in her lap. Fowler saw that well enough. Garreth watched his eyes widen and heard his breath catch. "Let's kill him and be done."

Grandma Doyle shook her head. "You newcomers to the life are still so full of human impatience. Besides, killing is merciful. After the way he's slaughtered our brothers and sisters, do you really want to be merciful?"

Lien appeared to consider. "No!" She fingered the stake. "I want him to suffer! Let me give him a taste of how this feels."

Fowler spat a curse.

"I'll handle this me own way, thank you. Mr. Fowler."

He craned his neck to look at Grandma Doyle

again. Garreth wondered what he could be thinking, lying there with these two half-seen figures talking across him. At least there was no doubt what he felt. Hatred twisted his face. "Who the bloody hell *are* you?"

"Those of the blood call me the Grand Dame because I came to this life late in years and I've lived a long time. If there's a quarrel to be settled or a problem to solve, it's me they come to for the settling or solving. You, Mr. Fowler, are a problem in need of settling."

"Go to hell."

She laughed with a note so authentically bitter and savage it sent a shiver down Garreth's spine. "We're already there, Mr. Fowler. Prepare yourself to join us."

Fowler stiffened. "What—"

"Hold him for me, girl . . . up on his knees with his head pulled back. You don't have to be gentle."

"You—" Fowler began.

"No!" Lien spat. "I won't have him one of us!"

"Didn't you say you wanted him to suffer? What worse suffering than to be trapped among those he hates, unable to escape because he's one of us."

"I'll escape," Fowler snarled. "I'll see all of you destroyed."

Grandma Doyle laughed. "You think so now, but it's different once you've made the change. Even though you hate us, you'll protect us . . . because suddenly you're as terrified of the stake as we are. You'll even protect Mada."

"No!" He writhed wildly, fighting the bonds on his wrists and ankles. "I won't be cheated out of destroying that creature! No matter what I am, I'll find her and kill her, and then I'll see to it that the whole world knows you exist! They'll have to believe me with a live specimen in front of them!"

"*Live* specimen?" Lien said with a snicker.

He cursed at her.

Grandma Doyle sighed gustily. "Enough of this yelling. Mr. Fowler, be still."

Fowler froze in response to the command suggestion Irina had given him.

Grandma Doyle and Lien slid out of their chairs to kneel beside the writer. While Fowler's eyes bulged in horror and hatred, Grandma Doyle bent low and closed her teeth on his throat.

Irina's second command took effect. Fowler went like a statue again.

Garreth limped out of the kitchen. "Great work, girls. Now let's get him out of here."

14

The cars were the big problem. They had three to take home, including the ZX still at the Cannery, but only two people fit to drive. Garreth finally put on his grandmother's coat and cautiously drove her and Fowler in Fowler's car, parking a block away from Harry's house where they waited for Lien to come back from dropping Irina off at the Cannery.

"Are you sure you can manage him?" he asked while helping Lien and his grandmother manhandle the limp Fowler into Lien's car.

His grandmother tossed her head. "Since when did the Irish ever have trouble handling the English?"

"Irina is right behind me," Lien said. "You just watch for the front door lights to go on at the house."

Garreth climbed back in Fowler's car to wait nervously. The ZX passing him a minute later helped only a little. For all his confidence when explaining the plan, he could think of a dozen ways for it to go wrong, all of them disastrous. If it went wrong in the next few minutes, only Irina stood between this wacko and the two women.

To distract himself, he imagined what was happening at the house. They would be tucking Fowler into bed on the earth-filled air mattress, rigging heavy drapes over the kitchen windows, and filling tankards with horse blood.

An hour later yellow flickered in the Takananda door lights, barely visible because of daylight.

It's showtime.

Taking a deep breath, Garreth started the car and gunned it down the street. In front of Harry's house he swerved into the curb with brakes squealing. The front wheel ran up over the side of the driveway so that he ended with both right wheels on the grass. Slamming the car door added another loud sound to attract the neighborhood's attention, then he charged up the front walk, trying not to limp.

"Open up!" he yelled, hammering on the front door. "I know you're bloody well in there. Open up before I break down the bloody door!"

Lien jerked the door open. "Mr. Fowler," she said loudly in a tone of outrage. "What is the meaning of this?"

He pushed at her. She pretended to resist, then fail. As the door slammed behind them, a grin replaced her frown. "We had an audience. I saw drapes move in at least three windows. You'd better hide before Fowler comes down and sees you. Use our room or your grandmother's room."

Garreth shook his head. "I'll be in the living room. It's closer to the kitchen." Though not as close as he preferred to be. "Where's Irina?"

"Out on the patio."

Also farther away than he liked. Too much could happen in the seconds it would take for either of them to arrive. Yet they could not risk being seen at this stage.

Lien rubbed her palms against her slacks. "Do you really think he believes Grania and I are vampires?"

"You know witch hunters; they see their bogeymen everywhere." He smiled wryly. "Fowler's got to be so bent by this obsession with Lane that if the encouragement we've given him hasn't blinded him to rationality already, making him think you're trying to bring him into your bloodsucking brood will keep him too distracted to examine the facts closely."

Grandma Doyle whispered down the steps, "I'm going to wake him now."

Lien nodded. "I'll call the police."

Garreth hurriedly hauled himself upstairs and into the darkened living room.

From there he heard his grandmother go into his room. "Mr. Fowler, I know it isn't sunset, but you've rested long enough. We have things to do."

He imagined Fowler sitting up and staring around, trying to orient himself, feeling the pallet under him. "Where am I?"

"Where we can watch you, of course," Grandma Doyle replied. "We're not finished yet; that is to say, you aren't."

"You've untied my hands and feet." Fowler made it an accusation.

Grandma Doyle chuckled. "Of course. How can you walk downstairs otherwise? But Mr. Fowler, don't be thinking of trying to run away. When the day comes I can't handle a young pup like you, human or otherwise, I'll turn in me cape and fangs. So up with you. Here's your coat. That's it; put it on. Now come along."

Garreth waited tensely in case Fowler resisted, but the writer apparently decided to play along for the time being, waiting for the chance to escape. From the darkness of the living room, Garreth watched Fowler follow Grandma Doyle downstairs.

As soon as the stairs blocked their view of the living room door, he limped quickly to his room and changed clothes. The pallet had to be hidden, too. Garreth cached it under the conventional mattress.

Lien's voice came up from downstairs. "What would you like to eat?"

"I'm not hungry."

"Really now, Mr. Fowler," Grandma Doyle said. "Do you think we plan to drug you? Nonsense. Your blood's no good to us polluted."

"I'll have a glass of water," Fowler said.

Water ran.

The bedroom looked right. He left and worked his way soundlessly down several steps to where, if he sat down and peered around the edge of the steps, he could see the kitchen door. The opening framed his grandmother sitting on a stool at the work island counter.

"A refill," Fowler said.

Grandma Doyle raised her eyebrows. "Still thirsty? Queer. I've only taken once from you. But here; see if this stops the craving." She pushed the tankard she held down the counter.

Nice move! Garreth grinned. The thirst was not one of the suggestions Irina planted but his grandmother had taken beautiful advantage of—

"No!"

The scream jerked Garreth onto his feet, raising the hair all over his body. It sounded like an animal. Skin crawling, he vaulted the railing. Pain shot through his injured hip and the leg buckled under him, sending him sprawling.

"*No!*"

Grandma Doyle ducked just in time to avoid the tankard flying at her.

"Garreth!" Lien called.

Cursing, he scrambled for the kitchen on his hands and good leg.

"You did it," Fowler screamed. "You've turned me into—into— You bloody bitches! *I'll kill you!*"

Fowler lunged into the frame of the doorway, his hands stretched for Grandma Doyle's throat. Garreth hurled himself at Fowler. Grandma Doyle jumped back, pushing a stool into Fowler's path. It hit the writer the same moment that Garreth's shoulder caught him at the waist in a flying tackle. Men and furniture went down in a tangle.

Irina came tearing in through the dining room door.

Snarling, Fowler clawed at Garreth's eyes. Garreth caught the writer's wrists before the nails more than scraped his forehead. A knee jerked up toward his groin. He dodged it just in time, but then almost lost his grip in a sudden twist of Fowler's wrists. The man bucked and writhed under him, fighting with animal strength. *Or a madman's.*

"Irina, get a choke hold on him!"

"I can't reach you down there."

Damn. He abruptly released Fowler's wrists, but only to change his grip to the writer's lapels. Then, heaving sideways with all his strength, he smashed Fowler's head into the cabinet. Fowler went limp.

The doorbell rang. "Mrs. Takananda, it's the police."

Cursing, Garreth scrambled to his feet, leaving Fowler sitting slumped against the cabinet. Look at this place. A struggling Fowler had been in the script but not a bloody kitchen! Crimson splashes were everywhere: counter, floor, walls, even on the ceiling, not to mention on everyone, too.

The bell rang again. "Mrs. Takananda?"

"We will have to use the blood," Irina said.

Garreth thought fast. "We need a source for it then." His stomach lurched. There was only one logical source. *Shit.* He hated knives. "Lien, throw me a knife." Looking around, he noticed the tankard lying by the dining room door. "Get rid of the tankards!"

"Mrs. Takananda!" The uniformed officers pounded on the door.

Grandma Doyle scooped up both tankards and threw them in the dishwasher.

Catching the kitchen knife Lien tossed him, Garreth set his jaw and before he could chicken out, quickly drew the blade across his forearm. Blood spurted through the slash in his sleeve. He clenched his teeth against the pain. God, he hated knives. "Let them in," he gasped. "Irina, you might as well stay out of it."

"Yes."

While Lien ran for the door, he wrapped Fowler's fingers around the knife, then pulled it loose again and tossed it across the room to where the tankard had lain. Irina retreated through the dining room.

Lien jerked the front door open. "Thank God! He's crazy!" She raced back toward the kitchen. "He came storming in here accusing us of hiding that Barber woman. When Garreth tried to make him leave, he snatched up a knife I had on the counter and attacked."

The uniforms stopped short in the doorway. "Christ!"

Garreth looked up from making a tourniquet of his belt. "'Who'd have thought the old man had so much blood in him.' Hi, Hingle, Rahal."

"Mikaelian?" They glanced at Fowler, then obviously deciding he would keep for a bit, came over to peer at Garreth's arm. "How bad did he get you?"

"It hurts like hell." He rolled up the sleeve for a look. And grimaced. He had not intended to cut quite so deep.

Rahal whistled. "That's going to take a few stitches. Better get a bandage on it."

He had barely finished saying so when Grandma Doyle pressed a folded dishtowel over the wound.

Fowler groaned.

The officers whipped around toward him. They pounced, handcuffing his hands behind his back. "Who is this turkey anyway?"

"You won't believe it. Graham Fowler."

Their jaws dropped. "The writer? Why the hell—"

Fowler screamed. It sounded even more animal than the last time. Hingle's and Rahal's expressions suddenly became those of men discovering they held a bomb.

"They've killed me! Kill them!" Fowler lunged to his feet and at Grandma Doyle. The officers hung on grimly. "Kill the vampires before they turn you into one, too!"

"Jesus," Rahal muttered. "You should have warned us to bring a butterfly net."

Fowler twisted to stare at him. "You think I'm mad, but I can prove they're vampires. The old-looking one bit me last night while Sergeant Takananda's wife helped her. See the mark—"

"Sergeant Takananda's wife is a vampire?" Hingle asked in a flat voice. "Right."

"She *is*, you bloody fool. Have a look in the fridge. There has to be some container of blood in there. They were drinking mugs full of it when I came into the kitchen. They tried to make me drink it, too. I threw it back in their faces. That's what all this blood is. Now will you look at the bite mark on my neck?"

Hingle rolled his eyes. "All I see is a hickey."

Fowler hissed. "It's a hematoma, you ass. That's how they hide the bite. There are punctures in the middle of it. There's more, too. I stabbed Mikaelian in the neck and hip with a wooden stake. Check him for marks. Even though it was only last night, he'll be practically healed."

It would not do to let them see his neck. "Why, Mr.

Fowler, everyone knows the stake is supposed to go through the heart while the vampire is sleeping in his coffin. Shall we check the bedrooms upstairs for coffins?"

The officers snickered, then shook Fowler's arms. "Let's go."

"No!" He jerked back against them. "Listen to me! They know where Lane Barber is. They're protecting her, though, because she's one of them. You have to make them tell where she is. Then we can destroy her and the rest of them. I'll help. I know how to kill them."

"Like you killed Richard Maruska and his room-mate and Leonard Holle?" Garreth asked.

Fowler's mouth thinned. "You know bloody well only Maruska was a vampire. The others were just—"

The front door banged open. "Lien!" Harry came pounding down the hall with Girimonte right behind him. "I heard the call on the radio. What's wrong? Whose car is that on the lawn?" They stopped short in the doorway just as the uniforms had. Harry sucked in a sharp breath. "Good God. Garreth, what happened?"

Holding onto his arm, Garreth shrugged. "It's crazy. Fowler came in here accusing Grandma and Lien of knowing where Lane is but protecting her because they're all vampires."

"You're one, too," Fowler spat. "That's why you don't eat."

Garreth raised a brow at Girimonte. "And you've been accusing me of being anorectic. See how wrong you are?"

She shrugged. A corner of her mouth twitched. "Ignorant me."

"He's also suggested he's responsible for our murder binge."

Her eyes narrowed. "Really. Can you give us enough to make probable cause so we can get a warrant to search his hotel room and check his clothes?"

He nodded.

Fowler shrieked and exploded into struggling violence, flinging himself back and forth, aiming kicks at the uniformed officers. "You bloody thick *fools! Listen* to me!"

The officers wrestled him against the counter. Rahal said, "Takananda, will you or Girimonte ride along with us? I'm not having my partner alone in the back seat with this loony tune."

"Van, you go," Harry said. "I'd like to tend to things here."

Girimonte nodded. "Sure."

Hingle and Rahal started Fowler toward the door. Garreth expected him to struggle, but he walked meekly. At the front door he stopped short, however, and looked back. "I'll be back. Don't forget, I have your powers now. I can just walk out of the cell when I please. Mada isn't dead, no matter what you say, Mikaelian. You can't fool me. She killed my father and I won't be deprived of my vengeance. I'll be back; I'll find her; and I . . . will . . . destroy her. Then it will be your turn."

He marched out of the house between the uniformed officers. Rolling her eyes, Girimonte followed.

Harry waited until the door had closed behind them, then, looking around the kitchen and at Garreth, said, "I think someone better tell me what the hell's been going on."

As briefly as possibly, Garreth told him.

Harry listened with his face turning steadily grimmer. At the end of the recitation, he let his breath out in a hiss. "I could strangle each and every one of you, even you, honorable wife. Garreth, how could you let Lien and your grandmother—"

"Since when do I let me grandchildren tell me what I can and can't do?" Grandma Doyle snapped.

Harry retreated a step. "It's a wonder someone wasn't hurt. Seriously hurt," he amended, glancing at Garreth. "Christ. I don't want to even think about trying to sort out the case against him. It's either a frame or something we can't use. You are going to clean up that apartment before he talks someone into checking it, aren't you?" He sighed. "Let's hope we find enough physical evidence in his clothes and luggage at the hotel to tie him to Holle's murder."

"You shouldn't have to worry about going to court with a defendant who claims he's hunting the vampire who killed his father," Garreth said.

Harry ran a hand through his hair. "That may be our salvation. If he's judged incompetent, he'll be locked up where he can't hurt anyone, without the risk of a trial and all its publicity."

"This is your humane alternative?" Irina said from the dining room doorway. "Madness?"

Garreth cradled his injured arm more tightly and sighed tiredly. Was there ever a good solution in conflicts between humans and vampires? In the end it always seemed to be a choice between evils. "At least he's alive."

"Unlike Mada."

Garreth sucked in his breath. He felt the violet eyes fixed on him behind her glasses. In accusation? Had she guessed?

"You mean Barber really is dead?" Harry asked. "How do you know?"

"We know when our brothers and sisters die," Irina replied. She continued to face Garreth.

She did know! But instead of dismay, relief filled Garreth. Someone else knew. He was not alone with the guilt anymore. He nodded. "I—"

"We can't always tell how or where, of course," Irina interrupted. "Considering Mada's nature, her death was perhaps justifiable homicide." She stared at Garreth.

He stared back. The implication was clear; she felt sure of what he had done but wanted to dismiss the matter. He said slowly, "Maybe even self-defense." At least she ought to know that he had not just killed in revenge.

Harry glanced from one to the other of them. "I wouldn't be a bit surprised." He put an arm around Garreth's shoulders. "That closes her case then, Miksan."

Garreth caught his breath. Harry had put it together, too. So had Grandma Doyle and Lien, he saw in a quick glance. They looked back at him, nodding at Harry's words. Those nods, like Harry's arm, told him that they intended to say nothing more about it, either.

Warmth flooded him, filling even places that had been bleakly empty the past two years. Savoring it, he nodded back at them all. "I guess you're right. That's the end of it."

15

He dreamed of life. A bridge stretched before him, massive and solid, its steel girders and cables glowing a pulsating blood red in the darkness. Strange. How had he failed to see that this was what linked him to humanity? Not that fragile wooden one with its combustible floor . . . ties of need and blood, blood shared and blood shed. Why, too, had he seen himself at one end and humans at the other when, in fact, they all milled together in the middle? Harry was there, and Lien and his grandmother, as well as a mass of relatives and friends from Baumen and San Francisco, all shaking his hand or hugging him.

Irina circulated through the group, too, catching his eye from time to time, and smiling.

Serruto extended a hand. "It's good to have you back. Is it true you're leaving for Baumen soon?"

Garreth nodded. "I have a personal relationship to wrap up. Not everyone can be told what I am. I also need to tell Anna that we uncovered information indicating Mada was killed and her body dumped somewhere in the Rockies. I'll have some of her belongings with me and they can send for the rest. I'll also give Anna the name of Mada's bank and her account numbers, so they'll know where her money is after they're able to declare her dead."

"And after that?"

Garreth shrugged. "I've met a woman who would like me to travel with her. There's an estate outside Moscow she wants to show me, among other places. She says I have a lot to learn and she'd like to teach me."

Serruto's brows hopped. "She sounds like an older woman."

"I think you could call her an older woman, yes. She doesn't look her age, though."

Girimonte slid up beside him, puffing one of her long, elegant cigars. "You heard what we found in Fowler's hotel room, didn't you? Climbing rope, suction cups, and a glass cutter. Fibers from his shirt also match some found on Holle's window, and particles from the soles of his running shoes are like material from the shingles on the roofs of Holle's house and the one next door. His cable ties fit the marks on Holle's and the count's wrists and ankles as well. Too bad he's so wacko he'll never stand trial."

"Too bad," Garreth lied.

Fowler had come to the party, too. He spotted the writer's tortured face beyond the edge of the crowd. With his wounds healing up, Garreth felt sorry for the man . . . another victim of Lane's excesses.

Where was Lane? Surely she had come, too. He searched through the crowd. Yes, there she was, but not among the others. She stood alone at the far end of the bridge, calling something.

The sound reached him only faintly through the voices around him. For several minutes he strained to hear, then realized that he really had no interest in anything she said. Garreth turned away, back to the party, and when he looked in her direction again a while later, she had disappeared.